*Who said mixing work and pleasure was a bad idea?*

For Kenley Carmichael, getting fired for sleeping with the boss's husband is almost funny—at twenty-eight, she's still a virgin. Not that her now ex-boss would believe it—Kenley's got the face and figure to attract plenty of men, even if she's never found the right one. A job at New Haven Custom Boats is a chance to start fresh and learn a whole new skill set. Trouble is, she can't stop wishing her incredibly hot new boss would introduce her to some decidedly un-businesslike pleasure . . .

Zane Jackson needs a new assistant, but when his pregnant sister hires her replacement, she chooses a girl who reminds him of the kind who broke his heart in high school. Zane might not be that shy boy anymore, but sweet, sexy Kenley makes him feel every bit as awkward as he did then—and even hungrier to kiss her. She's the perfect woman for the job—but he wants her to be so much more.

Interoffice dating can only lead to trouble—unless it leads to true love . . .

# Help Wanted

*An On the Job Romance*

# Allison B. Hanson

LYRICAL SHINE
Kensington Publishing Corp.
www.kensingtonbooks.com

LYRICAL SHINE BOOKS are published by

Kensington Publishing Corp.
119 West 40th Street
New York, NY 10018

All Kensington titles, imprints, and distributed lines are available at special quantity discounts for bulk purchases for sales promotion, premiums, fundraising, educational, or institutional use.

Special book excerpts or customized printings can also be created to fit specific needs. For details, write or phone the office of the Kensington Sales Manager: Kensington Publishing Corp., 119 West 40th Street, New York, NY 10018. Attn. Sales Department. Phone: 1-800-221-2647.

Lyrical Shine and Lyrical Shine logo Reg. U.S. Pat. & TM Off.

First Electronic Edition: September 2017
eISBN-13: 978-1-5161-0337-9
eISBN-10: 1-5161-0337-8

First Print Edition: September 2017
ISBN-13: 978-1-5161-0338-6
ISBN-10: 1-5161-0338-6

Printed in the United States of America

# Also by Allison B. Hanson

*Never Let Go*

*Nick of Time*

*When Least Expected*

# Chapter 1

After slamming her car door, Kenley stormed into the restaurant, madder than a hornet. When she'd first found out, her initial reaction was disbelief, but fortunately her brain quite efficiently turned the confusion into an easier emotion to express. Anger.

"I can't believe this," she muttered to herself while scouring the room for her support system.

Two blondes looked up and waved her over. She already felt a little better as she walked across the dining room to meet them. Good friends could fix anything. Well, good friends and whiskey.

The waitress rushed over and asked for her drink order.

"Jameson, neat."

"Ken, it's eleven in the morning," Vanessa reminded her.

"Thanks. But I didn't get fired because I couldn't tell time," Kenley snapped.

"Right, then." V backed off as the waitress scampered away.

"I'm sorry," Kenley moaned into her hands. She hated feeling helpless. "I didn't mean to snap at you. I'm just so pissed off."

"So what happened exactly?" Rachel was obviously still confused by Kenley's mayday text. Kenley couldn't believe it herself.

Rachel and Vanessa had been her best friends since high school and had stayed in their hometown of Madison, Connecticut, while Kenley sought adventure in Manhattan. Both were married, stay-at-home moms with school-age children, which was the reason they were available to come at her distress call for drinks so early in the day.

Kenley didn't begrudge them their lives. She knew being home with kids was not an easy job, and they had problems just like everyone else. They were just different kinds of problems than she faced now.

"I got fired," Kenley said while searching for the waitress. Where the hell was her drink?

"You said that, but *why*? You're the best worker they have."

"My stupid witch of a boss accused me of sleeping with her husband at their New Year's party."

"But...?" Rachel still looked confused, and rightfully so. "That's not possible."

"It's possible, Rach, just not *probable*," Vanessa pointed out the distinction.

Yes, it was possible for Kenley to have slept with her boss's husband at a party. It wasn't probable because she hadn't slept with *anyone*. Yet. Given the fact she was twenty-eight and still a virgin, it was highly unlikely she would finally give it up at a holiday party with a married man.

"Why didn't you tell her you were still a... you know?" Rachel looked over her shoulder as if the Virgin Police would overhear and arrest her.

"Why should I have to? It's none of her business."

"That's right! Screw her!" Vanessa blurted and took a sip of her margarita. Now, who couldn't tell time? "She wouldn't have believed you anyway. Look at you."

As instructed, Kenley looked down at herself. It did seem unbelievable, even to her. Not that she was God's gift to men, but she was at least *doable*, as her friends had told her many times.

She'd been a cheerleader in high school. Just that sentence alone should have taken her V-card. Through college she'd dated a lot. Just enough to move on before it got to that point. She'd done everything else, just not *that*.

Now, looking down at the tight skirt and fitted, button-down with some cleavage showing, she could see how someone might mistake her for a husband-stealing party whore. But looks could be deceiving. Didn't everyone know that?

Only the two women at the table—and their spouses, because it was apparently the law to share everything with one's spouse—knew the truth about her.

It wasn't like she would have held on this long on purpose. It wasn't a matter of morals or that she was holding out for some sexy, romance-novel highlander pirate to take her maidenhead. It just had never... happened.

While Rachel and Vanessa were losing everything at seventeen and eighteen, including their minds, Kenley was sitting next to her mother's bed hoping for a miracle that never came.

She was in college before she stopped seeing her peers as immature idiots who took everything and everyone for granted. By then it would have been awkward to admit to a guy who just wanted to hook up that he was her first. Guys didn't hang around long enough to be special when she wasn't putting out, so it became a vicious circle. Bringing her to this point in her life where she had been fired for being sexy, even though she didn't have a true concept of what that really was.

Irony was an asshole.

"You should take some time off. Just relax. Go on a tropical vacation," Rachel suggested.

Kenley made a show of looking under the table.

"Sure. That sounds like a great idea. Now, where did I put my rich husband to pay for everything while I'm lying on the beach drinking? Oh, right! I don't have one. I support myself." She was most likely going to have to give up her expensive, miniscule apartment in Manhattan and move back home. Another small part of her withered up and died.

"What's that supposed to mean?" Rachel asked, her brow raised. While Kenley might not begrudge their ability to go where they pleased at eleven in the morning, she might have been slightly bitter about the major financial back up that came from being married to a well-off man. Even if Vanessa's well-off man was Kenley's older brother.

"Nothing." Kenley rubbed her forehead. "I'm sorry."

"You need to find a better job. You were going nowhere at that place anyway," Vanessa said. "You did everything for her, and she held you back so she wouldn't have to find someone to replace you. You should find a job here so you can move home and be closer to your niece." Her best friend/ sister-in-law made it sound like a benefit—which it was—but it was also surrender to her failure.

"I like living in the city." In the city she was just another anonymous fish struggling to make it upstream. She was so busy she didn't realize what she was missing.

"This is your chance to get out and live." Rachel sounded like an 80s cruise ship activities director.

"Does this have anything to do with me, or is this about you feeling trapped?"

"Who knows? It will be good for both of us." Her friend shrugged as Vanessa pulled out her phone.

Kenley's drink finally arrived and she downed it before the waitress left. With a wince and a cough she held up the empty glass.

"Another, please," she wheezed. The waitress—who should have been impressed—looked annoyed as she trotted off to fetch another drink.

"I don't think getting wasted is going to help your cause," Rachel warned.

"I will be happy to test your theory, as I have no other plans at the moment."

"Ooh! Here's something that would be perfect for you." Vanessa held out her phone, expanding the print on the screen.

"It's in New Haven." Kenley frowned as reality reared its head. If she didn't find another job in Manhattan right away, she would have to move.

"It's at the marina."

"What's the position?" Kenley leaned over to get a closer look. Maybe this was what she needed. "It would be a fresh start. And it's only an hour and a half from Manhattan. Not on the other side of the world. Plus I'd be closer to you guys."

"It would be nice to see you more often." Rachel pouted out, working her over with guilt.

"If I'm still friends with the two of you after you were both pregnant at the same time, I think I've proven my loyalty." Kenley plucked the cherry out of Vanessa's drink and bit it from the stem as they chuckled. Where was her second drink?

"You're right. You need a fresh start where you can meet the man you'll give your heart as well as your…" Vanessa didn't finish the sentence, she simply pointed to the cherry stem in Kenley fingers.

"What is this dream job in New Haven?" She changed the subject.

"Like I said, it's at the marina. It looks like they repair and restore boats."

"I don't know anything about boats."

"You don't need to. They're looking for an Executive Production Coordinator."

"That sounds like a fancy name for a secretary," Kenley said.

"What was your title at your last job?" Vanessa asked with a look.

"Assistant Director of Programs."

"And what did that mean?"

"Secretary."

"See? It's perfect. And it says it's a growing company with occasional travel required."

"Ooh, travel. It would be like having mini-vacations while getting paid," Rachel said excitedly. "And maybe the guy will have a yacht."

"Yeah. I'm sure it will be exactly like that." Kenley downed her second drink the moment it was placed on the table.

* * *

"Executive Production Coordinator? Are you crazy?" Zane complained as he pointed to his computer screen. "What the hell does that even mean?"

"You have to put the bait out there," Sidney told him in that big-sister tone he'd hated all his life. "You can't put an ad out for a person who can do everything, including pick up your nasty work boots from the shop because you have them fixed instead of buying new freaking boots like a normal person."

"I like these boots. They're broken in," he defended.

"They're just plain broken." She rolled her eyes. It had no effect on him anymore. She could roll her eyes until they fell out of her head, and he wouldn't break a sweat. He was immune.

"I still don't see why you can't work for me part-time." He tried using his adorable little-brother pout. Apparently it had lost its effectiveness around the time her eye rolling had stopped working on him.

"*Part*-time? I don't even work *full* time. I work *over* time, Zane. I want to stay home with this kid." She pointed at her giant stomach for emphasis. "I want to be a mom. I can't do that if I have to fly off to God-knows-where at the drop of a hat to handle a client's insurance claims, or oversee transport of a moldy old boat. Besides, in another month I'm not going to be able to fly until after I have the baby. Doctor's orders," she sang the last part.

"Uh-huh. I want a second opinion."

Sidney's OB-GYN was also her husband. It was both convenient and creepy.

"Come on, Zane. This arrangement was only meant to be temporary anyway. I was supposed to stay on until you got up and running."

"I know." It was true. He hadn't wanted Sidney to work for him at all back in the beginning. He'd wanted to do it all on his own, but now he didn't know what he'd do without her. "Just make sure the person can read my mind. You know how I feel about verbal communication," he grumbled as he closed down his laptop to leave.

"You're going to have to work on that."

He sighed and checked his phone for the time. "I gotta go."

"Have fun. Tell the guys I said hi. Maybe you should talk to a woman. Go out on a date."

Zane narrowed his eyes at his sister. "I've had enough bossing for one day."

She put both hands up in surrender.

When he got to the Blue Star Bar, Josh and Paul were already there.

The bartender gave him a nod when he sat down, and he nodded back. This was their silent exchange that meant he wanted a beer. Verbal communication was overrated.

"How are the kids?" Zane asked Josh.

The answer was a giant smile as he held out his phone, scrolling through photos of his children. They hadn't changed much from the photos he'd shared two weeks ago.

"My oldest is riding her bike without training wheels," Josh shared.

"Next she'll be asking for the car keys," Paul said. Since Paul worked for Zane, he'd just seen him at the office an hour ago. But this was guy time.

"Or introducing you to her boyfriend," Zane added.

"Shut up." Josh looked a little green at the thought. "I'm going to make sure she knows all boys are idiots."

"Trust me, girls know that from birth," Paul pointed out.

"How are the women folk?" Zane asked, knowing that was the next stage of the conversation. Paul was engaged and Josh had been married for years.

The smile on Paul's face echoed the happiness that had been on Josh's. "Taylor's busy with the wedding. I try to help when she asks what flowers I like or if I want a black tux or gray, but honestly I don't care about the details. I just want to marry her and go on the honeymoon." Spoken like any man anywhere.

"I'm planning a romantic getaway for Bree's birthday." Josh beamed. "My mom is keeping the kids."

"You're not planning on number three are you?" Zane teased.

"We're not planning anything. But if it happens, it happens. If it doesn't, we're already blessed." Josh smiled and took a sip of his beer. These men sure seemed a lot happier than Zane.

"What's new with you?" Josh asked.

"I'm looking for a new assistant to replace my sister."

"Couldn't talk her out of it, huh?"

"Nope."

"Well, good luck," Paul said with a wince. Paul had worked for him for the past three years and was his top mechanic. "I swear that woman is a superhero."

"So you think I should put an ad out for a superhero instead of an executive production coordinator?"

"What is that?"

"It's the title Sid came up with to describe all the things she does."

"'Goddess' sounds more accurate."

"Goddess of bossing me around."

"Let me guess. She suggested you go out on a date," Josh said.
Zane nodded.

"She's not wrong. When was the last time you went on a date?" Paul asked.

A date. He hadn't dated anyone in months. He'd gone out with a woman during one of his jobs in Alabama. But when the job was over so were they. He hadn't bothered mentioning it to his friends. It hadn't been important. "I own a business. I don't have time to date."

Such was the life of the sole proprietor. Too busy for anything remotely fun, but somehow it was rewarding nonetheless. He loved tearing into a new project, seeing something old come back to life and become useful and beautiful again.

New wasn't always better, except when it came to wiring. In that case, new was better on the inside when covered up with a classically restored exterior. He prided himself on returning a crusty old sea vessel to its magnificent splendor. And though it paid quite well, he measured his success by the size of the owners' smiles when they saw their boats after restoration.

His sister had helped him keep things straight for the past five years. Now he would be on his own. Strike that: he'd be stuck with some stranger.

* * *

After waking up on her brother's sofa with a hangover that could kill a dead person, Kenley decided she couldn't stay unemployed for very long. Not only was it economically unfeasible, it was also dangerous to her health.

"Hello?" Rachel answered on the second ring, sounding a little too chipper and a lot too loud.

"I just wanted you to know, after thorough analysis, your prediction that getting wasted was not going to help my cause is sound."

Rachel giggled. "You always were a lightweight."

"I feel like a lightweight sat on my head."

"Feel better."

"Thanks."

She managed to get up and shuffle to the kitchen where Vanessa was equally chipper and loud.

"What is with you people?" Kenley complained while rubbing her temple.

"Are you ready to start the first day of the rest of your life?"

"Actually, I'm ready to crawl into a hole."

"No. Don't do that. You need to get a résumé together and start sending it out. I'll help as soon I get Hannah on the bus," Vanessa said.

"Did anyone ever tell you you're a force?"

"It's come up. But I've heard the same thing about you. You just need to get the wind back in your sails." She paused, a smirk teasing the edge of her lips. "See what I did there? Boats. Sails. Get it?" She chuckled at her own joke as she held out a cup of tea.

"Very funny."

"You also need to get laid."

"Thank you."

* * *

As Kenley took the train back to the city later that day she tried to formulate a plan. Her friends had told her what she already knew. And what her checkbook would be screaming in a matter of weeks.

She needed a job. Her father and stepmother had downsized and moved to a fifty-five-and-older community. She couldn't stay with them. While Vanessa had offered her brother's basement domain for the short term, she didn't want to infringe on their romantic—and nauseating—lives.

After another cup of tea and some Tylenol, Kenley sat at her computer in her warmest pajamas to start working on her future. Three hours later she held up her two-page résumé.

"Make my life." She rubbed her palms together before she began sending it out.

A fresh start was just around the corner.

# Chapter 2

"Sidney!" Zane called for his sister as he looked around his desk. She'd covered the entire surface with crap. Trays and other matching things, with the sole purpose of organizing his stuff. He hated when she messed up his system. Not that *system* was really the word for it, but he knew where things were.

"What?" she bellowed rather than get up.

"Where is the bid for the Wheeler job?" he yelled.

"It's not Wheeler, it's Weller, and it's in your *In* bin," she yelled back. They sounded like their parents—yelling from room to room instead of actually going to speak to the other person. And he knew it was Wheeler. As organized as she was, Sidney couldn't remember anyone's name.

"Which one of these bins in my *In* bin?" he shouted.

"The one that says *in* on it."

"None of them say *in*." He held up his hands in confusion as she tromped into his office, looking indignant and huge.

"This one!" She pointed to the side of the bin facing the door, away from him. "Right here." She pulled out the file and all but threw it at him. "Have you looked at any of the résumés that have come in?"

"Um, not yet. I haven't had a chance." He'd *not had a chance* for the entire month since she'd placed the ad.

"You promised me you would look at them last week. You don't seem to understand the urgency here, little brother. I am going to have this baby whether you're in denial of that fact or not. If you don't stop dragging your worn-out work boots and hire someone, you're going to be doing everything on your own. Do you understand what I am saying?" She had The Tone. She meant business.

"Yes. I understand. Can't you just interview the people who seem the most like you and then let me meet them? You know, so I won't be so overwhelmed." He wasn't as worried about being overwhelmed as he was about the impossibility of finding someone who could replace his sister, but he couldn't tell her that or her head would grow to the size of her enormous belly.

"Right." Sidney narrowed her eyes at him as if she knew he was playing her. "You'd better like who I pick."

"I will. If they're anything like you, I'm sure I'll love them." He gave her a grin.

"You should stop talking now." Her stony look silenced him as she walked out. She'd thought he was joking, but he was actually being honest that time.

"Yes ma'am." He knew when he was pressing his luck.

\* \* \*

Kenley was almost at the end of her rope when she finally got the phone call on Valentine's Day. After moving in with Vanessa and her brother—with their exuberant child and vocal mating sessions—she was just about to ask her father if she could wear a disguise and move into their place at the senior community.

Hope was restored when Sidney, from New Haven Custom Boats, called. She had an interview.

It had been a month since she'd sent them her résumé. The woman apologized for the time lapse, blaming her brother who owned the company.

"I have an interview!" she screamed as soon as she found Vanessa in the kitchen.

"Yay. With who?"

"The boat place in New Haven. The one with the occasional travel."

"Awesome. I knew that would be the one."

"I don't have the job. I only have an interview, but it's a start. Freakin' Ruth has me job-blocked from every opening in Manhattan." Kenley was still in contact with her friend and coworker, Alyssa, who'd told her Ruth still had it out for her.

She'd also fired another person for sleeping with her husband. Alyssa'd had the right idea when she'd suggested Ruth fire her husband instead of her employees.

"Maybe this will be better. My last two interviews went well, and then they didn't call. Hopefully her evil hasn't spread to the New Haven area. I have my fingers crossed."

"This is it, Ken, I feel it."

"It would have been handy if you would have had a feeling that going to that party was going to cause a problem for me."

"Don't question the force." Great. Vanessa was channeling Yoda now. "What are you going to wear?"

"My black skirt and my—"

"No." Vanessa shook her head.

"What? I look good in that skirt."

"This is a marina. They're not going to want someone who looks like a supermodel."

"I don't look *that* good in that skirt."

"You know what I mean. You need to look professional, yet dependable and efficient and not too stuffy."

"So… my pajamas with my hair pulled up in a twist and a watch?"

"Black slacks, sturdy shoes, and a tailored shirt. Pull your hair back in a ponytail."

"Do you have a feeling about this?" Kenley asked.

"No. I just looked it up on my iPad." She held it up.

\* \* \*

The next day, after outfitting herself exactly as Vanessa ordered, and spinning in numerous circles so her friend could approve, Kenley parked in front of the building that housed New Haven Custom Boats, also known as *her future*. She was planning on charming the bejesus out of whomever she needed to in order to get this job.

As she walked to the door she could almost hear the choir of angels singing a harmonic "Ahhhhhh." And did a beam of sunlight just come down to illuminate the door? Maybe.

She opened the door and stood, stunned, in the room.

The lobby, which also housed the receptionist area, was not tiny, but it seemed so with the amount of large, tropical plants taking up the area, giving the room a rainforest appeal.

"Hello?" someone yelled from the hall—a woman.

"Hi. I'm Kenley Carmichael. I have a one o'clock interview with Sidney. I'm a little early." Twenty minutes, according to the watch she'd decided to wear.

"I'm Sidney," the very round woman said as she wiped her lips with a napkin. Kenley assumed she was pregnant, but knew better than to say anything until it was confirmed. It was quite an embarrassing lesson to learn.

"It's nice to meet you. I didn't mean to interrupt your lunch. I could just sit and wait until you're finished." Sitting was going to be an issue since every square inch of horizontal space was covered in foliage.

"Come on back to my other office. We also call it the lunchroom. Now that I'm eating for two I spend more time there than my desk." She rubbed her large belly affectionately. Kenley smiled, having guessed correctly. This time.

"Have a seat," Sidney gestured to a table. There were file folders everywhere and on the edge of the table sat a salad and a giant hamburger. "My husband is an OB-GYN so he insists I eat right. The salad is me keeping up my end of the deal. The burger is none of his concern."

Kenley laughed and made a gesture of zipping her lips and throwing the key over her shoulder.

"So the job consists mostly of office work. Paying our suppliers and sending out customer statements. My brother handles customer invoicing himself. You may have noticed the large building out back. It's a covered slip for working on boats here. We service local boats. But our main focus is restoration. Depending on the size of the boat and the location, it's not always possible to bring the boat here to restore, so the team works on it offsite. Occasionally only the motor is shipped in or other pieces of the craft."

Kenley nodded.

"We have a small team that stays onsite to handle local calls and repairs. And three other guys make up the restoration team. I keep their schedules straight and make sure everyone gets paid. Sometimes I go out to a job to help with insurance work or quotes if the others are tied up."

"I wouldn't mind traveling."

"Okay, Kendra, tell me a little about yourself." Oh no. Should she correct her for saying her name wrong? Would it matter? Probably.

"Actually, it's Kenley. I know it's a weird name. I was adopted. My parents decided to keep my given name." She winced, not meaning to use the orphan card to get a job. She was nervous and it made her babble.

Sidney burst into tears, and Kenley cursed herself for correcting her.

"I'm so sorry. You know what? You can call me anything you want. Kendra is fine. I like the name Kendra, love it even. Please don't cry."

"I'm sorry. I just can't imagine a little baby being left alone in the world."

Kenley had been almost three when she was left alone in the world, but she had the sense to keep quiet.

"I'm not a very emotional person usually, it just comes on me at times." Sidney worked to gain control of herself while wiping her eyes with another napkin. "Go on, Ken-LEE." She enunciated the name correctly this time. "I apologize. I have it right here in front of me, but along with the hormones comes pregnancy brain." She rolled her eyes at her condition.

"Oh, believe me, I understand. My two best friends were pregnant at the same time. I think I should have gotten a medal—a plaque at the very least."

"You don't have kids?" Sidney asked, tilting her head to the side in that way that says, *You're old enough to bear children, why have you not produced any yet?*

"Uh, no. But I imagine you would want someone without any strings, so they could travel whenever necessary." Bravo.

"Yes. That would probably be easier for the person taking the position. Though I wouldn't say it would be a deal breaker." Of course not, because that would be illegal. Kenley only smiled.

"Okay, so I know you were adopted." Her lip trembled, but she held it together. "And I know you're no longer working at your job of six years at Hasher and Bourne."

"That's correct."

"And what happened there?" Sidney asked as if this were the easiest question ever. It wasn't.

Kenley swallowed and squared her shoulders.

"I've wanted to move back to New Haven for some time, actually. And I finally had the opportunity to explore that option recently."

"Were you fired?" Sidney asked.

"Yes. I was." Kenley's shoulders slumped as she let out a sigh. "I'm never going to get a job, am I?"

"Let's not jump to any conclusions just yet. I like that you didn't lie. You twisted it pretty well, but it wasn't a lie." Sidney smirked.

Kenley felt her lips pull up on one side. "I would prefer to call it *spin*. It's a marketing technique."

"You're pretty damn good at it."

"I didn't get past you."

"Well, I have my mommy powers kicking in, so not much gets by me these days." Sidney patted her stomach as Kenley nodded. "So since I know you won't lie. Did you steal from the company?"

"No." Kenley shook her head adamantly.

"Did you do something unethical?"

"No." She really hadn't.

"You can jump in here with the story at any time. I'm pregnant for crying out loud."

"Ah, yes. I remember this stage of the pregnancy from my friends. The guilting-everyone-into-anything stage."

"It's turning out to be one of my favorites." They laughed together.

"I was accused of sleeping with my boss's husband during a party at their home."

"And you didn't?"

"No. Even if I was a homewrecker, which I swear to you I'm not, I'd at least have enough respect not to wreck the home while in the actual home."

"And your employer didn't believe you when you told her it wasn't true?"

"I might not have handled the situation well. Instead of stating my case, and explaining I hadn't had an affair with her husband, I may have looked appalled and said something to the effect of 'There is no way in hell I would ever sleep with someone who looked like him.' Afterward, I realized she might have taken that as an insult, having in fact slept with him herself many times."

Sidney was laughing so hard she needed the napkin to wipe the tears away again. "Not your type?"

"He had these hideously hairy knuckles." Kenley shivered.

"Okay, so you didn't sleep with King Kong. What did you do for Hasher and Bourne for the last six years?"

And with that, Sidney moved on to the important part of the interview. The part where Kenley could prove herself a worthy employee. Which was exactly what she hoped to have the chance to be.

\* \* \*

Sidney waddled into his office with a file and a smile.

"Yes?" Zane waited.

"I want you to meet an applicant while I take the next appointment. Not that it matters. I want this one, so you're going to hire her no matter what."

"You know forcing me just makes me dislike the person already," he warned.

"I know, but you'll change your mind when you meet her. She's perfect. She's an extremely organized multitasker with no responsibilities, which would make it easy for her to jump on a plane when you have an emergency. You're going to love her, I promise."

"Can you just send her in so I can get it over with?" He held out his hand for the employment file sent straight from heaven. He would hire the perfect person and be done with it. After all, why would he need to waste his time on anyone else if she was so perfect?

"Her name is Kelsey Carpenter. I'll send her right in." Sidney pressed her palms together and looked up at the ceiling as if thanking God himself for sending this angel to work for him.

"Thanks." He plopped the folder down on the schematics he'd been wrestling with since the night before.

He opened the file as the woman walked in. Sidney hadn't even given him a chance to read a single word, or develop his own questions. He raised his head to see her standing there with a bright smile on her face just like the one that had haunted his dreams for years.

He choked and looked down at the paper.

"You're not Kelsey Carpenter," he said stupidly. This wasn't happening. Courtney Bishop had just walked into his office. He'd had a huge crush on her all through high school. And now she was here. But when he scanned the application for her name to see if she was married, he didn't see the words he expected.

"No. It's Kenley Carmichael. Sorry. Sidney kept getting it wrong and after she cried when I corrected her, I just thought it was easier to let it go."

No. This wasn't Courtney. Her voice was different. It was her hair and that billion-watt smile that made him think of Courtney. This girl was taller and didn't have a beauty mark on her chin.

"Yes. She's been getting a lot of things mixed up lately," Zane tapped the pages together and tried to focus on the print.

"It goes with pregnancy." She laughed.

"You have kids?"

"No. But I have friends who do." She winced as if her answer wasn't acceptable.

She tilted her head as he scanned her paperwork, not seeing anything. This woman had completely unnerved him. The way she'd walked in his office exuding confidence and flipping her blond hair over her shoulder. This woman might not be Courtney Bishop, but she was the type.

The kind of woman who thought she was too good for him. The type who wouldn't even remember his name or give him the time of day.

Back in high school it had been the classic tale of the dorky comic-book nerd in awe of the princess cheerleader. She had broken his heart every time she went out with one of the football players and she hadn't even known it.

Not that he'd ever had the courage to ask her out. Or spoken to Courtney like she was a real human woman.

Eventually, he grew into himself. In college he had the good fortune to attract a bossy girl who'd told him what to wear, how to cut his hair, and had forced him to wear contacts. Once he'd been transformed into the sexy guy she wanted, she grew bored and moved on to another struggling project.

He was able to relax into a middle ground and came out of college confident and ready to take on the world. Which he was doing just fine on his own, despite his sister's constant disapproval with his lack of a love life.

His sister's words from a few seconds ago echoed in his head. *You're going to love her.*

Sidney didn't know he'd already loved a girl like this a long time ago and she'd crushed him thoroughly. Not that he was blaming Kenley personally, but he was sure she had left some shy boy's heart in rubble too.

He picked up the paper in front of him and stared at it, trying to form the letters into words.

"Were you a cheerleader in high school?"

She looked surprised by the odd question, and rightfully so. But after a second, she nodded. "Yes."

He couldn't hire her. He couldn't go back to the Zane who felt helpless and insignificant in the presence of a pretty, unattainable girl. He would have to come up with an excuse to reject Sidney's request.

He nodded, more about his decision than about what was on the page. Then, realizing he should actually read it first, he focused on the words.

She had been at her previous job in Manhattan for a long time, with more responsibilities than the pay afforded. He glanced up at her, seeing her bite her lip nervously.

It was at that moment it hit him. Something he should have known all along, but somehow had overlooked.

Kenley Carmichael, as beautiful and amazing as she was, was still just a regular person. A normal person who now needed a job.

He let the anger and hurt wash away, and reassessed the situation. He would consider her as he would any other candidate. She would not be punished for the past, of which she was not an active participant. Nor would he favor her for being pretty. He would base his decision to hire her solely on her merits and ability to do the job.

Which, granted, should have been the objective in the first place.

As he read through her application and résumé, it became increasingly evident there was nothing he could use to keep him from hiring her.

Then, there it was. The kink in her armor.

"It says you left your last job for personal reasons."

"Yes." She continued to bite her lip, but made no attempt to explain.

He let out a sigh.

"In my line of work, when someone puts down *personal reasons*, it either means he stole something, came to the job shit-faced, or he forgot to come to work at all. Either way, it usually means fired, not left for actual personal reasons. Is that what it means in this instance?" he asked, pointing at the paper on his desk.

He was almost giddy with the opportunity to send her off with her tail between her legs. Despite his decision to look at her fairly, he still had wounds that had been torn open at the sight of her.

She looked down at the floor and twisted her hands together.

"I did get fired from my last job. But not because I didn't come to work or because I had been drinking. I didn't steal anything either." She let out a determined sigh. "It was a misunderstanding."

"Do you care to elaborate?" he pushed for details he didn't deserve.

"Not really."

"I need to be able to trust the person I hire for this position completely. All cards on the table."

She looked stunned.

"Sidney said meeting with you was a formality. She told me she was the one who made the final decision."

"She thinks she is, but she isn't. You would be working with me. She won't be working here at all."

"Fine." She shrugged and looked up at the ceiling. "My former boss accused me of sleeping with her husband. I didn't do it, but what does that matter? She fired me and now no one will hire me because I'm wearing a big old scarlet A on my chest. Who cares about the truth, right? It's not nearly as exciting as a scandal, or having someone to blame for her crappy marriage." She stood up and headed for the door. "I'm sorry I wasted your time, Zane. It was nice meeting you."

He should have been happy the interview was over so he could finally breathe, but all he could think about was the way her voice had sounded when she'd said his name.

# Chapter 3

Kenley was cursing and casting violent, powerless spells in the direction of her old boss as she walked to her car. She would not cry again over another opportunity lost because of that vicious woman. She wouldn't.

She pulled out her phone and called Rachel.

"It didn't work out," Kenley said as tears broke loose and ran down her cheeks. *Damn it.*

"Another one?" Rachel sighed. "I'm sorry, sweetie. Let's go get a drink."

"If we keep drinking every time I get turned down because I'm an alleged whore, we're going to have to start going to meetings."

"Fine, then come over here and we'll bake cookies." She offered a higher calorie option.

"See you soon."

Kenley drove slowly, letting the drive take even longer. She hadn't been lying when she'd told Zane it was nice to meet him. It was.

Despite his harsh demeanor, she'd found him to be adorable, in a manly kind of way. He had dark, shaggy hair that hung over his bright blue eyes. Kind eyes.

He seemed like the kind of guy she would have gone out on a date with, if she did such things. She wasn't good at dating. She'd started too late.

Back in high school her mother had encouraged her to go out, knowing Kenley was spending most of her evenings and weekends at home with her. But it had seemed ridiculous to go to a party or a football game when her mother's clock was winding down.

She hadn't wanted to look back one day and regret not spending as much time as she could with the woman who had taken her in and loved her as if she were her own. And today, as she made her way to Rachel's cookie factory, she realized she had been right.

"Damn it." Kenley wiped the tear from her eye and pulled into the driveway. She'd unleashed the tears, good luck getting them to stop anytime soon. She missed her mother every day, but she could honestly say she didn't regret giving up the dates, parties, or football games so they could share every minute they were given together. "Mom? Why is this happening?" she asked the empty car.

She would have liked to work at the marina. She would have liked to move to New Haven and start fresh, meet someone who would understand why she didn't want to jump into bed after two drinks. Maybe this stranger could get to know her, and she'd tell him about her predicament. He'd be understanding and would help lead her into that next phase of her life. The sex phase. Maybe she'd be so good at it right out of the box he'd ask her to marry him, just because he couldn't get enough. Did she even want to be married?

Sure it seemed ideal. Someone to count on. Someone committed to love you even in the mornings or during the flu. But she'd seen the other side. She'd seen her father utterly heartbroken as he watched his wife spend her last days in pain.

For some reason he'd signed up for marriage a second time. So maybe the good did outweigh the bad.

It would be nice to have someone to have dinner with each night. They could share stories about their workday. Maybe after dinner they'd snuggle in front of a fire with a glass of wine. They'd start kissing, and then he'd slip his hands into her sweatpants—not the ripped sweatpants with the missing drawstring, but a sexy pair she didn't own yet.

"What are you doing? You look like you're thinking about licking someone." Rachel knocked on the glass by her head, startling her out of her unrealistic day dream.

Kenley got out of the car and hugged her friend. Rachel didn't ask for details about the ill-fated interview. They made cookies and talked until Kenley felt better.

With a giant pile of cookies, Kenley went back to her temporary home and played dolls with her niece. After helping tuck her in and taking her turn with a bedtime story, she went out to the garage where her worldly possessions were stored. It took her three tries to find the box she was looking for, but she finally pulled out her photo album. She found a photo of herself when she was probably five. In the picture Kenley was wearing her mother's heels and struggling to carry her briefcase.

She'd liked pretending she was going to work.

Feeling inspired, she hung the photo on the door of her makeshift room in the basement so it could motivate her in the morning.

As she curled up on the sofa she thought about normal things. How long would she have to sleep on her brother's sofa? Why had she spent three hundred dollars on a ski jacket when she didn't even ski? Stupid. Stupid. Stupid.

But when she was done berating herself for her poor planning, she thought about Zane and the missed opportunity with him. If he'd just given her a chance, she would have proven herself. He would have been more than pleased with her performance.

This thought sparked a different kind of remorse. He was a big, muscular man. Strapping even, if virgins were allowed to use such a word.

She slipped off to sleep remembering the look on his face when she'd first walked into his office. For a moment he looked as if she'd made his day by just being there.

* * *

"I'm leaving today and I'm not coming back," Sidney snapped as she flopped down on the sofa in his office. "I had her in the bag."

"I'm sorry." Zane had apologized twenty or more times since Kenley had run out of his office the day before. He knew Sidney wouldn't abandon him. He was their mother's favorite, and Sidney wouldn't want to deal with the wrath if he told her Sidney was picking on him.

"You're not sorry. You're stupid and stubborn and"—she let her shoulders fall—"damn it! I can't think of the other word I want to use, but it starts with an S for emphasis."

"Look, I know you thought she was great, but I wasn't convinced she was going to be a good fit. And since it's *my* company and *I'm* the one who has to work with this person, *my* opinion is the only one that matters."

She looked him over, studying him, reading his mind in that way that she did.

"Stop it," he said, holding up his hands as if to block her powers.

"Stop what?"

"Stop looking at me."

"Why? Are you going to tell Mom on me?"

Maybe. "No. I have work to do. Let me know when more applications come in." He tried to sound both busy and firm.

"Before I go to the trouble of screening any other potential employees, maybe you could tell me what it was about Kelsey you didn't like." She raised her brow at him.

"For starters, her name wasn't even Kelsey, it was Kenley."

"Okay, that was my fault, not hers. What else?"

"I just didn't get a good vibe." The vibe was more than good. Too damn good.

"I'm sorry, we're hiring someone based on *vibes*?" she asked, eyes wide. "Do you have some kind of device I should use to measure a person's vibes?"

"I'm going to be working closely with this person. They're going to be like an appendage. It has to be a good fit, and this wasn't."

"You were able to tell it wasn't going to work out in the ten minutes she was in your office?"

"What do you want me to say?" He raised his shoulders. He didn't want a constant reminder of how his life might have been different if he'd had the balls to ask out Courtney Bishop. And he surely didn't want to go back to feeling like the nerdy kid in awe of the princess. She'd even been a cheerleader. He could practically smell it on her. *Eau de Too Good for You.*

"I'd like you to say I can hire her. She'd be so easy to train, and she could start right away."

"It's not about you."

"Fine. Give me the application and I'll file it." She held out her hand, and he shoved the papers toward her.

"Hmm. It is Kenley," she noted as she headed for the door. Then she stopped and turned around. "Didn't she kind of look like that girl you had a thing for in high school?"

Shit. He let out a sigh and shrugged.

"Maybe a little." Way wrong thing to say. He should have pretended he didn't know what she was talking about. That always worked. Why had he fallen for her trap? Her eyes flared and she stepped closer, tapping the folder.

"So you're not going to hire her because she reminds you of the girl who rejected you ten years ago?"

"You wouldn't understand, and I don't want to talk about it. It doesn't matter, because I'm not hiring her." As forceful as he'd made it sound, Sidney flopped back down on his sofa and scowled at him.

"Listen up, little brother. You're being an asshole, and I'm pretty sure it's illegal in some way. Discrimination or something."

"You can't discriminate against someone because you don't like them."

"Why didn't you like her? Was she nasty to you? Pick on you?"

"No."

She twisted her mouth to the side, which was her common expression when she was trying to figure him out.

"I hope you don't expect me to leave until you've explained yourself, because it's not going to happen." He knew her well enough to know she really wouldn't leave until he told her the truth. Plus, he wasn't sure if she could physically get herself to her feet. She was enormous.

"Fine. Okay. It's going to sound ridiculous, but she did remind me of Courtney, who may have broken my heart." His face was hot. Why was his office so fucking hot? It was the end of February for Christ's sake. "And forgive me if I don't want to walk into my office every day and be reminded of that feeling. It's too painful."

Sidney did a great job of keeping the laughter in. She even looked compassionate.

"I'm sorry," was all she managed to get out.

"So you see why I might be uncomfortable working with her."

Sidney tilted her head to the side while she thought it over.

"Nope. Sorry. That's not going to cut it. She's qualified. She's available to start immediately, and she's very pleasant. If there's a problem it would be on *you*, not her. Why should she be punished because you used to be in love with a girl who looks like her?"

"I wasn't in love with her," he corrected quickly. He was so in love with her. He used to pretend his pillow—never mind.

"Are you sure about that? Because most people don't have this kind of issue over a ten-year-old crush."

"She makes me feel like an awkward teenager again."

"Again, your problem, not hers." Drat. It was time for a compromise or else she wouldn't stop until he'd caved. He couldn't cave on this.

"She was only the first interview. Let's see who else comes in, and if we don't find anyone better, I'll reevaluate on Thursday when I get back."

"Fair enough." She smiled and left his office without another argument.

"Damn it." She'd agreed too easily. Somehow he'd made a fatal error.

\* \* \*

"Really? No one else? Not *one* other person?" Zane asked his sister after finishing the second interview on Thursday afternoon.

"Nope. Sorry."

He should have known no one better would apply. His sister had made up her mind, which meant the most perfect candidate could have come in and offered to work for free, and Sidney would have passed the person over just so Zane would be miserable.

The only other interviews she'd set up were one with an eighty-year-old woman who didn't like to fly and a girl out of high school who'd kept checking her phone the whole time.

He wasn't surprised to come in on Friday morning to find Kenley's application back on his desk with a sticky note that said:

*Hire this girl or you'll be sorry. She's perfect and she's not Courtney.*
The truth was, he couldn't argue.

Kenley *was* perfect for the job. She had a degree in business, had years of experience and stellar recommendations, with the exception of her last boss who said she was unethical and incompetent. When Zane had asked the woman why it had taken her six years to figure that out, the woman hung up on him.

Unable to put it off any longer, he took a deep breath and picked up the phone to call the woman—who would be a constant reminder of his past inadequacies—to ask if she would work for him.

Never, when he was a dorky kid back in school, would he have expected basic social hierarchies to shift so he would be in the position of power over one of the elite.

Long live the king. And God save his heart.

* * *

Kenley pounded on the punching bag even after her hands hurt. She had taped a photo of Ruth at the top of the bag so she could pretend she was beating up her old boss.

Ironically it was a picture of her and her husband taken at the New Year's party. She decided it was only fitting since both of them needed a good smack upside the head.

"He's not even good-looking," she yelled as she punched the bag over and over. "You've ruined my life!"

During her rant and assault on an inanimate object her phone rang. When she didn't recognize the number, her heart started pounding for a new reason. Was someone calling for an interview? After the disaster with Zane two weeks ago, she'd put out about a million résumés. She only needed one to get her in the door.

She shook off her boxing gloves as quickly as she could and picked up the phone.

"Hello?" She only then noticed she was out of breath. "I was working out, nothing else," she added stupidly in breathy pants.

She heard a man chuckle on the other end of the line.

"Is this Kenley Carmichael?"

"Yes." She worked hard to calm her breathing so she didn't sound like a whacko.

"This is Zane Jackson from New Haven Custom Boats."

"Yes?" She couldn't help but sound confused. He'd made things perfectly clear when she'd retreated out of his office.

"I was wondering if you were still available for the job. If you aren't, it's fine. No worries."

"I'm still available."

"Oh. Okay." He almost sounded disappointed. "Then I'd like to offer you the position."

"Really? I mean—thank you! Thank you so much. You won't regret this, I promise."

They briefly went over her salary—which was more than fair—and he told her to be at the office at eight on Monday.

"No problem, and thank you for believing me," she said when they'd wrapped up the business portion of the phone call.

"I don't have a husband so I figured I wouldn't have anything to worry about one way or the other."

"Right." She frowned. "See you on Monday." It would have felt better if he'd hired her because he believed she'd do a good job, but getting out of her brother's basement was the most important thing.

"Actually, I won't be there when you come in, you'll need to get with Sidney. I made sure she knows your name."

"Thanks," she said again before they hung up.

She screamed with excitement and hit the bag a few more times out of joy, realizing too late she didn't have gloves on anymore. She winced, but was too happy to let the pain deter her.

She tore down the photo of her old boss, ripped it up into small pieces, and threw it into the trash on the way to the shower. There would be celebrating tonight.

She started by calling her father, who was happy and reminded her how many times he'd told her everything would work out. He put her stepmother on the phone, who asked all the important details.

"Do they have good benefits?" she asked, much like Kenley's mother would have had she been alive. Kenley felt blessed that she'd had two wonderful women in her life who loved her as their own, even though neither had given birth to her. Long ago she'd stopped wondering about the woman who had.

"Yes."

"Are they paying you well?"

"Yes. And they gave me a week vacation to start."

"That's nice."

When her parents were as thrilled as she was, she got off the phone to call Rachel, followed by Alyssa, from Hasher and Bourne, and anyone else she could think of.

Vanessa invited her out for a celebratory drink.

That night when they got back, Kenley tried to calm down enough to get some sleep. She found that while alleviating the worry of a paycheck was definitely something to be happy about, she was more excited about the actual job.

Of all the companies she'd applied to, this seemed like the nicest place to work. She couldn't help but think it had something to do with it being owned by a handsome man. Something about Zane Jackson's eyes made her think he'd be a sweet guy when he wasn't trying to be intimidating. She was actually looking forward to getting to know him.

* * *

"We have a new Sidney," Zane told Paul and Brady as they walked down a dock in Mississippi toward their next job. While Paul was generally based in New Haven, he was the engine guy and often came out to give a quote. Brady handled transportation and Zane did everything else.

"No way she'll be anywhere as good as Sidney," Paul said.

"What's she look like?" Brady asked at the same time.

Zane stopped walking to stare at Brady momentarily. The man was blond and large, with tattoos. He was ex-military and hooked up more than he actually dated. Possessiveness twisted in Zane's stomach. It was stupid. No doubt, Kenley the Beautiful would be all over the attentions of someone who looked like Brady. But he should at least attempt to protect his new hire from heartbreak.

"It doesn't matter what she looks like. She's an employee, which means she's off limits."

"I know. I'm just wondering if I'll have something nice to look at when I work with her."

"She's—don't look at her," he ordered, sounding like a crazy person.

"What is this?" Paul asked while squinting and pointing at Zane.

"This is nothing. This is me being protective of my workers. If she was trying to ogle one of you, I'd put a stop to it."

"Please don't put the stop to any ogling on my behalf. I personally love to be ogled." Brady laughed. "Besides, Sidney already told me you used to be in love with a girl in high school who looks like our new girl so I'm not going to crowd your plate."

"Oh." Paul whistled. "So you broke down and hired her? Are you going to be able to handle it?" He looked genuinely concerned, like the good friend he was.

"Freakin' Sidney. When that kid comes out looking like a demon, my theory of her being the devil will be proven," Zane grumbled.

Brady was laughing too hard to speak, so Zane went to talk to the owner of the boat instead.

Of course he could handle it. He was not that stupid boy anymore. He could work with this woman and not turn into a drooling idiot.

She was no one special. Just an employee.

# Chapter 4

Kenley sang along with the radio for her twenty-five minute commute to work on Monday morning. It was nice to be able to use her car again. She hadn't been able to keep it in the city, so it had been her parents' spare car.

She found herself clenching the wheel. Occasionally, she would glance over at the car next to her and smile. No one smiled back.

Apparently they weren't starting new jobs today. They weren't beginning careers as Executive Production Coordinators with a growing company. They didn't have a sweet, sexy boss with a gorgeous smile and kind blue eyes, and muscles, and—

"Knock it the hell off," she scolded herself for getting dreamy about Zane.

By the time she pulled in—thirteen minutes early—she had already decided she would start looking for an apartment in New Haven as soon as possible. She needed to get out of Vanessa and Eric's house. While she loved her brother, seeing him every day was too much. Not to mention how she was growing tired of changing doll clothes over and over at the demand of her six-year-old niece.

"Good morning," Sidney greeted her when she walked in.

"Morning," Kenley answered as she looked around the transformed office space. It was more office than rainforest now.

"I already had my husband come move my plants to our sunroom."

"Ah." Inside Kenley was dancing with glee. She didn't have any plants and was convinced she would have killed the monstrous foliage in a matter of days.

"They were mine. Zane always hated them, but I just added more when he was away." She shrugged it off.

"Is he here?" She tried to hide the hope in her voice as she glanced toward the hallway leading to his office. He'd said he wouldn't be in, but maybe his plans changed.

"Nope. He's going to be out for the next two weeks. I'll be training you all on my own. The Friday after next is my last day, so you'll be going solo after that."

"Okay." She hid her disappointment and forced a smile.

They spent the morning going over the hiring forms and taking a more extensive tour of the huge building attached to the smaller office. It was empty of humans except for the two of them and Paul, who was up to his elbows in a greasy engine.

He seemed nice. He mentioned he was getting married, twice. Was he worried she was going to try to seduce him? He gestured at the boats surrounding him. They all had catchy names painted in artistic fonts.

Back inside the warm office, Sidney gave her a list of the other workers along with their cell numbers.

"So basically, if you can't get Zane on the phone and it's important, call Paul. Paul has an office in here, but he spends most of his time out on road or in the shop. If you can't get Paul, then try Brady. If Brady doesn't answer you'll just have to wait, because none of these other guys know much about the business end of things."

"Got it."

"My guess is Zane will be more likely to take your calls than he was to take mine." Sidney gave Kenley a knowing smile and Kenley wondered what that meant.

"So do customers come in?" Kenley asked, mostly to change the subject.

"Locals will stop in to schedule service or pay a bill. We have some cash in the box in Zane's office. We take checks if you get a copy of their license. And you can run a credit card on this little gizmo that snaps in the tablet. Most everyone else will call ahead to make sure Zane is in, and make an appointment. Over the years, people have learned how sporadic his schedule is."

Surely he had to spend some time here working on boats and running his business. She hoped, as Sid showed her how to fill out a service ticket and where to put them.

"Paul has the emergency line, so those calls go directly to him. If he's out of the area, he'll transfer the calls to one of the other guys who stay here. You shouldn't need to worry about that. If you get a call that someone is dead in the water, transfer the call to Paul." Kenley nodded.

Lunch was brought in from down the street, and she and Sidney chatted like old friends. When they finished, Sidney started up the computer system to show her payables and receivables.

"You'll make copies of all the bills, and put the copies in the proper job folder so Zane can review them when he bills out the customer. He takes care of that. He knows what he quoted and won't send out a bill for more unless there's a good reason. You'll apply the customer's payment to their account when it arrives and take the deposit to the bank when needed. Zane approves the original invoices for supplies and expenses, and then you can enter them for payment."

"Got it."

"Here are a few to start."

They spent the rest of the afternoon in training. They covered how to enter a payment and when to run statements so Zane could review customers who hadn't paid. At the end of the day she was shown how to lock up and set the alarm.

Her head was swimming as she drove to Vanessa's. She was mentally exhausted, but it was a great feeling.

By the start of the next week, Kenley was feeling pretty confident with her position. She also had an apartment lined up only a half mile from work, which meant she could walk when the weather warmed up.

Zane called twice to check in with Sidney, but Kenley hadn't talked to him since he'd hired her. It seemed odd not to see her boss on a daily basis. It might also have been that she wanted to see him. A little. To thank him in person, of course.

* * *

Paul called as Zane was closing up for the day to head back to the hotel. He'd been doing a repair on a hull.

"Hey, did you see the email Kenley sent regarding the bid in Kenosha?" Paul asked. They were both hoping to get the job on the '69 C&C-Belleville Frigate 36.

"Yeah. And then she left a message to make sure I'd seen it." Zane didn't mention how hearing Kenley's voice made his stomach flip. For as much as she looked like his old crush, her voice was lower where Courtney's was high and flinty. He'd listened to her message twice to make sure.

"I can get that if you want me to. You said you needed to be back in the office next week."

Friday was Sidney's last day, which meant next week it would be just him and Kenley at the office together. Alone. He was actually looking for a way to get out of it. Not that he'd be able to get out of it forever, but he needed another week or so to adjust. The ridiculousness of the situation made him snap in anger.

"I can do it, Paul."

So what that Kenley was attractive and had a nice smile? He'd dated tons of pretty women. Okay, maybe tons was a stretch, but several at least. None of them inspired this kind of reaction.

It was because she reminded him of Courtney. He needed to find a way to move past it. Maybe once he got to know Kenley he would be able to separate her from the pain of his adolescence. But not yet.

"Sidney told me she wasn't staying one minute past five on Friday. She's not going to come in next week," Paul reminded him.

"Sidney will understand and she'll cover for me." She always had his back when it was important.

"Okay." Paul didn't even try to cover his laughter. "Good luck with that." While Zane still had his phone out, he called his sister.

"Why are you calling my cell?" Sidney complained. "You should be calling Kenley since she is going to be handling whatever it is you need."

"Give me a break—"

"Here, I'll put her on."

"What? No. Don't put her—" Too late.

"Hello, Mr. Jackson," Kenley said. Hell.

"Please don't call me Mr. Jackson. We're the same age." According to her paperwork, her birthday was two days after his.

"Sure thing. Some people like the formality because it makes them feel important."

"I know I'm not important. Have you met my sister?" Kenley laughed at his joke, a warm throaty laugh that made him twitch in a good place. *Note to self: Don't ever make her laugh again.*

"So what can I do for you today, Zane?" she asked in that sweet, sexy voice. Yep, he was completely hard now. Hearing her say his name, and asking what she could do for him had all kinds of ideas hovering at the tip of his tongue. But he couldn't say any of those things, and she was waiting for an answer.

"Uh, I know Sidney wanted this Friday to be her last day, but I was hoping she could stay a little longer. I won't be back in town until next Thursday."

"Oh. Hold on." He listened as Kenley relayed the request perfectly.

"What?" There was a shuffling sound before Sidney took over the call. "You said you would be back," she accused.

"I know, but you also know how many times that plan falls through. I need to take care of that bid in Wisconsin before I can come home."

"Paul can do the bid."

"It would be better if I do it."

"Fine, then do it. You don't need me here."

"We can't expect Kenley to—"

"Kenley is a big girl. She can handle it on her own. To be honest, I really don't need to be here as it is. I could have turned everything over to her by day three."

"But Sid—"

"But nothing. She's going to be here all by herself most of the time anyway. Might as well start next week. Friday is my last day. Five o'clock." And with that she hung up on him.

"Just great," Zane complained to the phone. His sister was leaving him to fend for himself with Kenley. God help them.

A little after six his phone rang from a number he didn't recognize.

"Zane Jackson," he said officially, expecting a customer.

"Hi, Zane. It's me, Kenley." She didn't need to say her name. His body's response to her voice was all he needed to identify her.

"Oh. Hi. Are you still working?"

"No. I wanted to talk to you in private." Oh God. The word *private* made him twitch again. He was doomed.

"Yes?" His voice sounded funny.

"Well, this Friday is Sidney's last day, and I wondered if you were planning anything."

"Planning anything?" He didn't understand.

"You know, like a party or some gift to show your appreciation for her pivotal role in getting your business off the ground."

"Did Sidney tell you that last part?"

"Why yes, she did. Many times actually." They were laughing together.

"It's true, though. I would have had a difficult time if it weren't for her. I guess I didn't really think about a party or anything since I won't be in town."

"I can take care of it if you'd like. I just need to know the budget."

"You wouldn't mind?"

"I don't mind."

"Can we keep it under five hundred, will that work?"

"Yes. I can do that. Thanks."

"Thank you. I can't imagine what would have happened if we didn't do anything for her. I'd never hear the end of it."

"I got your back," she said, and a vision of them in the shower, her rubbing her soapy chest against his back, snapped into his mind.

"Okay, then. Thanks. I kind of have to go." He had been walking, but now walking seemed impossible with the sudden tightness in his jeans.

"Sure. I'll see you next week sometime, right?"

"Yep."

"See you then." He couldn't see her. Not when he literally sprang up like a fourteen-year-old at just the sound of her voice. What was he going to do?

The next evening, he received an email from Kenley detailing the going away send-off. Paul, Brady and four other guys would be home to attend. Kenley had ordered a cake. She'd gotten Sidney a simple diamond necklace, and there was a link to a website where he was to record a message saying goodbye.

This woman was scary good.

He clicked the link and straightened his shoulders for the camera.

"Hey, sis. So this is really it, I guess. You helped me get this place off the ground and I can't tell you how much I appreciate all your hard work. I'm so happy for you and Tim, and I'm looking forward to spoiling my little niece when she gets here. I'm going to miss hearing you nag at me about my awesome and beloved work boots. I'll be sure to wear them over to your house when I visit, which I hope will be often. Take care, and from the bottom of my heart... thank you." He closed the link before he did something stupid, like cry.

On Friday, he got the call from his sister. He could only tell it was her from the name on his caller ID. She was nearly incoherent with sobs.

"Oh my God, Zane. This is the nicest thing you've ever done," she managed to get out. "I wish you were here so I could hug you."

"I'm so sorry I'm missing that," he joked. "As for the party, it wasn't really—"

"Your idea? No kidding," she interrupted. "I've known you my entire life." Oh no. She was reminiscing about their past. Reminiscing always led to her telling the vomit story. "You threw up on my favorite doll." Yep. That was the vomit story.

"Yes. I remember." Only because she wouldn't ever let him forget.

"I know you didn't plan the party. Still, it was sweet that you okayed everything and were a part of it. I'm going to give you points for that."

"Thanks."

"This girl is going to change your life if you let her. She has a lot of great ideas. I know you're not one for change, but you need to embrace it. Don't be a dick."

"Don't be a dick. Got it." He wasn't the only person in the world who didn't embrace change. Not many people actually liked change. Only the freaks.

"I love you, and I'm going to miss talking to you every day."

"I'm going to miss you too. I'll stop by to check in next week when I'm in town."

"I'm eating your piece of cake."

"Enjoy."

When he got off the phone he sent a text to Kenley at the number she had used to call him.

"Great job," he wrote, adding a smiley emoji. Her response was a winky face, which made him twitch again. Surely it wasn't a good sign to be turned on by a winky face.

* * *

Kenley had plenty to do. It was Wednesday, her third day on her own, and Zane would be coming into the office the next day. She wanted to make a good impression so he wouldn't regret hiring her.

She stayed a little later than necessary, not looking forward to going home to unpack. Her new apartment was bigger than her old apartment, which meant there were huge voids of space her wallet was yet unable to fill.

Being only twenty-three minutes from her friends and family was nice, except it made her very aware that they all had lives. Even her newly retired parents had classes and trips scheduled. Vanessa was always on her way to ballet for Hannah or helping with some fund-raising event.

Despite the physical closeness, she found herself just as alone as she had been when she lived in the city.

She planned to go out and meet new people. Maybe even find that special guy, but so far she hadn't explored any farther than the restaurant across the street.

She wanted to blame her lack of social interaction on the weather. But with April just around the corner, she would be out of excuses.

Despite having set her alarm clock early and picking out her outfit the night before, Kenley was running late the next morning. The morning Zane—her sexy boss—would be coming into the office. March had decided to go out like a lion. A rabid, angry lion.

Not wanting to go to work with pink, wind-chilled cheeks, she drove. The sleet covering the roads made the short trip difficult and she stopped mere inches from the building as she slid into the parking lot.

She arrived only six minutes before she heard Zane coming in the back door. The coffeepot was filling as Kenley cheered it on, wishing it to brew faster.

He paused as he passed the door to the lunchroom.

"Good morning," she called. "Coffee will be ready in a minute."

"Thanks."

When the uncooperative appliance finally burbled out its last drop she filled the cup that said World's Greatest Uncle—a gift from Sidney in anticipation of his new role—and then froze.

She didn't know how he took his coffee. She should have asked Sidney. Now she was going to need to ask him, and she would seem incompetent.

Zane walked in and looked surprised to see her holding his mug.

"Sorry. I don't know how you take it."

"I take it myself, thanks. It's not nineteen seventy, where I expect you to bring me coffee." He smiled.

"Fair enough." She smiled back. Her stomach fluttered with nervous energy. "So what do you want to do first?" she asked.

"I'm guessing we have quite a list."

"A bit."

"Sidney always just told me what I was doing."

"Do you want me to do that? Maybe we could have multiple choice?" she suggested. "Would you like to start with incoming bids, payables, or marketing?"

"I would like to do payables first, because I hate them. Then incoming bids. I'll let you deal with the marketing because I hate that even more than payables."

"Good call. I actually like the marketing. I'll need a budget."

"I can do that. After I see how much money I have left when we're done paying everyone."

She smiled and gestured toward his office.

He picked up the pile and flipped through it. Then he pulled a file folder from his drawer to double check the copy was where it should be.

It was time for her to shine.

"What is this number?" He held up the bill for lumber and pointed to the number on the corner.

"Yes. I wanted to go over that with you. I made a change I think might streamline customer billing."

"I handle customer billing," he said immediately.

"I know. But this is a step that can make it easier for you. May I?" She pointed to his laptop.

He moved away so she could sit at his desk.

"So let's say you were ready to bill out the Murray job. You would pull it up in the system, and enter the line items manually. But your software already has the ability to integrate the two. When I enter the invoice to be paid, I simply code it to the corresponding job and it enters the line for you there." She pointed, feeling a little like Vanna.

"It enters the actual cost on the line. Then when you adjust it, it calculates the markup directly to the side. So you can easily see your profit on the job." She tapped the keys, showing him what happened if he made it lower or higher. "Also, once you've finished, all you need to do is click this button that says post, and it will be sent to my computer where I can print it out and mail it. This means you would be able to do it from another location, not to mention the time you'll save not having to keep track of copies in a folder." If she had a tail it would have been wagging.

"Don't you think you should be here a little longer before you start changing everything?"

The harsh tone in his voice caught her off guard. She expected him to be excited, maybe even pick her up and carry her around the room, cheering her name. But he was clearly not happy about the new efficiencies.

"I'm sorry. I was trying to make things easier."

"Meaning my sister was too stupid to find ways to make things easier?"

"God no. Of course not." How had he come up with that?

"But yet, here you are only a couple of weeks in, and you're already *improving* on everything."

"I'm sorry. I didn't intend—forget it." She was flustered and upset, almost to the point of tears. She'd wanted to impress him, instead she'd offended him.

Rather than break down in front of him, she squared her shoulders and pointed to the stack of invoices. "If you just want to okay those and give them back to me, I'll enter them for payment using the old method."

When he didn't say anything she turned to escape.

"What is this?" he asked, stopping her in her tracks. She turned to see the invoice for the new freight company she'd hired. She thought going with a less expensive company was a no-brainer, and had made the change on her own. No doubt he wouldn't be happy about this either.

"Um. I found a smaller independent freight company that specializes in boats. They're actually cheaper, and don't need as much lead time."

"Don't you think you should have discussed this with me?"

"I should have. I'm sorry." Her cellphone rang from her pocket. She tried to ignore it, but he narrowed his eyes on her. So much for her thinking he was sweet under the tough exterior.

"If you could keep personal calls to a minimum while you're at work that would be great."

"Yes. Sorry." She fled to the front office and answered the call.

"How's it going with the big guy there?" Sidney asked.

"Um. Well. I think I messed up." Her voice cracked, and she bit her lip to keep from crying.

"That son of a bitch," Sidney said. "I knew he wasn't going to be able to handle this. What did he do?"

"Nothing. I made some changes without discussing them with him, and he was perfectly within his right to call me out on it."

"It is your job to make decisions that make the company more efficient, Kenley. If it were up to Zane, he'd still have a pager instead of a tablet and a smartphone."

"Still, it's his company."

"What changes did you make?" she asked. For the next few minutes she briefly explained. Sidney seemed impressed, not that it helped her situation at all.

"Chin up. He's not great with change or admitting when he's wrong."

"Who is?" Kenley joked.

"He'll come around. I'm sure of it." Something in Sidney's voice sounded a bit ominous.

She hoped Sidney was right though. Having just spent the last six years dealing with a horrible boss, she hated to think of how awful this job would be if she couldn't get along with Zane even for the first day he was in the office.

She'd have to find a way to win him over. It was the only option.

# Chapter 5

Putting Kenley in her place wasn't nearly as much fun as he thought it would be. She didn't understand the hostility he had bottled up for the last ten plus years. The resentment. How could she understand? She hadn't been the one who'd broken his heart.

As much as he tried to remember that, seeing her made him bitter.

He'd hurt her feelings, and for what reason? Because she was attempting to make his business more profitable? Christ. That was her job.

"Damn it," he muttered as his cell phone rang. Sidney. Just great.

"What the hell is your problem?" she yelled as soon as he said hello.

"So she goes crying to you because I didn't like her idea?" It was a weak defense at best.

"*I* called *her* to check in, and I could tell she was upset. She didn't cry, but it sounded like she was probably pretty close to it."

The personal call he'd scolded her about would have been Sidney. Shit. He'd really made a mess.

"I didn't mean to upset her." He tried to defuse the situation.

"The hell you didn't. You didn't want to hire her, even though she was the best candidate. She's obviously proving that to be true, and you don't want to hear it."

He deserved this and more. He had acted like a child. A bratty, selfish child.

"I'll apologize," he offered. He'd pretty much come to this conclusion before his sister had yelled at him.

"Why didn't you like her idea? She told me about it and I thought it sounded great. You could work on things on the road so you wouldn't be bogged down with paperwork when you came to the office. Who likes to have a mound of paperwork waiting for them?"

"I just—"

"You just didn't want to like her idea so you came up with a lame reason to reject it. Simple-minded idiots do that, Zane. Are you a simple-minded idiot?"

"Not normally. I think I'm more a run-of-the-mill asshole right now."

"You know what I think?"

"I can't wait to find out," he muttered, away from the phone so she couldn't hear.

"I think you are being mean to this girl on purpose to make yourself feel big and bad because she intimidates you. That's not fair. You were a shy kid in high school. I remember how much you struggled to fit in. But go look the hell in the mirror. You're an adult now. A successful one. Your lack of confidence is not Kenley's fault. Don't punish her for something she didn't do. Besides, it was a long-ass time ago, so get over it already. I don't think your new niece would be very proud of you right now, Uncle Zane."

"Ah, hell." He hung his head. His sister knew just where to hit him. The kid wasn't even born yet, and she was already being used as leverage against him. "Fine, I said I would apologize."

"You should take her out for lunch."

"I—okay. I will."

"The next time I call this girl to check in she'd better tell me it's the greatest damn place to work or I'm coming in there."

"Yes. Got it. Bye." He hung up and looked over the changes Kenley had made to their system with an open mind. It was pretty nice. With a big sigh, he went out to Kenley's desk.

She glanced up, but didn't make eye contact.

"Why don't we go get some lunch?" he suggested, hoping it sounded casual.

"Should I take my things?" God, she was killing him.

"No. You'll be coming back. Or at least I hope you will."

She looked a little more relieved as she got in her drawer to retrieve her purse. She still wouldn't look at him, but that was fine. He needed a few moments to prepare himself for the big serving of crow he was going to have to choke down.

He held the door to Porter's Wharf and could have sworn he saw her cringe as she passed him to go into the restaurant. He'd done that. He'd yelled at her and made her skittish. He hated himself even more and he hadn't thought that possible.

She didn't know him at all, and so far her impression was that he was a nasty ogre.

It was still early for lunch as they were seated at an empty booth.

"Their burgers are the best. I swear my niece is going to come out a giant burger after all the ones Sidney has eaten since she's been pregnant." He tried to make a joke, but Kenley didn't laugh.

"I'm not very hungry." And he'd ruined her appetite too. Could he possibly feel any worse?

He set the menu aside and leaned down, trying to catch her gaze.

"I'm sorry about this morning. I'm not much of a morning person, and I was a jerk."

She glanced up and shook her head quickly.

"You weren't. I shouldn't have tried to change things—"

"Kenley, I was a jerk. There's no way around that. Let me apologize and take responsibility, okay?"

She nodded. "At least you didn't fire me for sleeping with someone," she said with a hint of a smile.

He jumped on the opportunity to continue the feeble connection.

"I'd have to be pretty stupid to fire you after seeing all the work you put into saving my company money. Fortunately, I'm only mildly stupid."

The waitress came and took their drink orders and left.

"So did Sidney call and yell at you?" She tilted her head to the side as she watched him.

"She did, but I had already decided I was going to apologize before she called."

"I'm sorry she yelled at you." He looked at her and saw how much she meant it. His gut twisted yet again with guilt.

"You don't have anything to be sorry about. I'm the one who messed up. I'm going to give your new system a try. After I got my head out of my ass, it seems like it might be a good move."

Kenley was trying to keep from smiling. Her warm brown eyes sparkled as she pressed her lips together. Full kissable lips. He was staring at them. He could feel himself staring and couldn't look away.

"What can I get you?" the waitress saved him as she put their drinks on the table and pulled out her green pad.

"Oh...uh. Did you decide what you'd like?" he asked, waiting for Kenley to go first. He was raised with *some* manners after all.

"I'll have the chef salad without onions, please." No onions? Was she going to be kissing someone later? He knew she wasn't married. He assumed she wasn't engaged because her left ring finger was bare. Surely she had a boyfriend. Maybe she lived with someone. Someone who didn't want to commit to her. What kind of rat bastard wouldn't commit to—

"For you sir?" The waitress was waiting.

"Oh. Cheeseburger and French fries." He needed to hold it together.

The waitress nodded and walked away, leaving them to their awkward silence.

"So are we good?" He went ahead and asked.

"Of course. No problem."

"If you have any other ideas, please don't be afraid to share them. I promise I'll react better the next time."

"I was thinking a parrot might liven up the place," she said.

He swallowed while he tried to come up with a diplomatic way to say, "Hell no." A *parrot*?

Just then she burst out laughing.

"You should see your face right now," she said, still laughing.

She was joking. With him. Like they were friends.

He laughed along, but inside his chest, his heart was waking up from a decade of slumber. Her laughter amazed him, her dimpled smile called him home. He was suddenly that stupid teenage boy wishing he had enough courage to ask out the pretty girl.

He was helpless all over again.

Exactly what he had been trying to avoid. He couldn't do this. He couldn't lose himself in this woman.

"Aw, shit. I just remembered, I have a conference call," he said as an excuse as he stood to escape. He was a coward, but he already knew that about himself. Now he also knew he was a liar.

"Oh. I didn't know."

"No, it's not your fault. It's something I set up myself. I should go." He tossed money on the table to cover their bill. "Finish your lunch and come back whenever. No rush."

"Okay. I'll have her pack up your food so I can bring it back with me."

"That would be great. Thanks," he called over his shoulder, already halfway to the door.

He couldn't do this. He needed to find a way to keep their relationship professional, but every time he saw her or spoke to her he was both turned on and flustered.

She had to be his employee. Nothing more.

* * *

Kenley watched Zane walk across the street. With his shoulders hunched over from the chill, he looked smaller.

His rejection still stung a little, but he'd apologized. He'd even called himself a jerk. She would let it go and start over. She needed to find a way to win him over.

It would have been nice to finish their lunch together. Not that it would have qualified as a date, but sitting across from a big, sexy guy in flannel was as close to a date as she'd been in a very long time.

Instead he'd run out of there like he was going to get caught by his wife. She knew there was no wife or girlfriend. Sidney had graciously supplied that information during her first day of training.

When Kenley's food came she looked over at the office, silently hoping Zane's call would end quickly so he could come back.

That didn't happen. It was probably for the best. She was wishing for things that couldn't happen. Sure he was attractive. But he was her boss. That was the most important thing. After the way she'd lost her previous job, she didn't want to set herself up for another miscommunication. She would have to rein in these lusty thoughts and keep their relationship strictly business. No flirting and daydreaming.

With her lunch hour up, she carried his food and change back to the office.

She tapped twice on his closed door before she entered and set everything on his desk. He was still on the phone, and he waved to her in thanks.

When she went back to her desk she found an email from Zane asking her to book a flight to Milwaukee for the next morning. He was leaving already?

She swallowed and did as requested, sending him the flight itinerary and the rental car voucher.

From his office, he wrote back. "You're the best." With a sideways winky face. She smiled stupidly at the emoticon, and then shook it off so she could get back to work.

An hour later Paul came into the office with a happy grin. He was shorter than Zane, but more muscular. He headed for the bathroom to wash up. He was a sweet guy who loved talking about his fiancée.

"How's it going so far?" he asked, drying his permanently stained hands on a paper towel.

"I think okay. Time will tell." There was no way she'd go into the details of her morning.

Brady came into the office then and leaned on the edge of her desk. She hoped the furniture could support him. He was huge with muscles.

Sidney said he'd been in the military, not that she couldn't have guessed that from his tattoos. Or the way he carried himself like a man who was confident in his ability to kill someone with his bare hands. Kenley found him to be a bit intimidating.

"Hey, beautiful," he said. He was a big flirt, but she had to admit she did like being called beautiful. "How's it going?"

Paul rolled his eyes behind Brady's back.

"She's doing a great job. We should let her get back to it," Paul suggested, sparing her.

"You only think I'm doing a great job because you both got paid on Friday." Brady winked at her.

"Keep it coming, and we'll get along just fine."

"You're easy men to please," she joked.

"You have no idea." Brady's look turned more devilish than payroll humor. He raised his eyebrows in a way that made her stomach flip. Crap. Their innocent banter had moved to the next level.

He was still leaning against the corner of her desk, and his leg was all but touching hers as he bent closer to look into her eyes. Oh boy.

She licked her lips, and then realized that was stupid when his gaze moved to her lips. Did he think she wanted him to kiss her? Did she? No.

She'd hoped for someone sweet who would be gentle her first time out of the corral. She needed training-wheels sex. She couldn't handle the ex-military playboy. He wouldn't be training wheels. He would be top-fuel dragster.

"Brady?" Zane's voice made Kenley jump as if she'd been caught doing something wrong. Brady didn't move from his position as he looked up at Zane with an easy smile on his face.

She heard Paul mutter something that sounded like, "Now you've done it."

"Got a minute?" Zane asked, his voice tight. Unfortunately she recognized this as his pissed-off voice.

"Sure, boss." Brady winked at her as he straightened. "He's sending me away tomorrow, but I'll stop in to visit the next time I'm home."

"O–okay." Why did her voice sound so breathy? "Have a safe trip."

"Will do." He tipped his ball cap in her direction, causing her to swallow loudly.

"Brady?" Zane repeated.

"Right behind you," he said with another wink at her. As he walked down the hall toward impending doom, she noticed he had a slight limp. Like a sexy cowboy from a movie.

Heaven help her.

\* \* \*

Brady followed Zane down the hall, preparing himself for battle. Or for a convincing rendition of it. He'd seen the way Zane acted around Kenley and knew he'd never take a shot unless he was forced into it. Brady was going to help the process along.

"What the hell was that?" Zane barked as soon as the door to his office was closed.

"I think it's called *laying the ground work*." Brady shrugged as if it made perfect sense, and held in his grin. He needed Zane to believe he was really interested in Kenley.

Not that she wasn't pretty. She was. She just didn't do anything for him. Mostly because she seemed like the type who would want a commitment. A nice girl.

He didn't do nice girls. He didn't have the time or energy to put into a relationship.

"No. No *laying ground work* with Kenley." Zane shook his head and pointed at Brady to make his point.

"Are you saying you're calling her? Because if you are, I'll back off. But if you're not going to make a move, I am. She's hot as hell." He made a move with his pelvis that made Zane's eyes widen. Maybe it was a bit too much. Zane looked as if he might have ripped Brady's head off if there hadn't been a desk between them. Good, it was working.

"Have you ever heard of a little thing called sexual harassment in the workplace? If she feels uncomfortable, she can file a complaint and I'll have to fire you."

Brady swallowed, hoping it wouldn't come to that. He needed this job.

"As a personal favor to me, I would appreciate it if you backed off."

"I don't remember owing you any favors." Brady crossed his arms over his chest and cocked his head to the side. In truth, Zane had done a lot for Brady. Hopefully, one day Zane would thank him for this.

"Fine, then I'll owe you one."

Brady shook his head slowly, enjoying himself. "Dude, she licked her lips," he explained. "You know what that means."

"I'm sorry. I don't. When I lick my lips it means they're chapped."

"It means a woman wants it when she licks her lips." In some cases this was true. But not with Kenley. That was why flirting with her was completely harmless. She would never try to take it to the next level on her own. Casual office flirting was the extent of their relationship.

"And there is research to prove this?" Zane said doubtfully.

"I've done enough research to know." Brady's lips pulled up on one side. He was the devil. But it was for a good cause.

"I'm—okay. I'm calling her, got it? She's mine."

*Gotcha.* Now, he just needed to set the hook and reel Zane in. "Really?" Brady laughed.

"Yep."

"And you're going to act on it?" he challenged.

"I'm just waiting for the right time."

Yeah, right. Like when? At his pace, he'd be working his moves with a walker. But this was progress. At least he'd owned up to it.

"All right. Good for you. I'll back off." *For now,* Brady added in his head. It wasn't easy playing the part of badass when he was actually a romantic at heart. Unfortunately he didn't have room in his life for romance. He had other responsibilities.

For now he would have to be content with casual hookups and office flirting.

* * *

Hearing the words *she's mine* come out of his mouth had made Zane feel kind of lightheaded. If only they were true.

But saying it was the only way Zane could think to end the nightmare of a conversation. It had worked. Brady had given up. At least for now. The relief Zane felt with this news was pathetic.

Zane went home to pack for a trip that was unnecessary. He could have easily handled everything through phone calls and emails, but he needed to get away.

After his failed lunch with Kenley and Brady's lesson on goals and lip licking, he came up with a strategy. If he could just stay out on the road, he might have a chance. And now, with her new system upgrade, she had given him the opportunity to do everything remotely. No need to come into the office where her presence would torture him constantly.

An even better idea came to mind. He'd been toying around with the idea of opening up another shop. He'd seen a place for sale in Ohio, on Lake Erie, that would be perfect.

It was a flawless plan, which could only mean it wouldn't work.

Project Avoidance was interrupted by his phone. Weston Archer had been his roommate in college. While they were only about two hours apart, they rarely had the opportunity to see one another. They both worked too much to have a life.

"Hey. How's things in Boston?"

"Good. How are you?"

"Good. What's up?" Neither he nor Wes were big conversationalists, which made them great roommates, but made it difficult to keep in touch.

"I want to get a boat."

"Sure. What size were you thinking?"

"Big enough that I could live on it for a few years."

"Your mother still nagging you to take over the business?" Zane guessed.

"Yep. I don't know what part of *I'm happy* she's not hearing. Maybe she doesn't care what makes me happy."

Zane would have argued, but he wasn't sure it wasn't true. The woman's priorities were out of whack.

"So do you really want to buy a boat?"

"My mother accused me of acting like an irresponsible playboy. I figure an irresponsible playboy should have a boat. The more pretentious the better."

"Shouldn't the irresponsible playboy also be either irresponsible or a playboy?" Weston was neither of those things. Despite all his money, he never acted like he was anything other than a friendly guy.

"Right. I'm working on that." Wes had dated a few girls in school, but he was far from being a player. "We'll start with the boat."

"There's a boat show coming up. I should be able to find you something there."

"Thanks. You can hang out up here when you deliver it."

"Sounds good." They hung up and Zane smiled, knowing he had another reason to get out of the office.

* * *

Kenley poured out the coffee from the day before and put a new filter in the machine. She didn't drink coffee and before she started the pot, she contemplated if anyone else would drink it. The chances of her being completely alone in the office for the third straight day were pretty good.

She still felt bad about the poor older man she'd trapped for forty-five minutes when he stopped in to pay his bill.

The service guys in back assured her they didn't need anything, not even her company. They had their own restroom in the shop, so there was nothing to bring them to the office.

At her last job people had stopped by her desk on an hourly basis to ask a question, pick up a report, or just to chat.

It had always seemed distracting. She never realized how much she would miss social interaction until she had none. Of course, even if Zane was in the office, it didn't mean there would be social interaction.

He wasn't one for interacting at all.

Zane had left last week for Milwaukee and, according to his last email, he was now in Baltimore. She'd called him a few times and left messages. He never called back, just responded with a brief text or email.

She understood the modern world didn't require face-to-face or even verbal communication, but she did. She was going crazy. She almost thought about getting a plant so she had something to talk to. Maybe that was how it had started with Sidney.

The worst part wasn't just that Zane wasn't there physically. It was also the emotional distance between them. She'd really felt like they were getting somewhere at lunch—before he had to run off.

She'd sent him a few funny texts and emails, but his responses were all business. She couldn't be upset by that, this was a business. But it was also sort of a partnership. It would be easier to anticipate his needs if she knew him better. Maybe in time.

"I'm going batty," Kenley confessed to Vanessa the next week. Paul had stopped in, and a few of the other guys came in to pick things up, but they weren't up for chatting. Brady hadn't even flirted with her, which was odd.

"I also think I'm unattractive."

"Why do you think that?" Vanessa laughed.

"The company flirt stopped flirting with me. He's taken on a big-brother thing."

"Wear something that shows off your boobs," she suggested.

"First, I don't want him to look at my boobs."

"Why not?"

"Because he's intimidating."

"But you want him to flirt? I don't get it." Of course she didn't. Kenley was losing her mind.

"I used to be flirtable, and now apparently I'm not."

"Oh–kay."

"Second, I don't know when he will be in next so I can't plan ahead to wear a shirt that shows off my boobs. I only have two boob shirts."

"Ah. I see. Wow. I think I need to go so I can have a real conversation with my six-year-old."

"I know. I'm pathetic."

"I don't think it's you, sweetie. You're still very attractive, even without showing your boobs."

"Thanks."

Kenley called Rachel next. It didn't seem wrong to make personal calls during the day. She was able to get all her work done and still have extra time. It seemed she'd never had enough time before, and now all she had was time. No matter how lonely and boring it was working at the office alone, it seemed worse being in her apartment. She'd talked to two guys at the grocery store, but neither encounter had progressed to a date. Apparently the theory that single men came to the grocery store to pick up women was a myth. It seemed they just needed food.

This pattern continued into the next week and the next.

No sign of Zane. His only contact was electronic, professional and a huge disappointment.

She did have a visitor one evening while she was closing up. But not the kind she was hoping for.

The three quick taps on the glass door made her jump, and seeing the police officer didn't help. She knew she hadn't done anything wrong, but that didn't slow her speeding heart as she unlocked the door and let him in.

"Can I help you?" she asked.

"Is Zane around?" He walked into the lobby and glanced down the hall expectantly.

"No. He's not here. He's out of town."

"And you're the girl who took over for Sidney?" he asked, looking her over with a friendly smile.

"Yes. I'm Kenley Carmichael. The new girl." She smiled up at him, though she wasn't really new anymore. He was about the same height and build as Zane, but with sandy-blond hair and green eyes.

"I'm Officer Scott Porter." He offered his hand and she reached out to shake.

"Are you related to the Porters—"

"Yes. My uncle owns the restaurant. Doesn't the office close at five?"

She let out a sigh and looked at the clock that said quarter of six. "Yes. I got carried away and didn't notice the time. I'm just going home to watch reality TV."

"Yikes." Scott winced. "We need to do something about that. I'll check in the next time I have a night off and I'll show you around."

Was he asking her out? It kind of sounded like an order.

"Thanks, Officer Porter."

"Call me Scott."

"Okay," she said, more because she was desperate for human contact than because she felt any real attraction to the policeman. He was cute enough and the uniform was hot, but she was more into T-shirts, flannel, and scruffy work boots.

She sighed as Scott stopped at the door on his way out.

"I didn't notice a car in the parking lot." New Haven was getting its money's worth with this guy on the force.

"Right. I only live a few blocks from here. I walked."

"It's a little chilly." He looked up at the dark sky. Two points for the incredibly perceptive officer. April was unpredictable and it had screwed her a couple of times. It was a good thing she'd purchased that ski jacket after all.

"I walk fast."

"Be careful. I'll check in later. We'll do dinner." Again, he wasn't really asking, and since he had a gun, she just smiled and nodded.

"Okay. Thanks." It was the best offer she'd had so far, so why not?

\* \* \*

The next night around eight she was still in the office. She had some time to make up thanks to the cable repairman who did not show up in the four-hour window he'd given her.

Zane was going to be in the next afternoon. She wanted everything to be perfect. She still had plenty of time to demolish a half-eaten container of ice cream. The first half had met its demise the night before.

As she straightened her desk to leave for the night she received a text from Zane.

"Seriously?" she said to her phone as she read the message. He wasn't coming home after all. "That's just great." She shut down her computer, grumbling the whole time.

The sound of someone coming in through the back door made her jump. She'd locked both doors at five when the business had officially closed for the night. The guys were gone for the night. Zane, Paul and Brady were all out of town. That only left the possibility of an intruder. Did Officer Porter have a key?

Breathing quietly became impossible as the sound of heavy footsteps came toward her. She picked up the only weapon she had available—a stapler—and prepared to bash in the intruder's head.

Except the intruder was Zane.

They both gasped in surprise.

"What are you doing here?" they asked at the same time. He motioned that she should go first.

"I was finishing up some things before I went home."

"Your car isn't out front." He almost sounded accusatory.

"Right. I walked."

"From Madison?"

"No. I moved here. I live on the next street, two blocks down."

"Oh." He rubbed his forehead, obviously uncomfortable.

Something occurred to her at that moment.

"You just sent a text that you weren't coming home?"

"Yeah. Uh..." He looked up at the ceiling. His expression could only be described as busted.

Kenley's heart seized. She understood what this meant. He was avoiding her. All this time, while she was lonely and wishing he was there, he was probably in the same town, hiding from her.

She'd guessed he was never really on board with hiring her, but she thought he'd at least give her a chance. If she could only prove herself, maybe they would get along. Obviously she had been wrong. Her second theory for his avoidance was even worse.

Had he seen how infatuated she was with him? Had she made him so uncomfortable he was desperate to stay away? She wanted to disappear.

"I see. Well, I should go." She put the stapler back on her desk and opened the bottom drawer to get her purse, her hands shaking.

"You're walking home in the dark?" He gestured to the front window.

"I'll be fine." She started for the door and then stopped. "I wanted to make a good impression." She shrugged and unlocked the door. This was beyond embarrassing. She used to be a strong woman, confident of her value as an employee, but thanks to Ruth she felt like a beggar, constantly trying to prove herself. And failing.

And now this man couldn't even stand to be in the same office with her.

# Chapter 6

Zane winced as he watched the expression on Kenley's face change from horror of an impending attack to a different kind of horror. She was embarrassed, and now she was leaving. He'd messed up again. He desperately needed to come up with some way to fix this.

"I got in late last night." Seven could be late. "And I had some other things to do today." Like hide from her. "I was planning to leave tomorrow again, so I didn't think it would matter if I was in town." Well, that sucked.

"You don't need to explain." She paused at the door, and then turned to face him. "Look, I know you didn't want to hire me. I know Sidney pressured you into it. I have an older brother, so I understand how sometimes it's easier to give in than to put up a fight. I get it." She looked down at the floor. "If you find someone you really want to work with, I'll train them before I go so you don't have to bother Sidney."

This was definitely not what he wanted, although it would make things so much easier. But he didn't want her to go. She must have sensed his delay as affirmation.

"However you want to handle it is fine. I can quit or you can fire me. It's up to you. I've been fired before."

"You don't like working here?" he asked. Maybe she wanted out.

"I do. I like it a lot, but I guess I thought…" She shook her head.

"What did you think?" He had to know.

"I thought we would be working together, like a team. It's stupid, but I really wanted to learn about boats. I wanted to belong here." She laughed. "I can't believe I just made this situation worse. God." She shook her head. "Like I said, it was a stupid expectation. I mean, this is your business. I'm sorry it didn't work out." She turned to leave again and his heart nearly stopped.

"Wait. I don't want you to go," he said more seriously than he needed to. "I mean, not tonight—you can obviously go home. But I want you to come back. Tomorrow." He sounded like an idiot.

"Sure. I wouldn't leave you hanging. I can stick around until you find someone else."

"I don't want anyone else. I want you." More than he should. "You're doing an excellent job. Everything's going according to plan and ahead of schedule. I actually like the new billing system. And you saved me a bunch of money by finding that other freight company to move our equipment and tools. I should have said something about that. Thank you."

"It's not like we've spoken."

"Right. I'm sorry about that too. I guess I just…" What was he going to say?

"I get it. You don't like change. No one does. Sidney was with you since you started your business so it's probably difficult to get used to someone else. Especially a stranger." She gave him the perfect excuse, and like a coward he took it.

"Still, it was rude. If you stay, I promise I'll do better. I'll make an effort to communicate and be here in person. So we can work together. Like a team." This idea put his stomach in knots, but he needed to do something drastic. This was his business. She was an asset he couldn't afford to lose. He needed her on his team as much as he needed Paul and Brady. He would only think of her in that aspect.

"It gets kind of lonely here all the time."

"Maybe we could get a parrot."

She laughed at his feeble attempt at humor. "I don't think that would be a good idea since I've killed a cactus."

"That takes some effort." His body responded to her laugh, but instead of running away, he stood there hoping he would eventually become desensitized to his reaction. If they were going to work together, he needed to figure out how to be close to her. And stay there.

"So I guess you don't need me to schedule your flight home."

"Um. No." He smiled. "I'm already here."

"So I see." She smiled back at him. Were they flirting? It seemed like it.

"Have you eaten?" he asked without thinking as she turned to go. The temptation was almost gone, but he'd called her back.

"No. I was going to go home and have a bowl of…" She waved her hand. "No."

"Do you want to go grab something to eat? My treat. I won't need to run out to take a call. We could get to know each other a little better," he suggested. What was wrong with him? Had he just suggested they go on a date? Before he had the opportunity to backtrack, he saw her eyes light up with excitement.

"That would be a great idea."

He couldn't believe he'd just asked her out to dinner. Did employers take their employees out for random dinners? He went for drinks with Brady and Paul. It must be acceptable. He swallowed and followed her out of the office.

Despite his expectations, dinner wasn't uncomfortable at all. Kenley seemed happy to forget about his appalling manners and sneaking around, so he let it go. They chatted easily about the boat he was working on and how he was going to be looking for a boat for Wes at the boat show in Montauk.

"That sounds like fun," she said.

"Would you want to spend a weekend looking at a bunch of boats?" He'd seen the frown when she thought she would be stuck in the office alone all the time.

"Sidney said she sometimes needed to go to take care of insurance issues and quotes. I'm prepared to learn how to do that. It is part of my job, right? I need to learn more about boats."

He frowned at the table.

"I'm sorry this job hasn't been what you expected. If you want to learn more, we can make that happen. I'll take you to the boat show. It's a two-day thing. I'm staying on my boat, but I'll get you a hotel room. Well, you can book that yourself with my card." He smiled. "I can show you what's involved in appraising a vessel. If we buy one, I'll be overseeing the project as a personal favor to my friend, Wes, but you can help me with it."

"That sounds great." She practically beamed with excitement and he felt even worse. She must be bored stiff if this prospect thrilled her so much.

"I'm sorry this job isn't more exciting. Why do you think I travel so much?" he asked.

"To avoid me."

Her honesty nearly made him choke on his drink. He set the glass down, his gaze on the table. He needed to make this right.

"That was beyond rude of me, Kenley. I'm so sorry."

"Do you want to tell me what it is I did that made you want to avoid me?"

"It's nothing you did. Nothing at all. I've not been dealing with things well. It won't happen again. I promise you."

"So I can stay?" she asked.

"Of course. You work circles around Sidney and you don't yell at me. Who wouldn't want to keep you?" Forever? Maybe in their bed? He was not desensitizing at the speed he would have liked.

When dinner was over they walked out into the chilly night air. Kenley pulled her jacket closer around her and turned to him with a smile.

"Thanks for dinner."

"Thanks for giving me another chance," he said. "Why don't you wait here, and I'll get my truck to drive you home."

"No. It's fine, really. I should walk." If she meant she needed to walk because of her figure, she was wrong. She was perfect. She had nice womanly curves in all the right places. Curves he shouldn't be noticing on his employee.

"I'm leaving tomorrow afternoon," he told her with a frown. Now that he found he could talk to her without feeling like a stupid, shy boy, he wished he could stay.

"For real?"

"Yes." He laughed at her expression. "I might be buying a small shop on Lake Erie. I'm meeting the inspector from the bank."

"Expanding? That's a good sign." He nodded. He'd planned to grow his company before now. It just hadn't worked out yet. He wouldn't tell her that hiding from her had been the catalyst to get him moving on the plan.

"So I'll see you in the morning before you head out?" She was still standing close to him, and when she looked up he saw it.

She licked her bottom lip. He swore he saw her gaze drift down to his lips before meeting his eyes again. He must have imagined it. His own gaze seemed trapped at her lips and then he abruptly turned away, cursing Brady for putting ideas into his head.

Whatever he thought he saw, or hoped he saw, he could be certain of one thing, Kenley Carmichael most certainly did not want to kiss him. And he surely could not kiss her.

He stepped back, chanting the word *employee* over and over in his head.

\* \* \*

Oh God. She'd almost leaned in to kiss her boss. It felt like a magnet was pulling her in, and she couldn't fight it. Fortunately, he'd turned away before she could make an even bigger ass of herself.

She practically skipped during her brisk trip home. As she lay in her bed, she couldn't help but replay her dinner with Zane. He'd smiled a few times, and each time it struck her right in the chest.

Her new boss was as sweet as she thought he could be. And his kindness came in a beautiful, sexy package. Sexy? She couldn't allow herself to think of him as sexy. He was her boss.

She knew very well what came from fooling around—even allegedly—with a superior. Unemployment, misery, and her brother's sofa.

It would be even worse if she lost this job. She really liked it. She enjoyed the challenge of finding ways to improve and be more efficient. And as much as she complained about the solitude, it was nice not having someone hovering over her second-guessing everything she did.

This job was perfect. She needed to make sure she didn't jeopardize it.

\* \* \*

The next morning Zane was there as expected. She tried to leave him alone, but couldn't help herself. Twice she came up with some lame reason to go into his office so she could interact. She bounced some ideas off him and took notes on future projects. She was doing it. She was establishing a business relationship with her boss.

Before lunch he came out to say goodbye.

"I'll be back next week. I'll let you know when I know."

"Okay. Do you want me to drive you to the airport?" she offered, not wanting him to leave yet. Now that they were working together so well, she wanted to keep up the momentum.

"No. But thanks."

"See you next week." She noticed a brief hesitation before he left, only to come right back.

"You're doing a great job. Please don't think I haven't noticed."

"Thank you." She blinked and watched as he left.

It felt as if he'd taken a big chunk of her with him. It was an overly dramatic thought, and made her laugh at the ridiculousness of it. She had a crush on her boss. She would have to find a way to keep that under control.

\* \* \*

A week later she was still working mostly on her own, but now Zane would actually speak to her on the phone. He gave her more responsibilities, which helped, but they still didn't keep her busy enough for her liking.

Her home life was just as bad. She'd worked long hours at her last job, and while she enjoyed the idea of having her evenings to herself to do whatever she wanted, she still didn't know what it was she wanted to do.

She joined a gym, but she could only work out for so long. Most nights she found herself sitting in front of the television or reading until it was late enough to go to bed without it being a disorder. She had never been so rested and restless at the same time.

"New Haven Custom Boats," she answered cheerfully the next morning.

"Hey, Kenley, it's me. Can you do me a big favor?" Zane asked.

"Sure."

"Go into my office," he instructed. She carried the cordless phone into his office.

"I'm here."

"Go to my desk. In the bottom left-hand drawer there is a box of pictures."

"Yep." She frowned at the shoebox stuffed full with photos. Some had fallen out, some were about to.

"In the front there should be a picture of a ratty green door."

She flipped through the beginning of the stack, noticing they were all images of boat parts.

"Green door. Brass doorknob?"

"Yes. That's it. Can you scan it to me? I think I wrote the size on the back. I need that too."

"Sure. I'll do it now."

"Thanks, I really appreciate it."

"No problem. When will you be in? I have two people who want to meet with you. Lawyer and insurance adjuster."

"Friday?"

"I'll see if that works for them and send you an email to confirm."

"Great. Talk to you later," he said before they hung up. She scanned the photo and sent it to him immediately, like the neurotic employee she was.

She took the photo back to his office and frowned at the mess, her OCD flaring up slightly. No way could she just shove the door picture back into the box and close the drawer.

"Damn it!" she huffed and took the whole box out to her desk to organize it. These were obviously pictures of things that were salvaged from boats to be used to restore other boats. She'd seen the racks of items on the far wall of the slip.

Over the next few days she scanned all the photos into a computer file and sorted them by tabs. Engines, hulls, windows/glass, navigation, brass, etc. She entered any notes from the backs of the photos. Then she loaded them all on the server. She spent her evenings at home learning how to create an app.

If nothing else, it gave her an excuse not to go with Officer Porter when he showed up at the door. For all the promises she'd made to herself about getting out there and trying to find a connection, she already knew she wasn't interested. She wished she did find him appealing. It would keep her from daydreaming about her boss, which she still found herself doing occasionally.

After finishing her project, she drummed her fingers on her desk and sighed. Now what?

\* \* \*

"Hello." Zane answered Paul's call as he walked into his office. It was good to be home.

"Did you hear from Josh? He says he's looking for a new nav system for his boat."

"Yeah, I heard."

"Did you want me to take a look and work something up?" he asked.

"No, I've got it. I'll look for something while I'm at the boat show. I'm taking Kenley with me so I can show her the ropes."

"Show her the ropes? She's into that kind of thing?" Paul teased.

"Very funny."

Paul was still laughing at his own joke. "Seriously, though. The two of you in a boat? Alone?"

"Yeah. So?"

"Overnight?"

"I'll stay on the boat and she has a room at the convention center." Why was Paul acting like this was a big deal? Maybe because it was a big deal. Huge. He and Kenley together. Alone, as he'd pointed out. This would be the ultimate test of his control.

"You know what they say about being at sea with a woman."

"It's bad luck?"

"That's only if you're crossing the sea. They say it's romantic."

"It's a boat show, not a tropical cruise."

"I took Taylor out on my boat one time and bam. We were in love."

"So you're saying if I take Kenley with me, we're going to fall madly in love and get married?" If only it could be that simple. He could see Kenley in a white gown, smiling at him. Tiny flowers in her hair, and—

Paul's laughter ruined his little daydream.

"No. You're probably safe."

"Thanks," Zane said with a frown as he employed the chanting again. *Employee. Employee. Employee.*

Zane was nervous about this trip. Over the last week he'd been talking to her on the phone instead of texting. A few times he was sure they were flirting. Not blatant flirting, but flirting nonetheless. The chanting wasn't working, so he'd switched to imagining how screwed he'd be if she quit. He tried to picture the lady who didn't like to fly, or the teenage text queen sitting in the office instead of Kenley. He didn't think they would care about keeping his job folders organized or cutting expenses like Kenley did.

Kenley had stopped in his office three times that morning, but it wasn't enough. He went out to find her. He had a question about something he already knew the answer to.

She was in the front office talking to someone. Thinking his eleven-thirty appointment was early, he went out to meet the person, but stopped in the hall when he heard Kenley whisper his name.

"Zane's in the office today," she told someone. Was that excitement in her voice?

"Who?" the other woman asked.

"Zane Jackson, my boss."

"What's he like?"

"Nice."

*Nice?* That didn't sound promising. Of course, it was better than hearing her tell her friend the truth, which was that he was a moody asshole.

"He draws the most amazing plans for boats."

"That's it?" He could see the other person's reflection in the glass as she frowned. "Nice? I see."

"No. You don't see. He's a really nice boss."

"Nice means ugly," the other person said. Before Kenley had time to respond, Zane took a few louder steps and coughed before he walked into the lobby.

"Hi, Zane. This is my sister-in-law, Vanessa."

"Nice to meet you."

Vanessa cleared her throat and said, "Nice to meet you too." She was blatantly checking him out. Unfortunately, it wasn't this woman's attention he wanted. Not that he should want Kenley's attention.

Thanks to the physical requirements of his job, and the gym, he was in relatively good shape. Maybe Kenley preferred her men bulky like Brady. Not that it mattered, because Brady had backed off after Zane claimed her. He wondered how long Brady would hold off if Zane didn't make a move.

He couldn't make a move. He was her boss. He squared his shoulders and prepared to do just that. Be the boss.

"Have you heard anything about the Oliver boat?" Zane got to the point of his interruption.

"No. I just checked on it again today. They said they would know soon." Zane had a buyer for that boat and a new motor waiting to be installed before he could flip it to his customer who demanded it be in the water for summer. It was already the middle of April. Time was getting tight. He frowned at her answer, but shook it off quickly and moved on to the next topic.

"So the show we talked about is in two weeks, would you be able to leave that Friday morning? he asked, seeing her face light up in surprise. "We'll be back on Sunday."

"Sure. No problem."

"Thanks." He nodded and gave her a smile. "Nice meeting you, Vanessa."

"Yeah. You too," she said, still staring. As he walked away, he heard her say. "Holy shit, he's hot."

"It doesn't matter. He's my boss. I can't lose this job." Was she having as much trouble keeping things professional as he was? He shook his head as he went into his office.

A few minutes later Kenley came in with a big smile on her face.

"So I really get to go to the boat show?"

"You seem to have a boat show confused with backstage passes to a premium rock concert, but yeah, I'd like you to come along to check it out."

"Will we be buying a boat?"

"We'll be looking for a thirty-foot cuddy for my roommate from college. The show actually starts on Saturday, but on Friday there's happy hour in the afternoon and a lot of deals are made then." He watched her as he mentioned the overnight stay again and was happy to see an extra flair of excitement. Or maybe he imagined it.

"It sounds so much better than being here alone for days on end driving myself crazy." She put her index finger up. "Which reminds me. Can I see your phone?"

"Okay." He handed it to her and watched her bite her bottom lip as her fingers swiftly slid over the screen. He looked away before her lips distracted him any more than they already had.

The smile was back as she turned the phone toward him and pointed.

"See this app with your company logo on it?" she asked as he stared at the screen.

"Yes."

"I thought it might be handy if you had all those pictures from your bottom drawer more readily available, so I put them up on the server. Then I got to thinking about how you would have to log in and fumble around with the tabs, so I figured it couldn't be that hard to design an app. I looked it up on the Internet and *voila*, you have an app with tabs to all the photos in that box."

"Holy shit!" He tapped the tab under brass, and scrolled through the photos. Her laughter made him look up. Standing so close, he could smell her hair. Strawberries and cream.

He got to a photo of a steering wheel he'd already used.

"This one isn't available anymore."

"I figured there would be things in there that weren't in stock anymore, so I made this little trashcan in the corner. Just slide it down there and it's out of the way."

"Very cool."

"Oh, and I thought this might come in handy. See this file icon here? Let's say you wanted to use a photo in a proposal to a client. You can label the file with the client's name and then slide it there. It moves the photo into the file so you can sort it later and attach it to the proposal. If you don't use it you tap that arrow and it goes back into the rotation."

"This is amazing, Kenley." He looked at her in awe. Kind and brilliant all wrapped up in a beautiful package.

He didn't see how she had time to do this and get the rest of her work done. Then he frowned.

"Did you do this on your own time?"

"No. Well, I learned how to make an app at home, but that's knowledge I can use for other things too."

"I'm going to pay you for doing this."

"No. It's really okay. I was bored."

"Still. I can't imagine how much it would have cost to have an outside company do this, so I'm going to find out and pay you." He wanted to compensate her for her efforts. He wasn't going to take advantage of her boredom. She was brilliant.

"You're too smart for this job," he told her with a grin.

"Yeah, well, you're the only person I could trick into hiring me after my scandal, so lucky you."

Lucky him indeed.

# Chapter 7

When Kenley got the confirmation that the Oliver boat was ready to be transferred, she knew it was going to be a problem.

The woman who owned the boat was only available on Wednesday. She knew Zane already had a meeting to settle on the Lake Erie property on Wednesday. She walked into his office to find out he'd already heard.

"I can't be in two places at the same time," Zane was complaining to someone on the phone. "I understand that, but I have to be in Galveston to purchase a boat I already have a buyer for."

He waved and smiled at her and then let his head fall back.

"I understand, but can we just move it to the next day?" He let out a sigh. "I know it's not your fault. Let me think about it and I'll call you back."

He hung up and took a sip of his coffee.

"Sounds like you're starting the day out right," she said as he rubbed his temples. "Can I do anything?"

"Can you split me in half? I need to get that boat in Texas now that she's finally ready to sell it, and you saw the settlement for the Ohio place is tomorrow as well."

"Yeah, but I think splitting you in half would be kind of messy." She got a smile out of him at least.

"Maybe you can tell me how I'm supposed to be in Galveston signing the papers on a boat and in Ohio settling on the new property."

She twisted her lips to the one side while she thought over the predicament. Which thing was the priority?

Both.

Which thing did he absolutely need to be there in person to do?

She smiled and held up her index finger to indicate she had an idea.

"You sign over temporary power of attorney to me. Then I can go to Galveston and buy the boat. You can go handle the settlement on the new place."

"I need to have the boat shipped out immediately."

"Brady can take care of that while I handle the purchase."

"You would do that?" he asked.

"Yes. It would be much easier than splitting you in two."

"Okay. That will work."

"I'll call your attorney so we can go have the paper drawn up, then I'll fly out."

"Tell her we need this quick."

She nodded.

"Thank you, Kenley. Really. I don't know what I'd do without you." His words held a sincerity that made her break out in goose bumps.

"Well, hopefully you won't ever have to find out," she said, before she realized how it sounded. Rather than retract it and make it worse, she turned and left his office as quickly as possible.

* * *

Kenley was in heaven.

Actually she was at JFK, but as she waited to board the plane to go to her first assignment, it was pretty damn close to heaven.

Most people wouldn't be this happy about flying out for a job, but she was excited to have the opportunity. She was going to do her best to make Zane glad he'd hired her.

* * *

Smoothing her black pants repeatedly during the flight, she hoped she wouldn't mess this up.

From the airport she took the rental car straight to the notary's office following the instructions on the GPS. And that was where her heaven abruptly turned to hell.

"I'm sorry. I know I said I wanted to do this, and you've come all this way, but I just can't. It was my husband's boat. We spent so much time on that boat. Earl and I and our two boys. I know I won't be able to take it out again, but I just can't stand to see it pulled out of the water," the elderly Mrs. Oliver said. Brady, who was standing next to the door, sighed. He had the truck ready to go. It was going to be a long trip home with no boat.

Kenley watched in horror as tears filled the old woman's eyes. She could feel her own eyes sting. It wouldn't be good to break out in hysterics when Zane was counting on her.

"Shit," Brady muttered and walked out of the office. He was probably going to call Zane and tell him they didn't have the boat.

She needed to do something. Zane couldn't take more stress on this job. Plus he might back out of the letting her go to the show next week if she was incompetent. She quickly came up with a plan.

"Mrs. Oliver? Can I show you something?" Kenley asked while opening her laptop. She turned it so the woman could see the screen. "These are other boats Zane has restored. Boats that were losing their battle with the sea. Zane was able to save them and make them beautiful again." The woman looked at the pictures with her lips pulled together in a frown.

"He does wonderful work, but I just don't think I can part with it."

Desperation made the next words fly out of her mouth.

"Are your boys interested in fixing it up?"

"Well. No. I did ask them if they wanted to, but neither of them have the time."

Kenley nodded. "I've spoken with Mr. Donovan—the man who wants to buy Earl's boat and have it restored. He was very specific about the year and model he wanted. He used to go out with his grandfather on a boat exactly like Earl's. He said the times on that boat were his greatest memories. At least until his own children were born. He wants to relive that happiness with his own kids." The woman continued to look at the screen. "Joel and Alex."

"This Mr. Donovan has two boys?" Mrs. Oliver asked.

"Yes. They live on Lake Ontario so they spend a lot of time out on the water. The youngest is six and can already water ski." The woman looked impressed. Mr. Donovan was pretty proud of the little guy. Zane had even posted the video on the company website. "I know you see this as the end of your boat, but it's not." She gave the woman a sad smile. "It's like a rebirth. Earl's beauty is going to get the care it needs. And a new family is going to enjoy her and make memories on her for years to come."

Mrs. Oliver nodded and looked at her hands for a long moment before raising her head.

"You're right. I'm just being sentimental. I'm ready now," she said surely and reached out with the pen to sign where she was told.

When the papers were pushed in Kenley's direction, she got a bit of a thrill signing her name on the line above Zane's name. It was stupid, but she couldn't help it.

She gave Mrs. Oliver a hug and offered to drive her over to the dock to see it one last time, but the woman declined.

Once outside, she found Brady pacing and talking on the phone.

"…what about that one in Wiscasset? It wasn't the same, but it was close." She walked up and tapped him on the shoulder with a smile.

"You can go get Mrs. Oliver's boat now," she said.

"What?" Brady looked at her with his brows creased.

Kenley held up the papers and pointed to the signatures.

"The boat is ours. You can load it up."

"But the lady changed her mind," he pointed out, still holding his phone.

"I know, and I helped her change it back."

"Did you beat her up?"

"No!"

"How—Oh, okay. Bye," Brady said into the phone. "Zane's calling you."

At that second her phone began to vibrate.

"Yes?"

"What happened?" he asked immediately.

"She had cold feet and I dealt with it. We're good to go. It's ours—I mean yours. You know what I mean." Apparently the signature thing was still having ramifications.

"I'm sorry it didn't go as planned," he told her.

"I used to work in mergers and acquisitions, Zane. Everyone has reservations, but if they've gotten to this point, deep down they really do want to sell. You just have to remind them why. How did things go on your end?"

"I have another property in Ohio."

"Good job."

"I hope I didn't make a horrible mistake."

"You didn't."

"Thanks for saving the day."

"Not a problem." She pumped her fist and gave a happy "Yes!" when she hung up.

* * *

When Zane got off the phone, a strange sense of calm coursed through him. Kenley wasn't just an employee showing up for a paycheck. She was a partner. He knew he could trust her to be there for him. He felt even more comfortable with her decisions than he had with his sister's.

Sidney always handled situations as she wanted to, which may or may not have been how he would have done it. But Kenley was like an extension of him. As if she could read his mind and handle things the way he would have if he'd been there himself. She acted on his behalf instead of with her own agenda. There was a trust there he'd never felt before with anyone.

He paid her well, but he needed to find a way to thank her for her trustworthiness. He wanted to show his appreciation. Pulling out his phone, he bought a ticket as he hopped in his rental to head to the airport.

What seemed like a great plan on the way from Ohio to Texas now seemed like a ridiculous gesture as he stood in the hotel lobby at almost nine o'clock at night.

Would she think it was too much? He fiddled with his key card, second-guessing himself. He paced for a few moments, until the desk clerk looked like she was about to call the cops. Deciding to take a chance he said, "Could you please tell Kenley Carmichael that Zane Jackson is here to see her?"

Hearing their names together in the same sentence gave him a stupid little thrill. Why was he here really? He wouldn't have come all this way and spent the money on a ticket to thank Paul or Brady for a job well done. He held out his hand to interrupt the clerk, but it was too late.

"This is the front desk. There is a Zane Jackson in the lobby to see you."

"The lobby?" Zane could hear Kenley's voice on the other end of the line and smiled.

"Yes."

"Of *this* hotel?" Yes, this was too much. Unfortunately he'd have to ride out the storm of stupidity.

"Yes."

"Please tell him I'll be right down."

"Yes ma'am."

It was only a few minutes later when she found him in the lobby where he was sitting in one of the fancy chairs, with his ankle resting on his knee. When he spotted her, a broad smile took over his face and he stood.

"Hey, how's it going?" he asked as if it was completely normal for him to be in Galveston.

"Good. Your boat is on a truck as we speak."

"Excellent." He glanced around the lobby. "Do you want to get a drink?" He pointed to the lounge.

She looked at the time on her phone and frowned.

"I'd better not. I have to get up really early tomorrow."

Zane fought a smile and failed.

"I won't tell your boss," he said, making her laugh.

"I have an early flight. I'll get a soda," she compromised and followed him to the bar. "So are you checking up on me?"

"No. I wanted to make sure everything went okay with the transport."

"So you're checking up on Brady?" She lifted her brow, calling him on the lie. He winced and fessed up.

"Okay. I wanted to double-check the paperwork before we left to make sure there wasn't an issue later." This was only partly true, but that meant it was only partly a lie. An improvement from a few weeks ago.

She laughed and nodded.

"You wanted to make sure I did everything right. Are you a control freak?"

"No. Maybe. It's your first purchase. What kind of boss would I be if I just threw you to the wolves without checking to make sure you were okay?"

"I appreciate your concern." She rolled her eyes as the waitress brought her soda and his beer.

"By the way, I talked to one of Mrs. Oliver's sons, and he told me you handled the situation perfectly."

She shrugged and gave him a smile. "This job is really important to me. I don't want to disappoint you."

"That's not going to happen." She was actually worried about that possibility? As if she was capable of disappointing him. She was the best employee he'd ever had. She cared about his business. And maybe even about him. "I have complete faith in you. You wouldn't be here if I didn't," he told her honestly. If he'd had any lingering doubts, they were long gone after today.

"*You* wouldn't be here if you trusted me." She tilted her head.

"Maybe I wanted to see your shining moment. Why should I miss out?" This was more truth than he'd planned to share.

"Really?" she asked, unsure.

"I know it wasn't easy working with me in the beginning. I was pretty much an ass. I wasn't really on board with hiring you, but I have to say, it's the best decision I've ever made." He hadn't really been involved in the decision at all. Bullied would be the better word. Still, the end result was that she worked for him, which at times—like right now—was a major inconvenience.

He couldn't date an employee. It was too risky. Especially if it meant something could go wrong and she'd leave him. She was too important to his business.

She smiled at his confession, and her cheeks turned a beautiful pink. Could it be the sexy cheerleader was a bit shy too? He couldn't let himself think of her as the sexy cheerleader. She was important to keeping his business running smoothly. That was it.

"I should get to bed. I don't want to miss my flight. I have a lot to do before our trip next week."

He stood as she did and walked with her to the elevator.

She pushed the three and he pushed the five as an awkward silence fell over them. The elevator was too fast for him to figure out what she could be thinking. He needed more time.

He stepped off on her floor and she looked up at him in surprise. What was he doing? Before he could change his mind, the lightning-fast elevator doors closed.

He watched as she swallowed and stared up at him. God, she was the most beautiful woman in the world. Maybe even more beautiful than Courtney.

Not sure what to do, he reached out to push the button to call the elevator back. But in that second her tongue darted out to wet her bottom lip. Christ.

One moment he was reaching for the button, and the next he was reaching for her. His body moved on its own, pulling her against him. His lips crashed down on hers, causing a little moan from her throat. Her breasts smashed up against his chest as his hand moved down her back. When her lips opened slightly, he pounced on the opportunity, sweeping his tongue inside.

He swallowed down her second moan as his erection throbbed painfully in his jeans. It was only then he registered her hands on his back, fisting his shirt.

A second later, he had her pinned against the wall, deepening the kiss. He couldn't believe this was happening. How many times had he fantasized about this since she'd walked into his office? Pretty much every hour of every day. And now it was real. He was kissing Kenley.

His employee.

Before he had the chance to pull away, she did. Looking up into his eyes she winced and said, "I'm so sorry."

He almost laughed, except it wasn't funny at all.

"Why would you say you're sorry? You don't have anything to be sorry for," he explained.

"I kissed you."

That time he did laugh.

"I'm almost a foot taller than you. If I hadn't bent down to kiss you, we wouldn't have kissed. That makes it my fault." He ran a palm over his hair. Shit. What did they do now? How badly had he messed it up?

"I'm the one who's sorry, Kenley. I'm the one who crossed the line."

"Oh." She blinked a few times and then looked... He wasn't sure. His best guess was impressed, though that didn't make any sense.

"Do you think we could chalk this up to being exhausted, and having a stressful day?" He hoped. "I don't want things to be awkward. I'll never let anything like that happen again. I promise.

She pressed her lips together and then nodded.

"I'll still get to go to the show?"

He smiled and nodded as he pushed the button to call the elevator to her floor. "Yes. Let's just pretend this didn't happen."

Kenley's fingertips trailed along her bottom lip and for a moment she looked sad. Maybe she didn't want to forget their kiss? But she'd pulled away.

Smiling at him she said, "What happens on the third floor stays on the third floor?"

"Yes. Thank you."

"No problem. I guess I'll see you back at the office?"

"Yes."

"And we're leaving next Friday?"

Hell. How was he supposed to spend two days with her? He'd promised nothing like this would ever happen again, but already he found himself wanting to pull her back into his arms. He nodded as he stepped onto the elevator.

"Eight a.m.," he said as the doors closed and he was hurtled up two flights to his own floor. As he stepped into his room he had to fight the urge to turn around and go back to her.

It just couldn't happen.

* * *

He'd asked her to forget about their kiss. The most amazing kiss she'd ever had in her life. That kiss had been going somewhere, and she'd stupidly pulled away.

At the time, she'd thought maybe she should warn him about her predicament. Surely a guy would expect a certain level of proficiency in skills she didn't have. Fortunately she'd kept her mouth shut. She could only imagine the look on his face if she'd blurted out, "I'm a virgin!"

Forgetting about the kiss was highly unlikely. In fact, as she got off the plane in New York, that kiss still consumed her thoughts. As she dropped her things off at her house and went in to the office, she found the odds of forgetting the kiss were quite impossible.

She wanted to do it again. And not just kiss him. But he'd promised to keep things professional. Maybe her subconscious had caused her to pull away from him. The part of her brain that liked having its own place, and food in the refrigerator. The part that liked having a job, and being an essential part to Zane's business.

She hoped that part would give the other part—the one that wanted to kiss her boss again—a good shake.

Zane didn't come in to the office at all that afternoon. She stayed until six and hadn't heard anything.

She frowned at her phone. Was he really doing this again? Hiding?

Deciding to do something about it, she sent him a text.

*I'm bringing cinnamon rolls in for breakfast tomorrow. How many do you want?*

She gathered her things, not expecting to get an answer. To her surprise, her phone chimed a few seconds later.

*If I said three would I sound like a pig?*

Her smile was huge as she typed a reply.

*No. Three it is.*

Before she got the door locked he responded.

*Thanks. See you in the morning.*

Kenley touched her bottom lip, thinking about the kiss. Again.

\* \* \*

Zane was already in the office when she got in the next morning.

"Good morning," he said with a smile that seemed forced. Something was up.

"Morning."

"I get three, right?" he asked with a grin as she held out the container.

"You get as many as you want."

She watched as he took a bite, his lips shiny with cinnamon glaze. How great they would taste right now. The sticky coating smearing between them—She stopped the inappropriate thought before it got out of hand.

"I have something for you," he said, quickly backing away. She realized she had been staring at his lips the whole time. "I saw it when I left yesterday and I thought of you." He held out a small velvet box.

Her heart seized, knowing the only thing that came in this type of box was jewelry.

# Chapter 8

Zane hadn't been sure he was going to give her his stupid gift, but he had to do something quickly. She'd been staring at his lips as if she wanted to lick the glaze off him. And he wanted her to. He wanted to throw her over her desk and lick her as well.

His jeans fit uncomfortably as he waited for her to take the box. He was getting used to it by now. It had become a near-constant situation when he was around her.

"It's to say thank you," he explained, feeling stupid.

"Really?" Her voice squeaked as she took the box and opened it. "Oh wow!"

He loved her reaction to his gift. She didn't seem to think it was creepy. She appeared genuinely pleased.

"This is so nice. It's beautiful." She was still smiling. "You didn't have to do this. I was just doing my job."

"See, I thought about that, but you do more than your job. You act like this is your company, too, and you treat every decision as if it directly affects you. That isn't your job, but I really appreciate it."

"You're welcome. My dad says I have loyalitis: an inflammation of loyalty." She laughed and shook her head. "This is really beautiful."

She looked down at the necklace again. The charm he'd seen at the hotel gift shop was a knot pattern. He didn't have a large selection to choose from once anything romantic was taken out of the mix, but when he saw the knot he thought it was perfect. It symbolized the way she kept all the loose ends tied up.

He smiled as she freed the necklace from the box and put it on. Seeing his gift settle against her collarbone made his heart twitch, and maybe some of his other parts as well. But that was getting easier to ignore.

* * *

His relationship with Kenley shifted significantly over the next few days. While they never mentioned the kiss, or moved to make it happen again, he could feel the tension growing. They flirted. Casual, friendly flirting. Nothing overtly sexual or inappropriate, just fun. But occasionally he saw her staring at him as if she wanted to take his clothes off. And the few times when she stared at his mouth while licking her lips was almost enough to ruin him and their tentative friendship.

He liked her.

He'd though she was beautiful from the moment he met her. It was the reason he'd tried to keep his distance. He remembered how he'd acted around Courtney. Like a junkie, eager for any bit of attention she would turn his way. But this was different. He knew Kenley as a person. He knew her heart and her mind. And every new thing he learned just made her more perfect.

She was also a kick-ass assistant. He would be lost without her. Everything ran smoothly and his entire workforce was less stressed. As much as he appreciated Sidney and everything she'd done to get his business started, he realized how much tension there used to be, now that it was gone. The constant bickering and struggle for power had worn everyone down. Including them.

One of his happier employees walked in and sat at the bar on Tuesday night.

"So you're still taking her away on your boat?" Paul asked with a smirk.

"Yes." Zane hesitated for a second, debating whether or not to talk to them about his issues. Josh was obviously waiting for an explanation. What the hell, why not tell them?

"I'm taking the new girl to a boat show. A work thing."

"Ah. The new girl," Josh said with a knowing smile. Zane glanced over at Paul, who was making an effort not to laugh.

"Asshole."

"What?" Paul said, knowing exactly *what*.

"The ocean is magical. Be prepared," Josh warned as he took a sip of his beer.

"I can't be fooling around with my employees." He frowned. "Right?" he added when neither of them responded.

"Bree helps me with my business. It's nice being able to share everything, and for her to understand what I do for a living," Josh said.

"But you were married before you started your business. Kenley is my employee. What if something goes wrong? It could ruin everything."

"What if it doesn't go wrong? It could be great." Josh was not helping.

"I think she's into you," Paul said. "Go for it."

"You're supposed to talk me out of doing something stupid," he scolded them.

"Did you just meet us today?" Paul frowned and shook his head while Josh laughed.

"It won't matter what you decide," Josh said. "When you get her alone on the ocean you won't be able to help yourself."

Right. The magic. He decided he didn't want to leave things up to magic. He liked Kenley, and he was definitely getting signals that she liked him too.

Instead of tiptoeing around the issue and hoping for the best, he thought it might be better to address it straight out.

He had a plan when he walked into the office Wednesday morning. It was a big step, but one he felt he was ready to take. He took a deep breath, gathering his courage as he walked down the hall to see her.

Hearing her voice slowed his steps. He didn't want to bust in there if she had a visitor.

"...none of your business. It was great and of course I'd like to go out with him, but if things don't work out I'll end up depressed and eating way too many cookies, like the last time. No, I definitely need to take things slow." He heard her say. When he didn't hear a response, he realized she was on the phone.

She was dating someone? And she wanted to take it slow with them? Zane looked down at the silly flowers in his hand. What had he been thinking? His stupid plan was to walk in there, hand over the flowers, tell her he had feelings for her and kiss her until she felt the same way. Get everything out in the open and hope it wouldn't end up wrecking his business. Instead, he left, throwing the flowers in the dumpster as he went to his truck and backed out.

It was for the best. Nothing good could come from him dating his employee. If something went wrong, she might quit and then were would he be? Yes, this was better.

Not having anywhere else to go, he went to visit his sister. That was a testimony to how desperate he was to stay out of the office.

"I'm glad you stopped by for breakfast, and now lunch, but don't you have a company to run?" Sidney asked as she put the dishes in the sink and came to sit next to him. She put her feet up as her doctor-husband had ordered.

"I own the company, so I can spend the day with my sister whenever I want to."

"Please." She flipped her hand at him, not buying it for a second. "What's going on?"

He hung his head, knowing if he told her the truth one of two things would happen. She would either give him some wise advice that would help, or she would make fun of him. The more he thought about it, the more likely it was that she would do both things. Making fun of him was a definite either way.

"Kenley is dating someone."

She was silent for a very long time. So long that he had to look up to see her expression. She was biting the inside of her cheek and looking at the ceiling.

Contemplation. Good. She hadn't gone right for making fun of him at least.

"I'm going to assume when you say she's dating someone, you don't mean she's dating you since you haven't grown a set of balls and asked her out."

Right for the jugular.

"She's my employee. It would be unprofessional to ask her out."

"Yes, because hiding out at your sister's house to avoid her is the epitome of professionalism."

"What should I do?" He decided to put it out there in the hopes she would cut to the chase.

"Grow some balls and ask her out."

"Other than that?"

"Let me ask you this: What is the worst possible scenario if you were to ask her out? Like your deepest, darkest nightmare?" She leaned closer, giving his answer her full attention.

"My deepest, darkest nightmare would be if her skin shed off and underneath she was really that clown from *It* with the teeth." He mock shivered.

"Okay, so the chances of that happening are slim. What's the next level?"

"Skin shedding off and she's Jabba the Hutt?"

"Let's say her skin stays on and she's not going to morph into something from an old movie. What are you truly afraid of?"

He took a deep breath.

"The worst thing would be if she said no, and was then so uncomfortable she had to quit and I never saw her again." He shook his head. "And then her replacement turned out to be Pennywise the Clown."

Sidney let out a sigh and crossed her arms over her enormous stomach. One thing about his sister, underneath all the ridicule and teasing she did actually take the time to think a problem through and offer valuable insight.

"It's a risk, Zane. The question is: Is she worth it? You used to watch Courtney from the sidelines and never did anything about it. Are you content to just watch from the sidelines with Kenley?"

"No." Just the idea of seeing some other guy pick her up to go off on a date made his skin crawl. "But I have no right. I'm her boss."

"Do you think you're the first people in the history of the world to have a workplace romance?" She sniffed and shook her head. "It happens all the time."

"What if I'm reading her wrong and she freaks out that her boss is hitting on her?"

"Do you think she's into you?"

Zane remembered back to the kiss. She had definitely kissed him back. She had been clinging to him. "And what happens when the workplace romance ends?"

"Who says it has to end?"

He gave her a skeptical look and held out his hands.

"Just because all your other relationships ended doesn't mean this one will. You're both adults. Talk to her. Make sure you agree to keep things separate."

"That sounds great, but I'm already struggling to keep things separate."

"Then you're going to have to do something."

He did need to do something. Get his act together and be her boss. She was seeing someone else. Time to move on and let it go.

* * *

Vanessa wasn't giving up on getting details about her weekend plans with Zane.

"I told you, it's business," she clarified.

"But you've waited so long. He's kissed you, *and* bought you jewelry. You should just jump him as soon as you get him alone. Let the last time count as your first date so you can get to the good stuff this time. You want to get to the good stuff with him, don't you?"

"Like I said, I'm taking it slow."

"You've been taking it slow for forever. Come on. This is your chance to live a little."

"I don't want to mess it up. He's my boss. This job is too important to me to throw it all away because my boss is..." She couldn't think of the right word. Yes, sexy came to mind, but he was other things too. He was kind and sweet. She touched the necklace he'd bought her and remembered the most important thing he was—an employer who valued her. She'd never had that before, and she wasn't going to risk losing that.

"Fine. But you'd better tell me everything when it finally happens."

"I'll spill every detail. I promise," she said, knowing it wasn't going to happen. She'd crossed her fingers before she said it. She may be an adult, but it still counted.

When she finally got off the phone, she decided she was going to put an end to all her anxieties. She was going to ask Zane out for dinner so they could talk about the kiss she had yet to forget. They'd been flirting and having fun, maybe he would tell her he felt the same way. Maybe she could have both things: the perfect job with a pleasant boss during the day, and a man who rocked her world at night.

But Zane wasn't there and when he finally showed up, he seemed to be in a bad mood the rest of the afternoon. She didn't say anything or ask him over for dinner. The flirty, happy Zane was gone, replaced by the miserable Zane who had hired her.

\* \* \*

The next morning she looked at herself in the mirror and gave her reflection a determined nod.

"We're going to handle this today. We can't go on like this. It's too tense. It will all work out." She wasn't so sure about that last part.

She left an extra button open on her blouse and put on lipstick. Surely taking these extra measures would be a game changer for her love life.

Zane wasn't in the office when she got in. She checked her email to find one from him saying he would be out most of the day.

She pouted at the screen and buttoned up the extra button before starting coffee for the guys and getting to work.

One of her duties was reconciling Zane's credit card, and she pulled up the bank's website with the pile of receipts in front of her. She wanted to be caught up before they left on their trip the next day.

One by one she coded each item and verified the amounts.

She paused on one of the last transactions on the screen. A transaction she had no receipt for.

"Meadow's Floral Shop?" she said with her head cocked to the side. She only deliberated for a few moments before she picked up the phone and called the shop.

"Meadow's Floral," the cheery woman said.

"Hi. This is Kenley calling from New Haven Custom Boats. I have a charge on our credit card from yesterday, and I need a detailed receipt."

"Sure. No problem." The woman helpfully offered to email the document to her without hesitation.

Two minutes later, Kenley was staring at a receipt for a dozen roses purchased the day before. She gazed at Zane's signature, unmistakably scribbled on the bottom line.

Her mind quickly mapped out a scenario. He had been moody the afternoon before, then bought flowers and wasn't at work today. Clearly he'd gotten into an argument with a girlfriend. Since he wasn't going to be in today, the flowers must have done the trick.

She sighed and picked up the phone to call Vanessa, hoping she could make her feel better.

"He has a girlfriend," she said right away.

"No way!"

"Yes. He bought her flowers yesterday."

"Are you sure? I thought his sister said he was available."

"Maybe he lied to her. He doesn't like her in his business."

"Maybe the flowers were for his sister or his mom's birthday or something."

"A dozen red roses? You don't take red roses to your mother on her birthday. Besides his mother lives in Florida."

"Right."

"He's not here today. They're probably off somewhere having all-day make-up sex." Kenley hadn't had the chance to have all-day make-up sex yet, but Vanessa and Rachel always made it sound wonderful.

"There are plenty of other fish in the sea."

She didn't want the other fish.

"This is for the best. It was a stupid idea to get involved with my boss. I need this job."

"Come on, Kenley. Work with me a little. We need to get you a man. Any man."

"I'm fine."

"We either find you a man or I buy you ten cats. It's up to you."

"I like cats. Maybe not ten. At least not all at once."

"God! You're unbelievable."

"Love you too." Kenley laughed and hung up.

She would not let this get her down. Maybe if he and this rose person had been arguing it meant she was a demanding witch Zane might want to replace with the woman who paid his bills. The woman he would be going away with the next morning.

Her stupid insecurities took that moment to chime in. *Why would he want a woman whose idea of seduction was opening an extra button?*

She flipped the newspaper to the pet section and began scanning for cats.

\* \* \*

Zane's pulse picked up when Kenley arrived five minutes early the next morning. Good looking, a brilliant mind, and punctuality all wrapped up into one amazing package. An amazing package who'd gone on a date that made her giggle.

Zane was still irritated with that information. She'd kissed him. Quite intensely, even. Of course, she was on board with his whole let's-forget-it-happened thing. He should have known.

"Good morning," he greeted her, trying to keep his voice pleasant. After all, it wasn't her fault she had a boyfriend.

"Morning," she said, sounding less than enthusiastic. She had circles under her eyes. Maybe she and the boyfriend broke up. He hated the thrill he felt over something that could cause her pain. But maybe he could help her with that pain. Make her forget what's-his-name.

She stood there on the dock looking at his boat.

"This is yours?" she asked.

He couldn't help the pride in his smile when he said, "Yes."

"You have a yacht." She let out a breath and shook her head. "Unbelievable." Since she said that last word more to herself, he let it go.

He loaded her small bag and helped her aboard as she thanked him. Ten minutes later, the trip so far consisted of him driving while she sat in the back of the boat looking out at the ocean in silence.

"Are you okay?" he finally asked, not able to deal with it anymore.

She shrugged. Obviously she didn't want to talk about it. The warm May day boasted perfect blue skies overhead. But with the cool breeze coming off the ocean, Kenley pulled on a sweatshirt and let out a sigh.

He told her what he was looking for in a boat. He briefed her on their plans. She pulled out her phone and typed in some notes. She seemed to be in a better mood by the time they arrived. He led her to the first boat he wanted to look at.

"It's beautiful," she whispered. He glanced over at her, taking in her golden hair whipping in the wind. He couldn't agree more. Except she was talking about the Trumpy yacht in front of them.

They got right to business. He gave her the lead to ask her list of questions. Even when the salesman attempted to ignore her, Zane directed the conversation back to Kenley so she had full control.

She did a wonderful job. She asked informed questions and seemed confident with her knowledge of the model. It was obvious she'd done her homework.

He'd left her alone while he went to pick up lunch, knowing she was capable of handling the salesman on her own.

When she had all her answers she shook the man's hand. "Thank you for your time. We'll be in touch," she said as she turned to Zane, indicating she was ready to go.

Once again he helped her into his boat, holding out the bag of sandwiches when she was safely aboard. He started up the boat and drove them out into the water far enough to give them privacy. So far there'd been no magic. They would only have a little more time for it to kick in before he moved around the point and moored at the marina.

"What did you think of that one?" he asked as he dropped the anchor and grabbed two bottles of water from the cooler.

"It was beautiful. As far as restoration, it wouldn't need much. The master bedroom was modernized and has an alarming number of mirrors, but other than that it's been left in original condition."

He'd seen the way her cheeks turned a glorious shade of pink when she'd seen the mirrors on the ceiling of the stateroom. What he wouldn't have given to take it out for a test ride and watch her respond from numerous angles.

Damn, he needed to buy bigger jeans.

His tension only built as he watched her lick the barbeque-chip residue from her fingertips. God, that tongue and those lips.

"I don't think it's worth the price," she said.

"Excuse me?" Oh. The boat. "Right. He's asking too much. We'd have to negotiate."

"Are you any good at it?" Her lips quirked up on the side.

"Asking for what I want?" He could only stare at her. "No. I suck at it."

An hour later they arrived where the boat show was being held. The convention center was within walking distance. He offered to carry her bag, but she simply pulled out the handle so she could roll it behind her. Chivalry was dead, killed by modern conveniences.

"Thank you for this opportunity, Zane. I really appreciate it," she said when they stopped outside her room.

"I really appreciate you taking the initiative. You've earned the opportunity. And I'll be happy to ditch jobs on you once you're broken in." He winked at her, it was the same kind of flirting they'd been doing the last week, but it didn't get the same response.

Instead she turned to unlock her door.

"I guess I'll unpack before I meet you downstairs?"

"Sure." And then she was gone. The door shut in his face.

* * *

Her hotel room was covered in rose wallpaper. Pink and red blooms taunted her. A reminder of the fact that somewhere out there was a woman to whom Zane had given a dozen red roses. Someone he probably loved, and had sex with.

"Damn it!" She'd had such high expectations for this trip, and it wasn't turning out at all like she'd planned.

Sure she was enjoying her job. She liked how Zane seemed fine to let her handle things on her own. He didn't jump in unless she asked him a question. She valued his opinion, and he was eager to listen to hers.

Now they would be going for drinks and dinner together.

She would rather stay in the overly floral room alone than go to an awkward dinner with the man she was falling for, but he would no doubt be concerned. She couldn't avoid him.

He hopped up quickly when she stepped off the elevator in the lobby. She hadn't changed because to do so would have implied this was a date, which it wasn't. But she had taken her hair out of the ponytail and put on a fresh coat of lipstick.

That was the extent of her efforts for a business dinner.

"You ready?" he asked with a strained smile. He was no doubt wondering why she was so cold to him.

She smiled a genuine smile, deciding to let it go. He hadn't done anything wrong. Okay, so maybe kissing her when he had a girlfriend wasn't the right thing, but it was really nothing.

"Yes."

She made an effort to chat, but it was difficult to hear with all the people crowded into the bar area. He introduced her to a few people. He conducted business easily, and she doubted what he'd said earlier about not being a good negotiator. He seemed to be doing a fine job of telling these men what he was looking for and what he was willing to pay for it.

Kenley paid attention, trying to pick up things she could use. By the time they were moving to the dining hall, Zane had bought a boat sight unseen and had plans to look at four more. She was impressed with his skill.

She was also finished with her first drink.

"Can I get a rum and coke?" she requested when the waitress came around. Then she worried two drinks might make her seem irresponsible. Did she care what he thought of her? No, she didn't. Kenley raised her brow at him in defiance. He couldn't tell her what to do. Damn. Yes, he could. That was what bosses did.

"I'll have a lager." He raised his brow at her, mimicking her rebellious expression. "We're grown-ups, Kenley. We can have a few drinks after work if we want."

She let go of the tension. He'd said after work, which meant they were no longer on the clock. While under normal circumstances having dinner with a man after work would be considered a date, she didn't allow herself to think of it that way.

He had a girlfriend. He was her boss. He was off limits.

They talked a little more about the boat they'd seen that day while they ate.

"So I was wondering," he said after they'd placed their orders. "Would you mind going out to Ohio and setting up the new office? Taking care of the files and things? Then maybe hire someone for there?"

Her eyes went wide with excitement. "Really?"

"It's not a big deal. You're running the office in Connecticut like a well-oiled machine. I'd feel better if you set it up so it would be easier for someone to take over. Plus I'm told my file system sucks."

"Sure. No problem."

"You can go whenever works best for you. I'm hoping to have it open for summer."

"Okay. I'll work it into my schedule." She almost hugged him, but played it cool.

Zane's crab legs were quite messy, so he excused himself the bathroom when they were finished eating.

She felt alone as she watched him walk away. It was stupid. On a normal Friday night she would have been alone, or maybe hanging out with Vanessa and her brother, but she wouldn't be with Zane.

Although, she'd never wanted anyone more than she wanted Zane.

She was in dangerous territory. She didn't know a lot about sexual relationships, but she knew that wanting someone she couldn't have wasn't a good idea.

# Chapter 9

He caught her looking at her necklace with a slight smile on her lips as he walked back to their table.

"So you like it," he asked, happy to see her smiling again. He wasn't sure what had been wrong earlier, but he was glad to see her back to her normal pleasant self.

"I do. It's so nice to be appreciated. I'm not used to it. My old boss just piled on more work."

"And then accused you of sleeping with her husband," he reminded her.

"Yeah." She laughed. "I'm kind of glad though."

"Really?"

"I probably would have stayed there my whole life."

"Because of the loyalitis," he teased, and she laughed.

"I wouldn't have known what it was like to have a job I actually loved."

Hearing her say the word *loved* made his heart do that twitching thing again. He couldn't do this. He couldn't pine for her from the sidelines. He wouldn't allow it. He was a man.

Before he had a chance to act, the lights in the room dimmed and the DJ in the corner announced that the dancing would be beginning with a classic. "Twist and Shout" filled the room.

"It's just like prom, huh?" He laughed.

"I wouldn't know. I didn't go."

"You didn't?" He couldn't hide his surprise.

"No. I was invited to my junior prom, but my mom was so sick. She was gone by my senior prom, but the people at school didn't seem important to me anymore."

"I'm sorry. I didn't know."

"It's fine. It's not something I talk about." She sniffed. "As one of my classmates pointed out, I shouldn't have been too upset since she was only my adopted mom. But she was the only mom I'd ever known."

He swallowed. "You were adopted?"

"Yeah. Didn't Sidney tell you?"

"No. She didn't mention it." It would have been nice to have a heads up so he didn't walk into an awkward conversation.

He could almost envision what it must have been like for her through her mother's illness. Struggling through school while hiding the pain. No doubt she would have been allowed to take a leave, but she hadn't. She was strong. Stronger than he ever was.

He always assumed the beautiful people lived perfect lives, but that wasn't always true. Kenley had faced a lot of heartache and still came to work every day with a smile on her face.

"I'm sorry for what you went through. And sorry someone was so insensitive. Of course she was your mother."

"Thanks. It's easier to know that now. It's harder in high school. I always feel like those four years were just practice for what happens in real life. Out here it's different. Back then, we were all so stupid. We didn't know what mattered."

She was right. And he knew what mattered now. Her. "I was kind of a geek in high school."

"No way."

"Yep. I was tall, but built like a stick until my junior year. I had trouble talking to girls and I spent most of my time drawing."

"Ooh. Artsy hipster."

"It's too bad that term didn't exist back then. Maybe I would have been cool in some way."

They laughed.

"Do you still draw? I like the pictures of the boats in your office." He couldn't very well tell her he'd done a sketch of her. He'd sound like a stalker.

"Occasionally."

"What got you into boats?"

"My dad had a boat when I was younger. It was the one thing my family did together. He had a sailboat and we had to work as a team to get it moving. There was no time for my parents' bickering." He shook his head.

"Sidney said your parents live in Florida now. Do you visit much?"

"No. I've never been down."

"You're not close to them?"

"Not really. They'll be coming up when my niece is born. It will be tense." He tilted his head. "Are you close to your parents?"

"Yes. When my mother died, my father was a mess. I didn't want to go off to school and leave him alone, but he insisted. And my mother had insisted before she passed." She smiled at the memory. "I came home for spring break during my junior year and he was acting all nervous when he picked me up at the airport. I didn't know what was up with him. When we got home he made me wait in the car until he mustered up enough nerve to finally tell me he had a girlfriend and she was living with him."

"That must have been a shock." He had lived through a similar shock with his parents. Though not as nice of a one.

"It was, and I didn't have much time to figure out how I felt about it. Just the few steps from the driveway to the door. But then I saw my dad's face when he introduced me to Belinda and I knew it was fine. She made him happy. And I wanted my dad to be happy."

"And you like her?"

"Yeah. She's great." She nodded. "The weird thing is she's not like my mother at all. They have completely different personalities. It's strange how someone can love one person, but can also love someone else completely different." Her father had found love twice, while some people never found it. It didn't seem fair, but he didn't say that out loud.

After the topic of love came up, they kept their gazes on everything else in the room besides each other.

A slow song came on, and couples migrated out to the dance floor, assuming the position. Men with their hands on hips. Woman with their arms looped around necks. There were a few couples that actually knew how to do a formal style dance. They wove in and out between the stiff-legged variety.

"Would you like to dance?" he asked. Her eyes widened in surprise. "Since you missed your prom." He quickly made up an excuse.

"Sure." He took her hand as they walked to the dance floor staying three feet from each other. There was a brief hesitation between them until he held out his arms awkwardly and she stepped into them.

He began turning them in a small circle to the sway of the music. He might not know how to waltz, but he could turn her in a small circle. She smiled up at him. Apparently he was doing well enough.

Now that she was in his arms, so close to his body that he could feel the heat of her skin, he became a bit more courageous.

"So how's your boyfriend dealing with you being away this weekend?" he asked.

Her step faltered, and she tilted her head to the side.

"I don't have a boyfriend." Her tone made it sound as if the idea was preposterous.

"Did you break up?"

"With who? I haven't had a date since Christmas."

"Oh." He reflected her look of confusion. "I thought—Never mind." He shook it off. Who had she been talking about on the phone?

"Does your girlfriend mind that you're away?" she asked timidly.

Was she joking? "I don't have a girlfriend."

"So the flowers didn't work, huh?" she said with a little smile. "Sorry."

"What flowers?"

"I saw the charge on the credit card."

He looked up at the ceiling, cursing his stupidity. Why hadn't he used a personal card so she wouldn't have seen the charge? Flowers obviously aren't a business expense anyway. He had been too nervous to think that morning.

He wasn't sure what to say next. He glanced around at all the other happy couples on the dance floor. He wanted that. He wanted to be a happy couple with Kenley and he'd waited long enough. He decided it was all or nothing.

"The flowers were for you. I was going to give them to you, and then ask you out. But I heard you on the phone talking about a date and taking it slow or something, and I ditched that plan."

Her sexy lips formed a perfect O and then she giggled.

"I was talking about you. Vanessa thought our trip to Galveston counted as a date."

"You said we were taking it slow?"

She shrugged and her cheeks flushed.

"We had been kind of flirting. I thought that was us taking it slow," she explained. She was adorable when she was embarrassed. He wanted her all the more.

"I think our attempt at flirting was more like taking things incrementally and painfully slow." They laughed together. For a second the moment seemed light, but too soon the awkwardness took hold of them again.

She was in his arms, she liked him, and she didn't have a boyfriend. It seemed like the obvious next step would be to kiss her or ask her out on a real date, or at the very least to say something charming.

He couldn't think of a damn thing. All the times before when he couldn't seem to remember she was his employee caught up to him in that moment when it was the only thing he could think of.

She didn't have anything to offer either. She tensed and watched the other dancers intently. When the music changed to a faster song, they sprang apart as if they were on fire.

He opened his mouth to say something at the same time she said, "I guess it's getting late."

"Yeah. I guess so." It wasn't even ten, but he could tell she wanted to get away. He needed to make sure they were okay. "Hey, about before."

"Yes?" She seemed eager to hear what he had to say.

"I don't want things to be complicated or awkward between us. You're a valuable asset to the company, and I'd hate it if I did something to mess that up."

"Right. I was thinking the same thing."

So that was that. He'd admitted he had feelings for her. She'd admitted she had feelings for him. But it didn't matter.

* * *

The moment was over. She'd messed it up. When he walked her to the elevator she was already planning to call Vanessa and tell her what had happened. Hopefully Vanessa would have some advice to help her. She really liked Zane, but between the fear of possibly losing her job and the terror of having to tell him she had never been with a man, she was barely able to speak. When she realized she wouldn't be able to call Vanessa with a dead phone, her shoulders slumped. "I just remembered I left my charger plugged in the boat."

She could only hope it didn't sound like a ploy to get him alone on the boat. It truly wasn't. She wasn't smooth enough to come up with an elaborate plan of seduction.

As they walked back to the boat in silence, she desperately tried to think of something to say to get the moment back. She didn't want to go back to inept flirting, or the miscommunications. She wanted him. And she needed her job.

He helped her onto the boat where she retrieved the charging cable from the deck. When she turned to leave he stood blocking the way. He stared at her for a long moment.

"Would you like some wine?"

"Wine?"

"It's in the refrigerator. It makes it look classy when I rent it out."

"Sure." She grabbed on to any reason to stay with him. Maybe wine would make it easier to tell him she was a virgin, but didn't want to be any longer.

She sat on the deck, listening to the sounds of him below in the galley.

Silently she braced herself for the next step. The final step. She wanted to be with Zane, and she wasn't going to let fear stop her again.

Zane handed her a glass and tapped his to hers. "To your first boat show."

She took a sip and then a nervous gulp.

He watched her over the edge of his glass as he took his sip and then set the glass down.

"The stars are bright tonight," he mentioned.

Stars. Talking about stars was something someone would do if they were trying to be romantic, right? Or was he into astronomy? She was so nervous her wine sloshed. Or maybe it was because she was in a boat. The soft sounds of the water slapping against the hull reminded her that this was real.

"So tomorrow we're meeting the guy about the cuddy?" she said, so she had something to talk about.

"Yes. He said around ten. If I can get a good deal, I think Wes will be happy with it." More silence.

"Are you going to build one of the boats you drew someday?"

"I've started on one of them. It's sitting in my garage at home. I guess boat building for pleasure doesn't feel much different than boat building for business."

That made sense. She twisted her fingers in her lap, grasping for something else to talk about. She was so nervous. How did people do this every weekend with strangers?

"Do you ever draw for fun?"

"I don't have a lot of time for any kind of fun, actually."

"Oh." Was that his way of putting her off? His eyes seemed to be luring her in. She didn't understand. She was so bad at this.

They found other things to chat about as they finished the wine and watched the stars. He told her he had a degree in engineering and how his roommate had wanted him to get a job at his family's firm in New York.

"I hated high school, and I always planned to move away. But after college when I had my chance, something brought me back to the area. I guess it's home."

"I liked living in New York, but it is nice being closer to Madison." Working with him.

When she couldn't put it off any longer she stood up to go to the hotel. Zane followed her as she got to the steps that would lead her to the dock.

She needed to do something. There would be no way she could go to sleep with these feelings zinging through her body. It just wasn't possible.

She needed him. Now.

* * *

"Do you—" Zane stopped when she paused at the steps that would take her off the boat. He couldn't say what he was thinking. He was just desperate to keep her close.

"Do I what?" she asked. The look on her face made him want to answer.

"You were right when you said high school was just practice for real life. I kind of missed a lot of practice back then." Special thanks to the wine for making the stuff on the inside of his head come out so freely.

"Me too."

"Maybe it's not too late." He took a step closer. She didn't move away, but she looked like a bunny being hunted by a wolf.

He opened his mouth to take it all back and apologize, but before he got the chance his lips were covered by hers.

"Yes," she whispered against him. Since his mouth was still open, it was easy for her to slip her tongue inside. His eyes were also still open, which was helpful in convincing himself this was actually happening.

The last time he'd told her it would be impossible for her to kiss him without him being on board. He had been wrong. She had definitely kissed him this time. She was braver than he was. She was the wolf.

His two-second delay went unnoticed as he quickly got in the game and kissed her back. Not only was he kissing her, but he was searching her body with his hands. He pushed her up against the wall of the bridge, making her moan as his body pressed to every part of hers.

This was just the beginning. There was no stopping in sight. He only had two questions at this point.

"How drunk are you?" he asked.

"I'm not," she answered.

"Are you sure?" was his second question.

"Yes." She managed to get out between gasps. She was really into it. He smiled against her lips while walking backward toward the steps that would take them below.

He kissed her for a long time before opening the door and leading her down. It was difficult to kiss while descending narrow stairs, so he helped her on the steps until she was safely against him once more.

At that moment, seeing her in his stateroom with the contents of his suitcase askew, he felt the impact of what was about to happen. Her lip curled up on one side as she unbuttoned the top button on her shirt.

There was no more resisting. He had to do this. In the name of every awkward teenage boy who was ever smitten with the sexy cheerleader, he had to. It was his duty. He was owed this for all the time he'd spent pining for an unattainable girl back in high school.

And then he noticed the way her hand shook as she moved to the second button and everything changed. This wasn't about the past or the girl he'd once thought he loved.

It was about Kenley. The amazing woman who was here with him now. He thought all this time he'd been attracted to her because she'd looked like the girl of his dreams. But somewhere along the way she'd taken over that spot all on her own.

There was only her.

She sat on the edge of the big bed, and he crawled over her as he made his way up to her lips again.

After his transformation from ugly duckling in college, he'd had his fair share of sex. He became quite skilled at it, giving him even more confidence as he grew into himself.

He decided to unleash all his best tricks on Kenley. Taking his time, he removed her shirt and jeans. But once he caught a glimpse of her sexy bra and panties, his movements became more hurried. Taking his time became a struggle.

She was as perfect as he'd fantasized. Her hard nipples pressed into his chest when released from her bra. He spent a good bit of his attention on them before taking off her panties.

And within a few minutes she was lying next to him, naked and breathing heavily. At some point his clothes came off, either her doing or his, he couldn't quite remember. The sound of their panting filled the space as he reached for a condom from the built-in nightstand and rolled it on. He was surprised to see his hands shaking slightly.

He gazed at the beautiful woman in his bed. It was like a dream coming true, and he couldn't help but take another long moment to appreciate it. To appreciate her.

With a smile at each other he lined up to her warmth, ready to slide into her. He touched her wet heat and then... resistance. He pulled back slightly, and tried again with the same result.

He looked down in confusion. Was he in the wrong place? He was a little buzzed, but not enough that he couldn't get Tab A into Slot B.

"I'm sorry," he said. Maybe he was nervous? He didn't feel nervous anymore, he felt determined. He wanted to be inside her. More than anything.

"It's okay. I'm fine."

He kissed her neck and then took his time making sure he was lined up at the exact spot. Pushing in again, he was faced with the same problem. It was as if he didn't fit, but he pushed on, unable to do anything else.

He heard her panting change from rapture to whimpers of pain and started to pull out again.

"No, please. Just do it. Please? Don't stop," she was begging him. Kenley Carmichael was in his bed begging him to have sex with her. He would not fail her.

When he pushed harder she cried out, and not in a good way. It was only when she relaxed, that he began to put the pieces of the puzzle together.

Was she a virgin? No, it wasn't possible. She was twenty-eight years old. Women who looked like Kenley weren't still virgins at twenty-eight. There had to be a law or something.

She kissed him and pulled him closer. All the emotions, mixed with this new possibility, and the physical sensations were too much for him to stop to ask questions. He looked down, seeing the trust in her eyes and the necklace he'd given her against her bare skin, and was overwhelmed.

"Don't stop," she said again. He had no intention of stopping.

He whispered her name and pushed into her fully, the heat almost too much to bear. The tightness around him was glorious. He continued and she began moving with him like she'd done this with him every night. He must have been mistaken about her inexperience before. He cast the thought aside, so he could concentrate on what was happening now.

Her tiny cries and moans were now from pleasure. He was making her feel good and that thought had him getting too close to the edge. He kissed her again as he rocked into her harder. Her orgasm came on quickly, and seemed to surprise her. But her moans of satisfaction continued louder, as he thrust into her those last few times that ended him.

He felt almost dizzy when he rolled off her and stared up at the low ceiling. He pulled her close to kiss her head and play with her hair. He'd been out of the game for a few months and now he felt energized. Not only had they had sex, but it had been mind-blowing sex at that.

People over-used that term. He was guilty of it himself. But this had truly been amazing. No exaggeration needed.

As his body calmed, he realized he was happier than he'd ever been after sex. He wasn't second guessing anything. There were no regrets. It was just her and happiness.

He'd had sex with the amazing woman in his arms, whom he respected and cared about. She was more than the physical part.

She was every part.

# Chapter 10

Neither of them said anything for a few minutes, which was good because Kenley had no clue how to make words. She was still floating in the new world, which was sex. Sex with Zane. Her own orgasms had never been like this—so intense and wonderful.

They lay there, touching one another, fingertips traveling over skin. Their legs still wound together, and she wished they could stay tangled up like that forever. She smiled at the sight of his fingers wound through hers, wondering what she should say.

She had no point of reference for all the emotions that arose after sex. Over the years, her friends had told her all the gory details about the act itself, but they hadn't explained this feeling. This sense of relaxation and happiness that made her want to purr like a cat.

Maybe not everyone felt this way?

She felt as though she should comment on his performance. She had nothing to compare it to, but she had to believe it was quite good since he was able to make her have an orgasm the first time out of the gate.

Eventually, he pulled his arm out from under her and rolled out of bed toward the tiny bathroom. The light snapped on and she watched his face as he looked down at himself, his brows pulled together.

Blood.

Not tons, but enough to reveal her secret. If she had successfully hidden her inexperience during their lovemaking, there were no doubts now.

He closed the door, giving her a moment to inspect things. Everything seemed to be in order on her end. No puddles of innocence or arterial spray. A few tissues from the built-in nightstand and all evidence was gone.

She was no longer a virgin.

She heard the toilet flush and then the water running, her cue to get in bed and strike an alluring and sated pose for his return. Again, she wasn't quite sure what to do, so she pulled the sheet across her middle, revealing her leg and one breast.

He stepped back into the room and looked at her in utter confusion.

"What's wrong?" she asked.

"I need to ask you something, and I want you to tell me the truth." His voice cracked on the word *truth*.

"Okay."

"Were you…? Did I just…?" He ran his fingers through his hair, and then tucked the towel tighter around his waist.

Kenley didn't say anything. Technically he hadn't asked anything yet. She allowed him to stammer.

"I mean it felt … and then the blood … and you looked like I hurt you, but that can't be." He met her eyes for the first time. "Can it?"

That was a question. *The* question.

"If you're asking if I lost my virginity tonight with you, then yes." She bit her bottom lip. "I did."

"Why didn't you say something?" He clenched his hair with his hands, his voice turning accusatory.

"What does it matter? Isn't this something you can brag about with your friends?"

"No!" he said with wide eyes. "It's something very important. Something you wait to do with someone special. Why *me*?"

"I'm twenty-eight. I was done waiting. I was willing to settle for someone who wasn't a dick." She sighed. It wouldn't help to get angry at him. "Besides, it *was* special. At least I thought so."

His eyes weren't any less frantic, and he didn't speak.

"It's not like I expect anything serious between us. I wanted my first time to be with a nice guy, and you're a nice guy." She shrugged, going for nonchalance.

"You could have said something." He seemed more upset about the secrecy than the deflowering. What a silly word. There was nothing flowery about it.

"You would have freaked out and not wanted to do it."

"Probably." He paced in the small space, ducking so his head wouldn't hit the ceiling. "Why me, Kenley? This is a lot of pressure."

"It's not any pressure. We can go back to work like friends."

"Shit! You *work* for me!" He held his hands up to the ceiling as if he just remembered this fact. The pacing became more like laps.

Kenley got out of bed and stepped toward him. She was still naked, and it hurt when his eyes darted away from her body like he was committing a sin by looking at her.

"I know I'm new at this part, but I guess sometimes the guy wants the girl to leave right away. Should I go? Would that be easier?"

"No," he said quickly. "I don't want you to leave. God, I'm not going to send you packing after I just..." He gestured toward her body, but still wouldn't look at her.

"Maybe I should go." She decided to make the choice for him. He was freaking out. She didn't want him to invite her to stay out of obligation.

She pulled on her clothes haphazardly while he stood there staring at the floor.

"I'm sorry," she whispered as she left the room. She kept going. Only when she was at the end of the dock did she stop. Her hands were shaking so badly she dropped one of her shoes on her bare toe as she fumbled to get it on. The fact that she could barely see through her tears didn't help matters.

She wiped the tears away before entering the hotel. Keeping her head down, she rode up to her room on the elevator. After fumbling with the stupid card for what felt like forever, she finally got inside her room.

Once inside, she dropped her purse on the table by the door and slid to the floor, letting the tears flow.

It wasn't about losing her virginity. By this point, she couldn't have cared less about how special and magical it was supposed to be. She didn't see it as a precious gift to be given to a deserving soul who would prove himself worthy by beheading dragons and saving the realm. It was just a thing, like getting her ears pierced, or her first hangover.

The thing that hurt was what she'd messed up with Zane. She knew him well enough to know how he would handle this. He would ignore her and keep her at a distance so he wouldn't have to deal with it. She cursed herself for not driving. Having to go back home in his boat—the boat where they'd been happy for a few moments—would be torture.

She wasn't sorry she'd picked him. He had been wonderful. If it had been a precious gift, then she was glad she'd given it to him. But now what?

A firm tap on the door behind her interrupted her from her sob fest. She quieted and froze, a defense mechanism usually employed by rabbits when being hunted by a fox. But she wasn't a rabbit, so it was no surprise when this method didn't work.

The fox knocked again.

"Kenley, please open the door. I'm not leaving."

With an exasperated sigh, she stood. For a second she contemplated her appearance—shirt buttoned up crookedly, jeans unzipped, hair mussed, makeup smeared by tears.

What did it matter?

She opened the door and watched his shoulders slump and his face fall in agony.

"Before you even think I'm crying because of what happened, I'm not. I'm glad it happened. Happy even."

"Yes, you look so happy."

"I am. I'm just upset about messing things up between us."

"I'm worried about that too. I didn't handle it right. I didn't want you to leave."

"Well, I did. I'm here now." She pointed to the very rosy room behind her.

"Right, but it's not that far. You could come back if you wanted." He pointed down with a small smile. "Do you want to?"

"Do you want me to?"

He let his head hang forward and then shook it slowly. "We're not good at this," he said.

"No. I guess not." She frowned and looked at his bare feet. How could a guy have sexy feet? It wasn't fair. Everything about him was sexy. From his muscled arms and shoulders to his bare chest and ripped abs. She had no idea all this was lurking under that scruffy flannel and faded T-shirt.

He put his finger under her chin and nudged her face up so he could look into her eyes.

"Just because we're not good at this, doesn't mean it's not worth trying to work it out."

A small smile threatened to break across her face. He leaned down and kissed her. Everything she'd felt before came crashing back over her. She hadn't realized she would want him so much, so soon, but she did. It was as if she had an on switch and he'd flipped it.

She deepened the kiss and pulled him toward her bed. He followed along willingly.

Slipping her hand under the waistband of his jeans made him moan. The power in that caused her body shake. His fingers fumbled, but he got her shirt open. She hadn't put on her bra in her rush to get away.

How strange—she didn't want to be away from him now. She never would have thought of herself as a flighty person, but this man made her crazy.

She kicked off her jeans at the same time he pulled off his pants. Then he froze.

"Hell. I only had the one condom," he said with a tortured expression.

"It's okay, I'm on birth control. To regulate my cycle." She was happy to finally get the chance to use it for its intended purpose. He murmured something that sounded like praise to God as she fell back on the bed. He moved between her legs and slid inside her in one movement.

It went a lot better this time. The tenderness was mild, there was no stinging, as she'd experienced the first time. And the pleasure made it worth it.

"Oh God," he whispered as he began moving slowly. She smiled up at him and he smiled back.

"It's okay?" he asked.

"Better than okay," she answered. "You can go faster."

"No, I can't. If I do, it will be over way too soon."

"Oh." She smiled wider, knowing it felt too good for him to control himself. She loved that.

"Really?" He chuckled as he noticed. "Now, I'm going to have to wipe that smug little smile off your face." He pulled out, causing her to groan from his absence.

"No. Please. I won't smile. Just come back." It was too late. He wasn't coming back. He was kissing her neck and moving down. Somehow he was able to play with one of her nipples with his fingers while sucking the other one into his mouth. She had to love a man who could multitask.

She couldn't keep her body still, it seemed to writhe and arch on the bed without her permission. A whimper escaped when he released her breasts. The moisture he left on her flesh chilled quickly in the cool room, but the rest of her was flaming hot.

She assumed he would move back into position, but instead he was kissing down her stomach. When he dipped his tongue into her belly button she jolted, knowing where he was heading.

"You don't have to—"

"Shut up," he said. She could feel his laughter on her inner thigh as he spread her legs.

"But I'm not sure—"

"Don't worry. I'm sure." He winked at her from his spot between her legs, and then before she could offer another protest his tongue swept up through her wetness and she involuntarily screamed and pulled away.

It felt too good. She wasn't prepared.

Zane laughed again, this time his breath spread over her center, causing yet another jolt.

"Watch me, Kenley," he said, and she realized her eyes were squeezed shut in anticipation. She opened them and looked down as he stroked her with his tongue again.

Her head fell to the side and her fingers clenched the sheets.

The tension she'd felt before was back. She knew wave after wave of pleasure was headed her way. She was so close.

Zane slid one finger inside her, stroking her internally while his tongue lapped at her again and again.

Somehow her hands had moved to his hair, and she was pulling him closer as she screamed out his name. The tremors began, and she knew she screamed again, but had no idea what she might have said.

She hardly had a moment to catch her breath before he was moving inside her again. Apparently she was going to catch up on all the years of sex she'd missed in just one night.

"Zane," she said breathlessly.

"Yes, sweetheart?" Oh. God. He'd called her sweetheart.

"Is it rude if I have more orgasms than you?" she panted while he laughed, the sensation of his laughter while he was inside her made her gasp with pleasure.

"Take as many as you can get." He kissed her lips, her cheek, her jaw and her neck.

It didn't take her long to test him on his generous offer.

Certainly she was being selfish. She should do something for him. She'd serviced a man before—she knew how—and while she hadn't really enjoyed it before, she thought that might be different now. With Zane. "Let me…" She wiggled again, but Zane kept her firmly in place under him.

"Stay still and come for me again, Kenley." At his words, she gave in. She pressed up off the bed, meeting each trust eagerly until her legs could no longer support her, and she slid back down to the mattress.

Zane's pace sped up and with a loud groan he pushed into her as far as he could before he collapsed. The heat he released into her like pulses of fire.

Her breathing was so loud. It might have been embarrassing except that Zane was just as out of breath.

"I can't believe I waited so long. Had I known it would be so great…" She shook her head, and he laughed.

"I've created a monster," he said, propping himself up so he was looking at her. She didn't shy away from his gaze. Instead she looked back at him, feeling invincible and happy.

"Is it always like this?" she asked. No way could everyone have sex like that. No one would ever want to do anything else. Nothing would ever get done.

He chuckled and shook his head. He didn't elaborate, and she didn't push for details. Being with him was enough.

"I still can't figure out how you made it this long without having sex. Every guy you dated had to be all over you," he said.

"I didn't really date much in high school. And in college they would drink too much and forget they didn't have sex with me, or worse; think they did." She frowned. "When I got out of school I was determined to find Mr. Right. But it wasn't easy finding someone who was the complete package. Especially when my list was extremely unrealistic. And then I started working right out of college, and was too busy to date. When I did, it was just one or two times at the most.

"I can't tell you how many times I almost went for it on the first date, just to get it over with. But I couldn't. I knew special was overrated, but I still didn't want to have regrets."

"And do you have any?" he asked as he brushed his fingers through her hair.

"No. Not one."

He leaned over and kissed her softly.

"We should get some sleep." He pulled her against him and put his face in her hair. Kissing her neck, he mumbled a goodnight and they drifted off together.

Hands down, it was the most amazing night of her life. Maybe special wasn't so overrated after all.

* * *

Zane woke before Kenley. She was curled up next to him, her long blond hair covering her face. Slowly, so as not to wake her, he moved the strands so he could look at her.

She looked like an angel, or a sleeping princess, or any of those things only guys who were whipped would think when they looked at a woman. Except this was different.

What would she want from him? What would he be willing to give? As he watched her sleep, anxiety crept in.

How long before she moved on to someone else, leaving him in shambles? Worse, he'd just opened her up to a whole new world. Surely she would want to explore it fully.

He'd nearly thought himself into a panic when his phone rang. It was on the floor in his pants, but he could hear it blaring his sister's ring tone. Hearing the theme song that accompanied Darth Vader's entrance made him cringe instinctually.

He snuggled in closer to Kenley as she shifted from the disruption. A call from the President of the United States wouldn't get him out of that bed. Not while he was sharing it with the most amazing woman he'd ever known.

But Sidney called again. By the third time, Kenley stirred and looked up. A happy smile crossed her face when she saw him.

"What is that?" she asked as the phone rang again.

"My sister is calling me. Just ignore it."

"Your sister who is having a baby any day?" she reminded him with wide eyes.

"Oh shit!" He jumped out of bed and tossed their clothes around until he found his phone. "Yes? I'm here!"

"It's about time. I'm about ready to burst here, and you can't pick up your goddamned phone?"

"Shit! I'm sorry. I was—" Well, he couldn't finish that sentence with the truth. "Not with my phone."

"Dr. Daddy says it's time. We're heading to the hospital."

"But it's not time." Her due date wasn't for another week.

"Try telling that to your niece. Don't worry. I'm close enough."

"Okay. I'm on my way. I'm out of town."

"You'll have plenty of time before Mom and Dad get here from Florida. You have to get here before them, Zane. I can't handle them and have a new life wrenched from my uterus at the same time."

"Yes. I'll be there as soon as I can to run interference."

"Thank you, Uncle Z." Damn, that got him every time. He got off the phone and turned back to Kenley, who was already dressed and packing.

"We need to go," she said, having heard the conversation.

"Yeah. I'm sorry."

"Don't be. You're going to be an uncle. It's going to be great." She zipped up her bag and tugged at her T-shirt. "I can contact the dealer and reschedule the showing for Weston's boat. Are we ready?"

He didn't know how he'd gotten so lucky that she was not only sexy, but also an amazing employee. Had he won the lottery?

"Thanks."

She checked out of the hotel while he went to ready the boat. The sun was up, shooting through the sky in vibrant pink. He put her bag below. The sheets were rumpled and his stateroom smelled like sex. He couldn't help but smile at the memories it incited.

He started the boat and helped her in when she got there.

"So are you ready for this?" she asked. For a moment he assumed she meant them. Together. "My niece is six and we spend hours changing her

doll's clothes. Over and over again. It's super fun. You're going to love it."
He chuckled at her deadpan tone.

"Yeah. It's going to be great. I just hope my parents don't ruin it." It
was nice to have hope, as unrealistic as it was.

"What's their deal?"

"They fight and make everyone around them miserable because they
are miserable. When they moved to Florida two years ago, we thought it
would be a break from the misery, but no. They call and complain about
one another. They should have gotten divorced when we were kids, but I
think they're both too stubborn to be the one to give up." He didn't go into
the details of his father's affair and how it had changed his whole view on
family. She wasn't ready for that.

"Sounds lovely."

"Oh, yes. And they're on a plane right now, headed our way."

"Can't wait," she said. Did she plan to go to the hospital with him? He
assumed he'd drop her off at her place. Why would she want to spend
hours in a hospital waiting room with him? But it would make it so much
better if she was there. But why would she stay, especially after he'd just
told her the hideousness that was his parents? He smiled over at her again,
as she shifted uncomfortably in her seat.

"How do you feel?" he asked.

"A little sore, but okay." He'd made her sore? A wave of primal delight
mixed in with his concern for her well-being.

"And how do feel about what happened with us?" He kept his eyes
straight ahead on the water.

"I feel fine."

"Are you regretting it? Are you sure you weren't drunk? Did I take
advantage of you?" He wanted to make sure he hadn't set himself up for
heartbreak—or an arrest warrant. She laughed at him.

"No. Calm down. It's all good. I'm good. Stop freaking out."

"This is a lot of pressure. I've never taken someone's virginity before.
I feel like I should present your father with a goat or something." They
laughed together.

"My dad might like that."

He reached over for her hand and wound his fingers through hers.

"Seriously, though. What do we do now?" he asked.

"We go wait for your niece to get here." It sounded so simple.

Maybe it would be.

# Chapter 11

Kenley loved the feel of Zane's rough hand in hers as they walked into the hospital. She needed a shower, but the excitement kept her from being self-conscious. For a little while at least.

As they took their seats in the waiting room, she realized she would be meeting Zane's parents and she hadn't even fixed her hair. They'd simply dressed and run out the door. She thought about changing on the way, but at the speed Zane had moved through the water, the ride was too bumpy. She'd thought it best to just stay seated and hold on.

"I'm going to the bathroom," she said as she took a silent inventory of the items in her purse. Unfortunately the lipstick, mascara and powder were unable to perform the magic required to make her look glamourous. She ran her fingers through her hair and sighed at the borderline-presentable result.

She studied her reflection, looking for any change. She was no longer a virgin. She'd had sex. Multiple times. Yet she still looked the same, though a bit rumpled. She hadn't known how she would feel afterward. She'd been so focused on getting to this point she didn't know what she wanted now. She wouldn't be opposed to a relationship with Zane.

They liked each other and worked well together. In more ways than one.

Still, she didn't want to read more into it than a good time. She knew sex didn't mean wedding bells. All these years her friends had teased her with the details of the physical sexual act, she found that had been the easier part.

Now she would be expected to know all the rules for their after-sex journey and she found she had no idea what to do. While she may have had sex, she was still a relationship virgin.

"God help me." She sighed, taking one last look in the mirror.

She'd have to win over Zane's parents with charm since looks were not in the works. Zane gave her a grin when she sat next to him. He didn't seem to mind that she looked disheveled. Maybe because he was the one who had made her look that way.

"You look beautiful," he said, making her face go hot. He'd gone to get food while she was attempting a miracle, so they shared a limp breakfast sandwich and a smashed Danish.

Two hours later he stopped in the middle of his lap in the waiting room. "Thanks for staying, but you can go home if you want. You can take my truck. I'll catch a ride."

"No way. I want to see the baby." She waved in a motion to tell him he should continue his circuit. "I'll be ready to call the florist the second they tell us she's here." Sidney had become a good friend during her training so of course she wanted to be there when the baby arrived.

She also wanted to be there for Zane, and she may have also been hoping they could go back to her place and have more sex after the baby was born. Maybe he was right about creating a monster. She couldn't stop thinking about him on top of her.

"I was thinking, it might be best if we don't tell my sister or the other guys," he whispered.

"Because Brady will be jealous you never paid him the same attention?" she joked.

"I just think it would be better to keep work separate from personal."

"Of course." That made sense. As long as she got plenty of personal time, she could be a regular employee during work hours. That thought brought her up short. She'd lost her last job for sleeping with the boss's husband. She hadn't done it then. But now she was. What kind of repercussions would there be if things didn't work out? She didn't think he'd fire her, but wouldn't it be awkward?

Another hour went by and other than a few updates from Zane's brother-in-law, Tim, everything was quiet. It just gave Kenley more time to think and panic.

Finally Tim came out with a smile on his face.

"She's here!" he said.

"Congratulations, man." Zane shook Tim's hand and patted him on the back.

"She's perfect. They're weighing her and cleaning her up then we'll get you in to see her."

"I'll be waiting," Zane said.

Tim's face went white and he backed away quickly, heading for the restricted area behind the nurse's station.

Kenley turned to see what the problem was at the same time she heard Zane mutter, "Oh shit. They're here."

A couple in their fifties walked steadily toward them. It looked like they were arguing as the bleached-blond woman's face pinched up in a scowl.

"Well, did we miss it? Your father thought it would be nice to upgrade the rental, which took twenty minutes. If I missed the birth of my first grandchild by twenty minutes, you are dead to me, Randy."

"Oh, it was more like forty-five minutes ago," Zane said, saving his father. "Kenley, these are my parents, Randy and Diane. This is Kenley Carmichael. She works for me." Kenley couldn't help but notice he'd moved away from her.

"It's nice to meet you both," Kenley said, extending her hand as she nervously tucked her bed-mussed hair behind her ear. She had no experience with the Walk of Shame, especially not in front of parents. Her face felt like it was on fire.

"Oh my God. You're diddling your secretary!" his mother said, sounding both appalled and annoyed. Kenley let her hand drop down by her side as her mouth fell open in shock.

"No, I'm not." Zane denied it emphatically.

"Do you see this, Randy? This is your fault. Fooling around with one's subordinates apparently runs in the family. At least your son isn't *married*."

"Just kill me already. It would be better than hearing this again. It was eleven years ago, for Christ's sake. A moment of weakness. What do you want me to do, cut my balls off and hand 'em over?"

"Please. What would I want with those shriveled up things?" She rolled her eyes. "Look, little Miss Secretary, Jackson men are incapable of settling down. You should run now. Save yourself."

Kenley could barely swallow, her throat was so dry. There was no way she could talk. Before Tim had come out with the good news, Kenley had been worrying about all the possible pitfalls of having an affair with her boss.

She hadn't even contemplated what would happen if everyone found out. She hadn't made it ten seconds. What if Brady and Paul found out?

"Mom, knock it off. We're not sleeping together. She's my employee, that's the extent of our relationship. I would never sleep with an employee." Zane sounded very convincing. If it weren't for the fact that employees generally didn't accompany their bosses to the hospital in wrinkled clothing, it might have worked.

While she'd been in total agreement that they keep their relationship a secret just minutes before, she found his dismissal hurt. She wasn't cut out for this kind of thing. She didn't know how to be suave and sophisticated.

She wanted to go back to how things had been in her hotel room. When it was just the two of them and nothing else mattered. She didn't want to think about how they would make it work in the office, and definitely not how it would feel to be accused of inappropriate behavior and actually be guilty this time. What had she done?

"You're making an ass out of yourself, Diane. Let the boy do what he wants. He's young. Don't get yourself strapped down, son. Nail everything that moves while you still can."

"Do you want him to get some sort of disease?" his mother went on. "And he's twenty-eight. That's not that young. He should be thinking about having a family. If he's capable of such a thing after being tainted with your genes."

Kenley backed away from the argument. It was easy to do since Zane was still insisting he hadn't diddled his secretary, and his father was patting his back proudly for doing just that. In another time she might have laughed at someone actually using the word *diddling*, but it wasn't funny yet.

Instead of going out the main entrance, she walked through the emergency room and found a cab waiting at the curb where it had just dropped someone off.

She could get her bag another time. She just needed to escape.

Zane had asked her if she had regrets, and at the time she hadn't. But as the cab pulled up at her apartment, she couldn't help but feel stupid and naïve.

The best night of her life had been nothing more than a one-night stand with her boss, and she'd just now figured it out.

* * *

As she showered she tried to calm down. She began sorting things into pros and cons. It was always a logical way to come to a decision when she was too emotional. So far everything on the list of whether or not it was okay to sleep with one's boss was in the cons column.

"Damn it!"

She pulled out her phone after getting dressed and pulling her wet hair up in a ponytail.

"Hey, how's it going?" Alyssa asked.

"I need cheesecake. Can you meet me at Junior's?"

"Of course. See you in a bit."

"Thanks."

* * *

He couldn't figure out where she could have gone. One second Kenley was standing next to him during the worst conversation ever, and then she was just gone.

He'd searched everywhere but couldn't find her. He'd called and texted. Nothing. Not that he could blame her for blowing him off. He'd fucked up.

He should never have encouraged her to stay with him at the hospital. Not when he knew the hounds of hell were descending. Of course she'd run away without a word. His parents were hideous.

And he hadn't been much better.

Had he really said he'd never sleep with an employee? In front of the employee he had slept with? It was his parent's fault. They made him crazy. He couldn't think straight. He couldn't imagine what Kenley must be thinking.

He hadn't wanted anyone in his family to know about Kenley. Not because he was embarrassed. Hell, she was wonderful. Any normal family would have welcomed her with open arms, not scorned her as some kind of illicit temptress.

As it was, he should have come clean when his mother called them out, but fear had held him back. Not fear of his mother or what they might think, but fear that if he announced their relationship formally it would mean more to him than he wanted it to.

He should have found out what she wanted. He should have told her how he felt. Instead she was gone and he was back to being the boss.

When he got called back to his sister's room, he waited his turn to see the little person who was his niece. She was tiny and loud, and he was won over instantly. He wished Kenley had gotten the chance to see her. Thinking of her standing by his side made his heart hurt.

"Did you know your brother is sleeping with his secretary?" his mother asked Sidney, who raised her eyebrows.

"You didn't," she said. He couldn't answer her.

While his mother and father talked in high voices to the baby, Sidney motioned him closer.

"Is it true? You slept with Kenley?"

"Yes." He let it out with a sigh. Why not admit it now? He'd been planning to tell Sidney at some point. Just not right away. Not when he could still smell Kenley's sweet perfume on his shirt. "And then I said I didn't, right in front of her. I didn't defend her to Mom and Dad. She made a run for it and I'm worried I might not see her again. What if she doesn't come back to work? What am I going to do?"

"If I hadn't had another human being pulled out of my uterus I would get out of this bed and beat you silly." He didn't know what was worse, the threat of a beating or any talk of his sister's uterus. He knew he deserved whatever punishment she dished out.

"I panicked," he admitted.

"You probably should have introduced her as a friend or a girlfriend, and not even told them she worked for you."

"Yeah. That would have been better. I didn't think of that." He frowned and tried to change the subject. "She's beautiful, Sid." He nodded toward the baby.

"I think so too." He relaxed, having managed to steer her to another topic. "You need to go fix this thing with Kenley." Or maybe not.

"What should I do?"

"Do you like her?"

"Yes."

"Do you want to be with her?"

"Yes."

"Find her and tell her how you really feel about her."

He let out another sigh.

"That might be a problem. I don't know how I really feel. I mean last night everything seemed clear, but now it's kind of complicated."

"Don't be one of those guys who wanted the girl until he got her, and now just wants to get away." He wanted to defend himself and tell her he wasn't doing that, but maybe it was true. Not because he wanted to move on, but because he was afraid he wouldn't be able to keep her and he'd find himself back in the position of wanting someone he couldn't have. He didn't want to go back to being that person again.

"She's my employee, Sid. What if it doesn't work out? It would be uncomfortable for both of us."

"You're assuming it's not going to work out. And even if it ends, it doesn't automatically mean you can't continue to work together. We had a stressful relationship and it didn't get in the way of our working relationship."

If she'd planned to make him feel better, she'd struck out. Working with Sidney—while easier in some ways—also meant he had to agree to things he might not have agreed to if they hadn't been related. It also meant seeing so much of her that the sound of her voice sometimes made him nauseous.

"You need to at least try. Go talk to her."

She was right. Regardless of what happened, he needed to make things right. After all, he'd taken her virginity. No. He hadn't taken it. He hadn't even known it was up for grabs. This was on her. She'd hoisted her virginity on him, ambushed him with it even.

He rubbed his forehead. Was he really blaming her for this? He needed to do better. He'd wanted this woman since the moment she'd walked into his office. He'd gotten her and now he was... what?

Terrified.

Once he'd come up with a plausible excuse as to why his parents couldn't stay at his house during their visit, he left the hospital to find Kenley.

He called again, and left a message.

"Look, I'm really sorry about what happened at the hospital. Can we talk? Please call me back. I'm sorry."

He pulled up in front of her apartment and knocked on the front door before going to the back. Her car wasn't there, but maybe she'd parked somewhere else.

After ten minutes, he decided she wasn't hiding inside her apartment. She really wasn't home.

He'd blown it, and now he couldn't even find her to make things right. As if he had a clue how to do that even if he did find her.

\* \* \*

"Are you sure you're not making a big deal out of this scene at the hospital as a reason to push him away because you're scared?" Liss asked before licking her fork clean. Once they'd both completed their fork-gasm, she'd told her ex-coworker the story. Leaving out the part about her being a virgin.

There was no reason to make her friend choke on perfectly good cheesecake.

"No. Of course not." Kenley made a snorting sound in an effort to make Liss feel ridiculous for considering such a thing. Though... "Yes. Maybe." She changed her answer. "I started thinking about all the things that could go wrong if it didn't work out between us."

"You're worried about losing your job?"

"Right."

"He can't fire you if you refuse to have sex with him again. It would be illegal."

"I'm not concerned so much about not wanting to have sex with him again. I don't think that will be a problem. It's more about the dynamic in the office. Maybe he won't fire me, but if it's uncomfortable, we'll both be miserable. Surely he wouldn't encourage me to stay under those conditions."

"I think you're talking to the wrong friend." Liss was not a relationship person. In fact, Kenley didn't remember a time when she'd dated the same guy more than once. Still, she didn't feel comfortable talking about it with Vanessa and Rachel who were cover models for *Marriage Weekly*. She didn't need the added stress of how to move things to the next level when she was panicking on the level she was already on.

"Do you know of anyone who's done this and had it work out in the end?" Kenley waited.

"No. No one."

"Damn."

"So what are you going to do?"

"I'm not sure." Kenley shook her head. "I sure liked the sex."

"Was it your first time?"

"How did you know?"

"You rarely dated, and you were the only female in the office who didn't complain about the strange noises and facial expressions of the guys you'd had sex with."

"I still have no point of reference on that front. I liked Zane's noises and facial expressions. Well, maybe not the horrified shock part."

"Congrats on reaching the new plateau."

"Emotions sure do mess up a good thing."

"Amen." She nodded as Kenley's phone buzzed again. She had been avoiding Zane's calls. She didn't know what to say yet. "Do you like this job?"

"Yes."

"Do you like this guy?"

"Yeah."

"Then you're going to have to talk to him eventually. Answer it while I go get us each another piece of cheesecake."

"You're the best."

Kenley picked up her phone, looked at Zane's name, and sighed. She was acting like the naïve virgin she had been the day before.

If they went public things could be uncomfortable if they didn't work out. But should they assume things would go bad? Could she risk it? She needed a job. It had been difficult to get a job after the first scandal. How would she manage an interview when there were two?

Armed with steely determination she answered on the next ring.

"Hello."

"Kenley, I'm so sorry."

"How's Sidney and the baby?" she redirected.

"They're fine. Good. Can I come over so we can talk?"

"I'm in New York. I needed cheesecake."

"Oh. I see." *Did he think cheesecake equated to DEFCON 2 in the relationship world?* "Will you be home later?"

"I'll be at work tomorrow morning."

"I won't be in tomorrow. I have a trip." Which he'd scheduled himself.

"I'll make sure to forward any messages."

"I think we should discuss this."

"I think we should just keep things professional going forward." She swallowed and gripped the phone tighter.

"Oh. Okay. If that's what you want." He didn't sound so sure, and she almost faltered. But she didn't want to risk her job on her irrational emotional state. Professionalism was the only option she could see. Sleeping with her boss had been a mistake. The best they could do now was put it behind them.

"I'll see you when you get back. Let me know if there's anything you need me to take care of while you're away." She fell back into her role of assistant who managed things efficiently and pleasantly.

"Sure. Thanks."

"Goodbye." She hung up and winced from the pain in her chest.

"You cut things off?" Liss set a plate in front of her.

"Yes. It's for the best."

"Are you sure that's what you want?"

"I'm not sure of anything right now."

\* \* \*

The next morning she opened the building and started coffee. A few of the guys stopped by to pick up paperwork before starting the day, each giving her a smile and a greeting as they drained the coffeepot. No one started a new one.

It was going to be one of those days.

Three days later she still hadn't seen or heard from Zane. She wanted to be mad at him for hiding, but she'd insisted they keep things professional and he was away on business.

On Friday morning she was ready to break down and call him, but then Officer Scott Porter walked in.

"Good morning, Officer," she said with a smile. She was so happy to have someone to talk to she didn't even mind that she didn't have any feelings for him. He was a nice enough guy.

"Good morning." He winked as he held out a small bag with a picture of a muffin on it. "Before you get all excited about me buying you a pastry, you should know I didn't actually pay for it. Nobody lets you pay for stuff when you're in uniform. I feel like a mobster or something."

She peeked inside to see a cinnamon roll.

"Thank you for sharing your protection pastry with me," she joked.

"I also wanted to see if you were free tonight. My shift is over at four. I could pick you up here at five."

She looked down at her jeans and button-down.

"You look great. We're not going to do anything fancy. Just dinner and get to know each other a little. What do you say?" He was actually asking her this time.

For a small second her mouth opened to say she was seeing someone. But then she remembered she wasn't seeing Zane. She wasn't seeing him, hearing him, or reading him by text or email. Other than receiving the invoices through the system, she might have thought he'd been kidnapped or something. Besides this man was not her boss.

She could go out with him, have a nice time, and not worry that it might affect her job. It didn't matter that she didn't feel a spark. He was safe.

"Sure. I'll be ready at five."

"Excellent. I'm looking forward to it." He backed toward the door. "Until then, have a great day."

"See you then," she called, knowing he wasn't the man she really wanted to see.

The day went by quickly. She only had a few minutes to spend worrying about her date with Scott. His method of ambush dating was a godsend.

At four thirty she stepped into the bathroom to check her hair and makeup. Good to go.

She was tossing her lipstick back in her bag as she walked down the hall and ran right smack into Zane.

Her bag landed on the floor with the contents scattered around his scruffy boots. As they both bent to gather her things their heads knocked together in a painful thump.

"I'm sorry," he said, his voice low and rough. It made her stomach flip in excitement. Unfortunately her stomach wasn't aware of what this man had done to her heart.

"I'm fine."

He put his hand on hers and looked her in the eye.

"No. I mean, I'm sorry, Kenley."

"Don't worry about it. While I don't regret what happened, I think it best that we keep things professional. I like my job and I like working for you. I don't want to risk messing it up."

He let out a breath and nodded.

"You're right. I'm still sorry about what happened with my parents."

"Don't worry about it," she repeated. After throwing the last of the items into her purse she passed him to go back to her desk. It was almost five.

Of all the times for Zane to show up wanting to apologize, why did it have to be ten minutes before her date was coming to pick her up?

But no. It wasn't ten minutes before her date was coming. Of course, Scott was early. He stepped inside the lobby, wearing jeans and a dress shirt. Out of uniform she could really look at him. He was cute. Tall and broad-shouldered. Much like Zane, who had followed her to the lobby and gave Scott a nod.

"Hey," Zane said with his brows pulled together. "Did we have plans tonight?"

Scott shook his head.

"Not with you. I'm here to pick up Kenley." He held out his arm like the perfect gentleman. "Are you ready to go?" he asked.

She wanted to say no and run back to Zane, but instead she shut off her computer and nodded.

"All set."

* * *

They were nearly out the door before Zane realized what was going on. She was going on a date. With Scott.

While Zane knew the officer wasn't a player, he'd heard more than enough tales of carnage and mischief when they went for drinks on the rare occasion they were both not working.

One thing was for sure, Scott Porter knew how to seduce women. And he had just walked out the door with Zane's girl.

Zane didn't know what to do as he stood at the glass door watching them. Scott opened the passenger door to his cruiser and closed it behind her. He gave Zane a smile and a wave as he passed in front of the car to get in the driver's side. This was really happening.

Should he run out there to stop them? Maybe some cool move like sliding across the hood and pulling her out of the car in one big swoop? Would she even want him after what he'd done?

Probably not. Truth be told, he didn't want to be with himself much at the moment. Fear had kept him from getting too close to Kenley. Fear that he would turn back into that pathetic puppy he'd been in high school. Fear that he wouldn't be enough to keep someone as amazing as her. Fear of the pain that would destroy him when she left him for one of the cool kids.

Apparently Scott Porter was one of the cool kids.

"Christ," he muttered as he stomped back down the hall to his office, and slammed the door.

* * *

As Scott had promised, they spent the evening eating and getting to know each other.

He had a lot of funny stories about his job, and he seemed captivated when she talked about herself. He even asked follow-up questions, proving he'd been paying attention.

"So let me get this straight, someone left you in a library when you were little, and the town named you after the book you were holding?"

"Yes. I was known as the library girl. I don't remember it. My only memories are with my adopted parents. I think my life turned out better than it might have if my real parents had kept me." She believed that to be true, though she did occasionally wonder why they hadn't kept her.

"Maybe I could run your DNA through the system and see if anything pops up."

She tilted her head to the side, thinking it over for no more than a few seconds before shaking her head.

"No, thank you. I have no interest in finding them. No reason to go looking for trouble."

"Smart girl."

By the time Scott dropped her off at her house, she knew a lot about him. Including the most important thing.

While he seemed interested in her, and he was both charming and adorable, he just wasn't Zane Jackson.

"Thank you for a great time," she said when they arrived at her door. There was no way she'd invite him inside. While she wasn't a virgin anymore, she wasn't ready to sleep with men on the first date. Especially not when she was still hung up on the first guy.

There might have been a warning, but she was distracted with thoughts of Zane when Scott bent close and kissed her on the mouth.

Her body instantly turned into a plank and she couldn't breathe until he stepped back. He was frowning down at her.

"Okay. Don't panic. Take a deep breath and relax. When you're ready I'm going to try it again."

She couldn't help but laugh at his reaction. Playing it up a little, she rolled her shoulders and cracked her neck as she shook her arms out like she did before a run.

"Okay. Go."

Even as he was taking a step in her direction she felt her body go rigid.

"Power through," he said as he leaned down and kissed her again.

Expecting it this time, she was able to kiss him back, but it was nothing more than lips moving against lips. It wasn't a kiss so much as a handshake with tongues.

"Hmm. That wasn't any better," he said honestly.

"Yeah. I noticed."

"Did I do something?" he asked.

"Oh no!" she nearly shouted. "It's not you. It's... I guess I'm still getting over someone. I'd hoped I already was, since we hadn't been together very long at all, but it seems I'm not."

He nodded as if this made more sense than the possibility that the problem could be his kissing skills.

"Well." He looked up at the dark sky for a second and then back to her. "I had a good time. You didn't get on my nerves, so maybe we could try it again. And at some point you might be over the other guy. What do you say?"

"I would like that," she said, though her heart was already generating a surplus of excuses. "Thanks again."

With a wave, she watched as he walked to the car and drove off.

She stepped into her lonely home wondering if she'd ever get better at this.

# Chapter 12

"I'll be bringing a few boats out to Ohio next week while you're there. Maybe we can grab some dinner." Brady watched Kenley's expression for some clue of what was going on. Zane had been acting weird all week. All he'd said when Brady teased him about the boat show trip was that it was cut short because Sidney had the baby. But something was up. Brady could tell.

"Maybe."

"Are you afraid Zane will have a problem with us having dinner together?"

Her cheeks turned a pretty pink and she looked away with a shrug.

And there it was. Zane and Kenley had had sex.

He nearly fell off the desk in shock. Zane had claimed her after Brady pretty much forced him into it. But he didn't think the guy would really make a move. Good for him.

Except they weren't acting very happy about it. Something must have gone wrong.

Before he had the chance to ask a bunch of nosy questions, his phone rang. He recognized the number and ducked out of the office to take the call.

"Hello?"

"Is this Brady Martin?"

"Yes. Is Hunter okay?" He didn't have the patience for a get-to-know-you if something was wrong with his little brother.

"He's fine. The doctor says he may have a mildly sprained ankle. He fell out of a tree."

"What was he doing in a tree?"

"He found a nest on the ground and wanted to put it back."

Brady pinched the bridge of his nose and took a deep breath. He paid these people a shit-ton of money to watch his brother and keep him safe. He should get a refund.

"It's protocol to contact you if there's an incident."

"You mean anytime you people aren't paying attention to your patients?" He knew it probably wasn't this woman's fault. She was most likely the person who got stuck making the phone call. But it pissed him off that he couldn't take better care of his brother.

"There are notes in his chart that you do not want him sedated or over-medicated. Would it be okay to give him something for the pain?"

"Something mild. I swear, if he can't say his name when I get there, I'm going to own that place."

"I'll tell him you're on your way," she said, ignoring his threat. Probably for the best.

"I'll be there in twenty minutes. You might want to wait about eighteen minutes before you tell him I'm coming. He likes to count down the minutes."

"I'll meet you when you arrive."

After she hung up, Brady realized he hadn't caught her name.

He pulled in at Elmhurst Adult Care Center twenty-three minutes later. Inside he found Hunter chatting to the two women at the desk.

"Are you sure he said he was coming? He should have been here. It's not Saturday. Are you sure he's coming?" Hunter's anxiety twisted Brady's stomach.

"Here I am." It never got old, the way Hunter's face lit up when Brady walked in the door.

"I wasn't sure you were really coming. You were three minutes late."

"Traffic."

"Is it Thursday?" Some might think it was Hunter's way of accusing him of making up the traffic, but no, he'd just changed topics that quickly.

"It is."

"Will I still go home with you on Saturday?"

"Yep."

"Two days."

"You got it."

Another woman walked out carrying crutches.

"Okay, Hunter. Can you try these? Keep your left foot off the floor if possible. Use the crutches to hold yourself up."

"Brady, I get to have crutches." To see the excitement on his face, you would have thought he'd won the lottery.

"I see that. Maybe don't climb any more trees."

"But the nest fell on the ground, and the bird would come home and it wouldn't be there."

The other woman stepped closer and held out her hand.

"I'm Dr. Walker. I just took over as director two weeks ago." He recognized her voice as the person who had called him.

"And how many of your patients have fallen out of trees in the last two weeks?"

\* \* \*

"Do you have a moment to discuss your brother's care?" Michaela asked, as she ignored his jab and tried to stand tall. She was on the short side, but she knew backing down from this huge man who was trying his best to intimidate her would get her nowhere.

"Yes." He turned to his brother and smiled. For a moment she wished he would have smiled at her. But of course he wouldn't. He was angry. She needed to diffuse the situation. "I'll be right back. Keep your foot up, okay?"

"You'll be back?"

"Yes. Right back."

"How many minutes?"

"I'm not sure. I'll let you know when I come out."

"Okay."

Michaela led the giant to her office and gestured to the chairs in front of her desk.

"So what's up?" Brady took possession of the room the minute he sat. He looked completely in control as he leaned back and crossed his arms over his chest.

"I wanted to discuss some options with you."

"Options?"

"Yes. I guess I wondered why Hunter was here."

"Why?" Brady looked at her like she was nuts. "Because when he was eleven he was thrown through a windshield and ended up in a coma for nearly two months before he woke up with brain damage."

"I've read his chart. I understand the injury. I'm just wondering why you haven't looked into assisted living or group homes."

"That's what this place is."

"No. This is a complete care center. It's for people who need more extensive care and rehabilitation."

"A pretty expensive one who allows people to fall from trees."

It didn't seem he was going to let it go anytime soon. "Do you know how he fell out of the tree?"

"I'm aware of how gravity works Mrs. Walker. I'm guessing he fell down." Oh, this guy was clever. If he wasn't so angry she might find him amusing.

"He went to the maintenance building and got a ladder. It was a step ladder, but he propped it against the tree and climbed up high enough to reach the limb. He actually put the nest back in the tree. He only fell on his way down when the ladder slipped away from the tree." She took a deep breath before adding. "And it's Dr. Walker, not Mrs." She would like to think she corrected him because she'd worked hard for the two letters in front and the three others behind her name, but if she were honest she just didn't want him to think she was married.

"Did someone videotape the scene instead of stopping it?"

"No. No. He told me every detail. He is capable of more than you think."

"Excuse me, but didn't you just say you've only been here two weeks?"

"Yes."

"I've been taking care of him for the last nine years. Don't tell me what I think."

"Fair enough. But when Hunter would have first come out of recovery he was undoubtedly worse than he is now. I understand he was placed here straight out of the hospital."

"I'd just got home from Iraq. I was dealing with some other things. I couldn't take care of him myself."

"I'm not judging. I just wanted to know if you've considered other options since he's improved."

The man blinked at her, and she braced herself for some rude comment aimed to unhinge her. Instead he let out a breath and tilted his head.

"I have to get back to work. If you could just say what it is you need to say, I'd appreciate it."

"Fine." She could do that. "Your brother is capable of more than you might realize. With occupational therapy and job placement, he could potentially become employed and learn to care for himself in an assisted living or group home situation. I understand it may be difficult for you to envision him being self-sufficient, but I want you to know it is possible and I'd like your permission to explore his potential."

"You want to put him to work?" It figured that was all he'd picked up from her statement.

"I want him to live the best life he can."

"You're saying I'm doing a bad job?"

"No. No! Definitely not. I've looked at his charts. You visit all the time and you take him home with you every weekend. I know he's not just being parked."

Brady's eyes went wide at the same time she realized her mistake. "*Parked*?"

"It's a term we use to describe someone who could be in a personal home, but a family member doesn't want to be bothered." She appreciated his look of disgust at the thought.

"I have to travel for work. I needed a job that paid well and had good insurance so I could afford the best home for him. The downside of that is I'm not around a lot or I'd have him with me more often."

"With some training, he might be able to stay by himself." Brady shook his head, but she cut him off before he could contest. "Hunter is a twenty-year-old man. He has a long life ahead of him. Is this place all you want for him?"

"I appreciate the optimism, but he likes it here and we're doing fine."

Time to get tough.

"I had hoped it wouldn't come to this Mr. Martin, but you've given me no choice." She straightened her shoulders, ready to fight fire with fire. She didn't want to be the wicked bitch of Elmhurst, but he needed a good shaking. "You mentioned needing good insurance. Even the best insurance doesn't pay for all of Hunter's care."

"Trust me, I'm aware of how much the insurance doesn't pay."

"Part of our process is patient evaluations for the insurance companies. Until now, Hunter has been reported as a long-term care candidate and your insurance pays the biggest portion of his care. If I change his status the insurance will decline to pay."

"Are you kidding me? Your incompetent staff let my brother fall out of a tree, and now you're *threatening* me? Is this some tactic to keep me from suing your asses?" He got up and walked to the door. She noticed a slight limp when he rushed out to where his brother was chatting with the nurses. Hunter's leg was not propped up. "Come on, Hunter. We're going."

"But it's not Saturday. It's only Thursday."

"I know. We're mixing it up."

Hunter smiled and waved at her as he followed his older brother out the door, carrying his crutches instead of using them.

"I get to go home with my brother on a Thursday." He spent most of his time at Elmhurst, but his brother's apartment was considered home.

\* \* \*

It was obvious something was wrong when Brady walked into the office. Kenley could feel the tension coming off the already intimidating man. He had a younger man with him who had to be related to him. They looked so much alike.

"I have a huge favor to ask," he said as he placed both palms on her desk and leaned over. "This is my brother, Hunter. Would it be okay if he sat in here with you until I get these boats loaded up? Then I'll take him home."

"Sure." Kenley didn't understand why he needed to be watched. Her confusion must have showed.

"Hunter, why don't you go wash your hands?"

"Do I need my crutches?"

"Does it hurt when you walk?"

"No."

"Then you can leave them here."

Hunter walked down the hall and went in the right door on the first try. He must have been here before.

"When I was in Iraq, our drunk of a mother wrecked her car and nearly killed Hunter while managing to kill herself. I've been taking care of him ever since he woke up from the coma. He's not dangerous. He hurt his ankle today at the home. I didn't want to leave him there."

His expression tensed on the last part, but she nodded.

"Sure. I'd love to have some company." She was sick of staring out the window, thinking about Zane.

"He won't be in the way. He'll be fine to sit and look through magazines until I'm finished." Hunter came out of the bathroom, waving his hands that weren't quite dry.

"Hunter, this is Kenley."

"Sidney is home with Baby Paige. We took her a stuffed rabbit last weekend."

"Right. I want you to stay with Kenley until I come back, okay?"

"How many minutes?"

"I'm not sure yet. I'll let you know."

"Okay." Hunter took a seat and picked up the first magazine. "Don't get in the car with Mom," he said with a wave to his older brother.

Brady let out a sigh and went through the door that would take him out to the shop.

Other than the occasional swish of a turning page, Hunter was as quiet as a mouse. It meant she was able to focus on her job, but it also meant she found herself staring out the window again, thinking about Zane.

When Brady came in to collect Hunter, he thanked her profusely.

"It was no problem at all."

"It was nice meeting you," Hunter called by the door.

"It was nice to meet you too."

When the brothers were gone, she locked up the building and headed out.

Following the directions she was given, Kenley pulled down a winding driveway to a large brick home. It looked as if it could easily house twelve people.

Sidney met her at the door before she even had the chance to knock.

"You're a sight for sore eyes," Sidney said, giving her a hug. "I haven't had the chance to thank you for the flowers."

"Of course. I understand." Kenley rubbed her hands together. "So where is she?"

"She's napping."

Kenley didn't hide her disappointment, letting her shoulders fall with an "Awww."

"That's okay. I'm sure you also came to visit me and will be happy to wait to hold my child."

"Yeah. I guess so." Kenley laughed and Sidney playfully swatted her on the shoulder.

"So how are things going?"

"Fine. Good." She hadn't come there to bash Zane. At least not unless Sidney started it first. "Brady brought his brother in to the office today. He's a sweetie."

"He is. It breaks my heart that a mother is capable of hurting her child. The worst thing is how he always tells Brady 'not to ride with Mom.'" Kenley had noticed that, but hadn't asked. "If he'd done just that when he was eleven, who knows what he'd be doing today. I'm sure it tears Brady up every time he says it. The poor guy feels terrible about what happened, but it wasn't like he could help. He was in a hospital in Germany when the accident happened."

"Why was Brady in the hospital?" Kenley asked.

Sidney looked a little surprised and then said, "He lost his foot in Iraq."

"Oh. I had no idea." She'd noticed a slight limp, but nothing to indicate it was that serious.

"I guess that's the point, that he's able to walk well enough no one would know it's a prosthetic." She shrugged.

"Brady is like a different person when Hunter is around. No joking or flirting. I didn't realize he could be serious."

"He's spent a lot of his life being way too serious." Before she could ask what Sidney meant, they were distracted by the sound of Paige's slight whimper on the baby monitor.

"She's up! I get to hold her."

Sidney rolled her eyes, but led her to the nursery. Once Kenley was settled in the rocker with the baby in her arms she felt the stress of the last week flow away.

"She's beautiful," Kenley said while sniffing her hair. "And she smells so good."

"Trust me. Sometimes she doesn't smell good at all." The sound of someone coming in the front door caused Sidney to stop laughing and go investigate.

Kenley heard the low rumble of his voice before he stepped into the room.

Perfect. Zane was here.

\* \* \*

To say Zane was shocked to see Kenley in his sister's home rocking his niece was an understatement. He'd been on the phone when he arrived and didn't notice her car.

Then he remembered he didn't have any reason to hide. Not that he needed a reason, obviously. He'd been doing a fair job of it since the night she'd gone out with Scott.

He knew that hadn't gone anywhere. For a cop, Officer Porter didn't seem to realize when someone was manipulating information out of him.

He'd been almost chatty about how he'd kissed Kenley—a statement that made Zane cringe—but it hadn't been right. They'd had no chemistry.

Zane knew for a fact, the fault wasn't Kenley's. The two of them had plenty of chemistry. Too much, in fact.

"Hi, Kenley."

"Zane." She managed to say his name, though she didn't look up from the baby.

While he knew his niece was adorable and could captivate anyone's attention, it was pretty obvious Kenley was uncomfortable.

She still did a great job at work, but she'd yet to speak, text or email him about anything other than business. He didn't know what to do. Or if he should do anything. Wasn't this what he'd been hoping for? That they could go back to what they'd had before without the tension? Except there was still a lot of tension.

He'd suggested they talk about what had happened, but she'd resisted. And he'd backed off, but maybe things still needed to be addressed.

He told himself every day this was for the best. It was bound to come to the same end. Eventually he would have done something to mess it up.

"Sorry. I didn't know I needed to make an appointment," Zane joked. Again, Kenley didn't look up.

"I should get going." Kenley moved to get up and Zane stopped her.

"It's okay. You don't have to leave on my account. I'm the uncle. I get to hold her anytime I want."

She passed a now sleeping Paige over to Sidney, who glared at him, but spoke to Kenley.

"You don't have to go. If you want, I can kick this big doofus out of my house so we can visit longer."

"I just remembered I need to go pick up a few things for my trip on Monday."

"Trip?" he asked.

"You told me to set up the office in Ohio. Is that not what you want?"

It was, but he had planned to stay in the office all next week so he could try to work things out with her. If he changed his plans now it would be too obvious.

"That's fine. I didn't realize."

"I put a note on your desk." A note he wouldn't have seen because he'd been away. He let out a sigh.

"Okay. Good. Thanks."

"I'll stop in when I get back next week," she promised Sidney, who put the baby back in the crib and walked her out.

He watched Paige breathing while listening to the murmurs downstairs. He couldn't make out the words, but it didn't matter. They were most likely complaining about him. After the sound of the door opening and closing, Zane braced for battle.

"Tell me this is not still about your stupidity at the hospital," Sidney snapped when she walked back into the nursery.

Zane put his index finger to his lips and pointed into the crib in an effort to silence the woman, but it didn't work.

"Paige is used to it. She had a front-row seat for the last nine months." He let out a breath and shrugged.

"We decided it would be better if we kept things professional."

Sid tilted her head to the side as if to contemplate his position.

"Good luck with that."

# Chapter 13

Kenley felt better on Friday as she opened the office and started coffee. She had plans this weekend with her family and friends. She wouldn't spend the whole time second-guessing her decision not to start something romantic with Zane. Not that she knew if he would have wanted such a thing. She'd ended it with him before he'd had the chance to end it with her. She paused with the carafe of water hovering over the coffeepot as that thought settled in.

She'd run away from Zane because she was afraid. It was not the first time she'd felt this way. It was ridiculous really. She'd been three when she'd been left at a small-town library. She didn't remember her parents or being abandoned.

But something inside her always wondered why she'd been left there. If she had been given up for adoption as a baby it would have made more sense. If her mother wasn't capable of caring for a child, adoption was a viable option. So why did they keep her until she was three and then give her up?

What had she done wrong?

She shook off the familiar irritation and continued with her day. A day that would be spent without Zane because he was—surprise—not in the office that day because he was going out of town to look at a boat. He could have really been going to look at a boat, but she knew how good he was at creating reasons to avoid her.

Brady came in with Hunter and she smiled.

"Hi, Hunter. Are you keeping me company today?" she asked as the brothers looked at one another.

"Would you mind?" Brady asked. "It shouldn't be all day. I have a delivery to New Bedford, and I'll be right back."

"I don't mind. It's nice having him here. It's so quiet and boring when everyone is out on the road." Not that Hunter had been a big talker the day before, but she was going to work on that today.

"I'd take him with me, but he's not great on trips."

"I like to stop at all the McDonaldses," Hunter supplied.

"Yes. *All* of them."

She couldn't help but laugh at Brady's pained expression. "It's really no problem. It will be fun."

"Thanks. You're the best." With that Brady gave her a quick peck on the head and then hugged his brother. "Listen to Kenley. She's in charge until I get back."

"I was in charge last night while you went to the store."

"Yes. But now Kenley's in charge."

"You were gone seventeen minutes."

"I'm going to be gone longer this time."

"How many minutes?"

"I'm not sure. I'll let you know when I get back." Hunter seemed to be okay with this answer, though she'd already heard it twice. And yesterday he hadn't said how many minutes he was gone. She didn't say that out loud though.

"Don't ride with Mom in the car," Hunter said while straightening his tattered magazines. This time Kenley noticed the pain that flashed in Brady's eyes at the comment.

It was obvious Hunter wasn't saying it to hurt his brother. It was probably something he'd been told repeatedly as a child and it stuck. Except the time it mattered most.

"I'll be back as soon as I can."

"But longer than seventeen minutes."

"A little bit. Yeah."

Hunter followed Brady to the door and then waved. With a sigh he came to sit in his usual spot and opened one of the magazines.

"Have you read those before?" She noticed there was one with boats. And two with motorcycles.

"Yes. They're Brady's, but he let me bring them here. He said to stay quiet."

"You don't have stay quiet all the time. Just when I'm on the phone."

"Oh." He looked around the space. "I could help you if you want. I used to water the plants for Sidney, but they're not here anymore." Thank God.

"Hmm. Well, I don't really have anything I need help with. Since I only have the one computer." She smiled and then had an idea. "Wait here a second."

"A second?"

"How about seventy seconds?" she revised, realizing he was a stickler for time.

He nodded and she rushed out the back into the shop and gathered up a number of brass fittings and hardware that needed to be polished before they could be used. She picked up a pile of rags and the polish and came back to the office with a few seconds to spare.

"Did you want to help by cleaning up these parts and making them shiny?"

"They aren't shiny."

"Not now. But if you put this stuff on them and then rub them, the dirt will come off and they'll be shiny underneath." She demonstrated with one of the cleats, and watched his look of surprise when the gunk was removed. As if she had been trying to trick him.

"I can do that."

"Sure you can. Here, we'll set you up at this table." She pulled the table from the corner and moved the papers from it. "Can you go get a chair from the lunchroom?"

"Yep." He ran off, eager to help. His ankle didn't seem to be an issue.

Once he was set on his task, he was a polishing machine. She'd come up with the job as something to keep him occupied, but now she felt kind of guilty for taking advantage of him. She'd had to go gather more items and it wasn't even lunchtime.

She decided this was an executive decision.

*How much would you pay to have your brass polished?*

As soon as she sent the text to Zane she realized how it might sound.

*Did you mean to send this text to me?*

*Yes. Hunter is in the office with me today. He's polished a bunch of fittings. I thought we should pay him. What do you think?*

*Hundred bucks?*

She did the math. Even if he was there all day it was adequate compensation.

*Sounds good. Thank you.*

*Thank you.*

He added a smiley face which made *her* smile before she reined it in.

As Hunter polished, she finished her payables, cutting Hunter a check along with her payment batch. She even put it in an official envelope.

"I need some more."

"Again? Why don't we go get some lunch?"

"It's not lunchtime yet."

"Right. But it will be lunch time in eleven minutes. I think it's close enough."

"Okay. Can we go to McDonald's?"

"There isn't one nearby. But if you like burgers we can get you one at the diner down the street."

"Okay. I like burgers."

She smiled when he took her hand as they crossed the street. He let go as soon as they were on the other sidewalk. Despite his slight impairment, he was very responsible.

They chatted while they ate. She asked him questions about his favorite movie and what color his bedroom was.

"I have two bedrooms. One at home that I sleep in on Saturday nights, and one at Elmhurst where I sleep all the other nights."

"So Brady picks you up on Saturdays and takes you back to Elmhurst on Sunday night?"

"Yep. Except when we go on vacation in the summer. Then I stay with him the whole week. Sometimes we go camping, and sometimes we go on a boat. You can come with us."

While seeing Brady with his little brother had made him less intimidating, Kenley knew he wasn't for her. Her heart belonged to the surly owner of the company, no matter how much she wanted to pretend otherwise.

* * *

Brady was prepared to apologize to Kenley as he rushed into the shop at ten past four. He hadn't planned to be that late, but of course he couldn't catch a break. Neither delivery had gone as planned.

Maybe he'd take her out to dinner to thank her for her help. He was all ready to make his invite sound friendly instead of flirtatious when he opened the door to the office and found his brother... working.

"What are you doing?" he asked Hunter, but looked at Kenley for an answer.

"He wanted to help, so I gave him something to do."

"Oh." He wasn't sure why he had a problem with it, but for some reason he did. "Well, we need to get going."

"Can we wait just two minutes so I can finish this one?" Hunter asked, taking his exploitation seriously. Brady watched as Hunter rubbed the hardware, his tongue sticking out the side of his lips as he concentrated.

It didn't take him the full two minutes to finish. When he was done he smiled and held it up to the light, taking in the sparkle from the freshly buffed metal.

"All done?" Kenley asked as she stepped over to the table.

"Yep."

"You did good work today. Here's your paycheck."

Brady's eyes widened in surprise. Brady wasn't expecting that. It was clear that Hunter hadn't expected it either. Brady knew his brother so well he could read every expression on his face as he went through them.

First was confusion. Kenley must have understood that one as well because she said, "You worked hard, so I talked to Zane and he said we should pay you."

The expression that took the place of confusion was one Brady saw only once in a great while. It was utter joy.

"Brady, look! I got a paycheck! I can pay bills now, like you!"

Brady chuckled at the route his mind took.

"How much is it? Maybe you could do something better than pay bills with your money."

He opened the envelope and held it up.

"A hundred dollars!"

Brady nodded and held out his hand. "I'll hold it while you go wash up." As soon as Hunter left he turned to Kenley.

"That was really nice of you."

"He did good work. At first I thought it would just be something to keep him busy, but he's very thorough and he seemed to enjoy it. I took him for lunch too."

Brady realized he'd jumped to the wrong conclusion. Kenley wasn't taking advantage of his brother, she was encouraging Hunter to excel in something.

"I'm not leaving until Tuesday, but I'll be in Ohio by Thursday afternoon to deliver the boats to the new shop. I'll take you out for dinner."

"Sounds good."

As he and Hunter drove to the bank so he could cash his very first paycheck, Brady realized he'd been wrong about the entire situation with Dr. Walker.

Now he'd have to figure out a way to apologize.

* * *

Zane took a deep breath before walking into his sister's house on Saturday afternoon. His parents were there, which meant he was facing the trifecta of people telling him all the things he was doing wrong with his life.

Only his niece and his brother-in-law were safe.

Unfortunately, Paige was napping and Tim had run out to pick up ice cream.

"There you are." His mother acted as though he were late, when there was no set time. It had begun. "Where's your girlfriend?"

"I don't have a girlfriend."

"The girl who works for you. From the hospital."

"She isn't his girlfriend anymore, because he scared her off," Sidney supplied helpfully.

"Good for you. Don't get strapped down, son."

"As if being married kept you from dating." His mother scowled at his father, and Zane lost it.

"Would you all just shut the fuck up?" He rubbed his temple as they stared at him in shock. He'd always been the quiet one who just took it. Where had that gotten him? Nowhere!

"Zane—" His mom started, but he cut her off.

"Dad cheated on you. It was a cowardly, despicable thing to do." He looked right at his father, who flinched. "But you didn't kick him out or leave him, so you made the decision to accept it. You need to stop bringing it up, and you"—he pointed to his father now—"need to stop giving me advice as if I would *ever* want to follow in your footsteps." Finally he turned to his sister. Her eyes were wide.

"I love you, Sid. I know you want to help me. You've always wanted to help me. But I'm a grown man. I messed up with Kenley. I know that. I'm working out how to fix it. I need to do this on my own. Please just let me figure it out for myself."

She wrapped her arms around him and squeezed him.

"Good for you." Her words were rough with tears. Great. He'd made her cry.

"Sorry I'm late. I had to go to three stores until I found the right ice cream." Tim took in the scene in his kitchen and frowned. Chances were good Tim had never seen his mother-in-law so silent.

Sidney wiped her eyes and went to hug her husband. "I'm fine. I'm just so proud of my little brother." She smiled. "He said a bad word in front of our parents."

The sound of Paige fussing on the baby monitor snapped everyone out of the surreal moment. Life went on. Peaceably. They spent their meal talking about the weather in Florida, Paige, and the new shop he was opening in Ohio.

There were no comments on his love life, and his parents didn't take stabs at one another. Overall it was a nice visit.

He found his father alone on the patio where he went to smoke.

"You heading out?"

"Yeah. I've been gone all week. I have a pile of laundry that won't do itself."

"You need a wife." His father chuckled at his own comment and pulled in a lungful of smoke.

"Is that all you think wives are good for?" Zane frowned. He hated facing the truth of who his father really was, but it was time. He'd spent too much of his life trying not to be like his dad. It was obvious he didn't need to worry. They had nothing in common.

"Relax. It was just a joke."

"It wasn't funny." Zane started to walk away and then stopped. His father smoked like a fiend and drank too much. He might not be around for long. "Can I ask you something?"

"Sure."

"Why did you cheat on Mom? Was it worth it? All this misery afterward?" He'd been a senior in high school and hadn't known why his mother was crying all the time. When Sidney had broken the news to him, his first instinct was to beat up his father. But his father had apologized to him. Told him he'd made a mistake. Back then Zane believed him, but now he wasn't so sure. "Tell me the truth."

Twin flumes of smoke exited his nostrils and he tilted his head to the side as if contemplating whether or not to answer. With a glance toward the door, his father nodded. "Yeah. It was worth it. Two reasons."

Zane folded his arms across his chest, waiting to hear them.

"I never loved your mother. I knew it when I proposed to her, but she expected it. My parents expected it. Her parents expected it. I thought it was the right thing to do. It wasn't. I didn't love the woman I had the affair with either, but for a moment it was nice not to have to pretend. So, yeah, I'm glad it happened."

He drew in another drag from his cigarette and put it out in the can he'd brought out with him.

"The other reason was it woke me up. I realized that while I don't love your mother, I do love you kids, and that I came really close to losing everything I'd worked so hard for."

"So you stay with mom because it's easier?"

"Yeah. I know it's pathetic and not fair to her. But she knows the truth and she's not made any moves to change anything either. If she ever asked me for a divorce, I'd sign in a heartbeat and wish her the best, but she never asked. And she never loved me either."

Zane shook his head, not sure if knowing this helped in any way.

"I know you hate it when I give you advice, and I realize the way I do it is all wrong, but the message is important. Don't settle for someone who doesn't make you happy. I've never been in love so I don't know what it should feel like, but I know what it shouldn't be."

That seemed reasonable.

"You shouldn't have to hide who you really are. You shouldn't be afraid of sharing every part of you. And you shouldn't want to rip your own ears off when you hear their voice. Instead, I think you should be excited to see her, look forward to it even. You should laugh together. She should know you as well as you know yourself."

"Mom knows you pretty well."

"That is familiarity, not love. She hates everything she knows about me."

Zane couldn't argue. It did seem like that. "What are you going to do? You can't live the rest of your life unhappy."

"Are you sure about that?" his father asked, tapping out another cigarette and lighting it. "You've been doing it so far."

Christ. His father was right.

\* \* \*

The familiar smells of the subway greeted Kenley as she stepped off the train and headed up the stairs. She hadn't missed the feeling of being crowded and jostled as she crested the surface of the earth into a new swarm of people on the street.

She hooked her thumbs in the straps of her bulging backpack and made her way to the building where she used to work.

Unwilling to go up, she waited for Alyssa on a bench outside. Alyssa's roommate was going away for the weekend, so that left the loveseat in their tiny apartment up for grabs. Kenley had jumped at the opportunity to hang out with her friend and get away from her thoughts.

"You are not going to believe what happened today," Alyssa said as soon as she saw her. She paused for a brief hug and then went on with the story. "Ruth was fired."

"No way. Why?"

"Mr. Hasher's stepson apparently wanted a job, and Mr. Hasher worked it out for him. Chuck didn't want to be treated differently, so he asked Mr. Hasher not to tell anyone about the relationship. It turns out he ended up working for Ruth. She ended up propositioning him, and when he turned her down, she fired him."

"Wow." There was no other word to describe the mound of shit Ruth had unleashed upon herself.

"I bet you could get your old job back if you wanted it. Hell, maybe you could even get Ruth's job. You were doing it anyway."

Kenley felt dizzy for a moment. Move back to New York? Away from Zane?

"I don't know."

"Come on. You hated that you had to move home. And just two days ago you sent me this text." Alyssa pulled out her phone and scrolled until she found the right one. "I can't wait to come stay with you this weekend. This new job is sucking my will to live."

"Right. But it's not the job really. It's something else."

"Your boss, whom you slept with." Alyssa smirked. "You see why that is so funny, right? I mean you were fired for sleeping with the boss's husband and now you've—"

"Yep. I get it."

"You need to let it go. Men mess up anything with thinking involved. They try to anticipate what we want and they don't have a clue. They're constantly tripping over their dicks." Alyssa rolled her eyes and pulled Kenley out of the way of a tourist. "Things would be so much better if people could just make appointments for sex like they do with the dentist. They could show up for their appointment, do it, and leave."

"As I recall, I usually leave the dentist in some kind of pain."

Alyssa ignored this and pushed her way through the mobs of people to the subway.

\* \* \*

After dropping off their stuff and changing into suitable club attire, they caught a cab to Alyssa's favorite hunting grounds.

Alyssa didn't date. Like she'd said, she approached the whole concept of men as she would a business proposition. She had a need, and the other party could fill the need. Once the transaction was completed, she moved on.

It wasn't that she was a slut. Or that she had some empty place she was trying to fill with sex. She just had the unerring ability to keep it from being emotional.

Kenley wondered if she was heading down that path. She knew from her glimpse at a sex life that tying emotions to the act made it more painful than a root canal.

She also knew she wouldn't find anyone at the club who stirred those emotions like Zane had.

\* \* \*

"Will they think I'm late?" Hunter asked as they pulled into the drive at Elmhurst on Monday morning. "I'm supposed to be back on Sunday night."

"This is not a prison. You're allowed to come and go as you please," Brady assured his brother.

"I always come back on Sunday night."

"I know, but we were having fun and I wasn't ready to bring you back last night." He also hadn't figured out what to say to Dr. Walker.

Hunter had asked when he would be allowed to work with Kenley again at least ten times over the weekend. He'd also spent a lot of time considering what he might do with his first paycheck. Every time Brady suggested a game or something fun, Hunter resisted, saying he wanted to pay bills or buy groceries with his money like Brady did. In the end, Hunter had given the money back to Brady so he could put it in Hunter's savings account.

Hunter raced ahead and was already telling the story of his paycheck when Brady caught up to him at the front desk. The women were smiling and telling him how proud they were of him, which made Hunter even happier.

"Is Dr. Walker available?" Brady asked the receptionist.

"Let me see." She picked up the phone and punched a couple numbers. "Hunter Martin is back. Uh-huh. His brother would like to see you." A pause and then a nod. "I'll send him right in."

Brady was already moving down the hall. "Hunter, I'll stop in your room before I leave."

"Okay." He went right back into the hallway without even looking up.

The doctor opened her door before he got the chance to knock.

"Please, come in. Did you really bring him back? I was so afraid you wouldn't and after what I did I couldn't blame you. I'm so very sorry. After you left, I realized what I'd done and I was so stupid. I can't believe I threatened you. I crossed the line and I can't apologize eno—"

"Enough," Brady said, finishing her sentence, and put up his hand to stop her confession. "Take a breath."

As she did what he said, he noticed the rise and fall of her perfect breasts. Yes, the doctor had breasts. He hadn't really noticed the last time. Mainly because he'd been angry, but also because she was the doctor in charge of caring for his brother, and therefore off limits as far as breast-noticing was concerned.

Now that he'd noticed said breasts, he couldn't help but appraise the rest of the package. From her silky blond hair to her bright blue eyes and those lips. Oh, those lips.

"Are you going to sue me?" she asked with a little wince that he found adorable.

He tried desperately to put her back into the off-limits, doctor spot, but he only noticed more enticing things about her. Most appealing was the fact she wasn't wearing a wedding ring.

Scanning her desk and the cabinet behind her, he found only pictures of her with an older couple he guessed were her parents, and a number of photos of a brown lab.

"I'm not going to sue you."

Her shoulders sagged in relief and a smile took over her face. He'd definitely not noticed the smile the last time. No way would he have forgotten it if he had. She had dimples. Perfectly matched on either cheek.

"Oh, thank you. Please have a seat." She gestured to the chair he'd sat in the last time and walked around to the back of the desk. He had a split-second view of her perfect ass.

He sat down, hoping he'd be able to get back up with the erection growing in his pants.

"How is Hunter?" she asked.

Hunter. Right. She was Hunter's doctor. The woman he needed to apologize to, and whom he hoped would have a plan to help his brother get a job. He couldn't mess things up for his brother because he was lusting over the hot doctor.

"He's great. That's why I wanted to talk to you."

"Are you taking him out of Elmhurst?" She worried her bottom lip and he shifted in his seat. He was trapped with her in the small room. The blinds were shut and the door closed. The smell of her perfume luring him in as intensely as the way she looked down at his lips. *Focus. Focus.*

"No. Not right now anyway. I wanted to apologize to you for losing my temper." Losing his temper most likely meant he'd lost whatever shot he might have had. Women didn't like scary guys. He was definitely scary. He remembered the way Kenley used to step away from him whenever he walked in the room.

"You had every right—"

"No. I didn't. You were looking out for my brother, and I was being stubborn. I thought over what you said, plus something happened this weekend that made me realize you were right. Hunter is capable of more in his life. I think it would make him happy to have a job. I have to say, the idea of having him living on his own and going to work terrifies me, but I'll have to work on it."

"You've been taking care of him for a very long time. It's going to be difficult for you to take a different role in his life."

He wanted to argue with her assessment, but once again he knew she was right.

"I'm willing to give it a shot. What do we need to do?"

She smiled at him again, flashing those dimples. Then she pulled out a file.

"The first thing would be the occupational therapy I spoke of. We would teach him some basic skills and evaluate the types of things that interest him. Then we can do a job shadow session. Where he would sit with someone and try the job to see if he enjoys it. Then we would move into job placement. I would suggest going slow with Hunter. While he's always pleasant, it's obvious any change from his routine causes stress."

Brady nodded, remembering how many times Hunter had asked if he was going home on Sunday night. He would have brought him back the night before, but he wasn't sure if Dr. Walker—Michaela, he'd seen on her business cards—was working that late.

"Would you ever consider having him live with you at your home full time?"

Brady sat up straighter. "I'm away a lot. There wouldn't be anyone to watch him."

"If it got to the point that he didn't need anyone to watch him?"

"He would be welcome, if that's what you're asking. My place isn't much since most of my income goes to paying for this place." He hadn't meant it to sound like an accusation but she frowned.

"I want you to know, I would never, ever do anything to change your insurance coverage for Hunter. He qualifies to stay here. I was desperate last week and I overstepped."

"You probably wouldn't have been so desperate if I hadn't been so hardheaded." He grinned at her and watched her eyes widen in response.

Thank God, it wasn't just him. There was something going on from the other side of the desk too. It meant he had a chance. He would start with a little flirting today. Maybe by next week he could step it up to asking her out.

He was still working out the elaborate plan when she stood and nodded.

"I'm so glad you're willing to give this a try. I'll set up the first session tomorrow, and I'll call you with the results." She stepped around the desk and he briefly checked out her curves.

"Thanks." He stood too. It was obvious she wanted him to go. Maybe he was making her uncomfortable. "I really appreciate what you and your staff do for my brother. I'm glad there are other people who care about him. I wish it hadn't taken me so long to realize I'm not in this alone."

She hadn't backed away like he'd expected. They were standing way too close. He could see the amber flecks in her blue eyes.

And then, as if it was the most natural thing in the world, he bent down and kissed her. It started out as a tender kiss of appreciation—both physical and professional. But then she engaged.

It was as if each touch escalated the situation. When her hands wound around his waist, he pulled her closer, pressing those breasts up against his chest. When her tongue reached out for his, he moved his hands down to cup her firm ass. In only a matter of a minute or two he had her pushed back on her desk, and his hand was under the edge of her shirt moving up.

At the sound of her gasp, reality forced him back. They blinked at each other for a second before she spoke in a rough voice. "What just happened?"

"Chemistry. A whole hell of a lot of it."

# Chapter 14

Kenley was already in a bad mood when she opened the office Monday morning. Her bag was packed and in the car. She would be leaving for the airport at noon, which was the only reason she hadn't called off.

"How was your weekend?" Paul asked as he filled his cup with coffee.

"Great." She must not have sounded convincing, because Paul chuckled and patted her shoulder.

"It will be okay." She wasn't sure if it would be.

When she'd gotten home the day before, she'd taken Scott up on his offer to try another date.

One thing was for certain, they would not be trying a third. They had no connection whatsoever. She found him attractive, but she wasn't attracted to him. She thought he was nice enough, but she couldn't wait to get away.

At least they both realized it was a disaster before trying to force the kiss goodnight. Scott had merely laughed at her door, and said, "Yeah. I know. This is never going to work."

She'd been both relieved and frustrated at his comment, though relief was definitely the main emotion. After striking out at the clubs with Alyssa, she was happy to come back to reality. Unfortunately her reality was a stabbing pain in her chest.

"No Zane again today? I thought he'd be in." Paul frowned as he looked up at the clock on the wall in her office. Yes, normally Zane would have been there by then. He was not.

"I'm not sure. He didn't say." Not that he'd needed to. Kenley was aware he was still hiding from her. After bouncing ideas off Vanessa and Alyssa, she wasn't sure what her next move was going to be, but it was clear she was the one who needed to make it.

After all, she was the one who'd said she wanted things to be professional. She was the one who thought their interaction could go back to the way it had been before. This was all her fault.

Her friends had suggested she walk into his office, take off her clothes and crawl up on his desk. She'd even practiced seductive glances in the mirror. The only thing she needed was the nerve. She hadn't found any yet, which also pissed her off.

Not that it mattered since he wasn't there.

"I thought he ran his schedule through you." Paul seemed determined to push her to the limit this morning.

"No." She shrugged as Paul pulled out his phone and moved his thumbs over the screen.

She took a sip of her coffee and swallowed. She was finally learning to drink the stuff. While she still wasn't crazy about the taste, she did enjoy the caffeine boost. Especially since she hadn't gotten much sleep the night before.

Paul's phone beeped and he held the screen up.

"He won't be in until later. He says he's working from home."

"I see."

"Is something going on between you two? You both seem tense lately."

"I couldn't say. You'd have to ask him."

"I did. He said nothing was wrong."

"Then I guess nothing's wrong."

"Okay." Paul collected his things and headed for the door, finally giving up. "When's your flight?"

"Four."

"Have a nice trip. See you next week." He tipped his imaginary hat and left.

Zane was working from home, which meant she wasn't going to get her chance to confront him about their situation.

She'd been prepared to sit down and ask him what he wanted. No matter how much it scared her. She knew they had to find a way to move past it or find another alternative.

\* \* \*

*This was too familiar,* Zane thought as he went into the office after making sure Kenley had left. He knew she would be leaving early for a flight and would be gone all week.

He wanted nothing more than to talk to her, to work things out, but when he'd pulled onto the street that morning, he'd kept driving and gone back home.

What if she was happy after her date with Scott? Worse, what if she had that after-sex glow? The same glow he'd seen while she lay in his arms, happy and sated. He wouldn't survive it.

Paul and a few of the guys had been there this morning. He couldn't risk going in and making a scene. Not that Kenley was the kind of woman to make a scene. And his excuse didn't explain why he hadn't gone in later in the morning after everyone else had left.

He sat at his desk and pulled the pile of mail closer. The top letter didn't have an address or a stamp on it. The only thing written on the outside was his name, "Zane." He recognized the writing as Kenley's, and ran his finger under the flap as his heart raced.

"Oh no." he said when he read the first line.

*This letter serves to inform you of my two-week notice. While I enjoyed my time working at New Haven Custom Boats, I have another opportunity I feel I need to pursue.*

"Another opportunity, my ass." She was a bigger coward than he was. And that was really saying something.

After reading the short letter three times, and not getting any answers, he pulled out his phone to call her.

He expected it to go to voicemail, but to his surprise she answered on the second ring with a brusque "Hello."

He didn't know what to say first.

"It's me. Zane." As if she would have forgotten him so quickly.

"Yes, I know. It says so on my phone." Of course it did. He was making things worse.

"I got your letter."

"I see. So you were in the office today. Did you sit on the street and wait for me to leave before you went in?" He winced and rubbed his temple.

"No." But he had driven by slowly to make sure she was gone. "I don't want you to quit. Can we please talk about this?" he asked, not caring if he sounded desperate. "I know we decided to keep things strictly business, but I wasn't doing that. I was staying away because I didn't think I'd be able to be near you without wanting more. And I know I'm not supposed to say that, but I really don't have anything to lose at this point."

"It's my fault. I thought if we kept things professional everything would be fine, but it's not. We can't go back to how it was. And things are too tense between us now. This is for the best."

"Are you seeing Scott now?" It was none of his business, and as much as he didn't want to know, he needed to know.

"I took this job hoping to interact with coworkers, learn from them, and advance my career with the company. It has become apparent that my supervisor does not share my goals. Besides, I've recently learned that my old position with Hasher and Borne is available, and it's been offered to me."

"You want to go back there?"

"I stayed very busy in New York. Busy enough to keep me from being alone every night."

She was alone every night. So was he. He hated it and knew she must hate it too. They should be together. Why couldn't he just tell her how he felt?

"This is about me not coming into the office or calling."

"This is about me wanting to be a part of something."

She could have meant the company, but maybe she meant something else. She wanted to be part of a relationship? With him.

"I have to go. They're calling my flight."

"Okay. Let me know if you need anything. We'll talk when you get back. Please don't do anything until we've spoken."

She didn't respond. She simply hung up.

He tapped the letter on his desk, his world tossing like a ship on stormy seas.

He'd be better off if he stopped thinking about her altogether. He should just let her go. She would be happy in New York. And he could hire a nice, competent replacement. Not that she would be easy to replace. She ran his office without a hitch. What would he do without her?

He knew the answer. Life would go on.

The only problem was, his life hadn't been all that great before she'd started working for him.

It was time for a change.

* * *

Kenley was glad to have something to focus on other than her broken heart and her stupid irrational thoughts. She was also glad to be out doing something instead of sitting in the office thinking all day.

Not only had she ended things with Zane before he ended them with her, but she'd run from her job as well.

Unfortunately, her high hopes for the day fell flat when she arrived at the new building bright and early on Tuesday morning.

They were obviously behind schedule, and the reason seemed quite clear when she found the men in the office instead of outside painting.

Two of them leaned on the counter while the other two slouched in the office chairs. They didn't even straighten up when she stepped inside. They knew she wasn't the boss so why should they be worried?

"Hello there, darlin'," the man behind the desk—her desk for the time being—said while his gaze scanned her from head to toe. She was wearing jeans, sneakers and a T-shirt with the company logo, but the way he was ogling her made her feel naked.

"You must be the contractors who were hired to power-wash and paint the dock and the building." They didn't even move after her blatant hint.

"That would be us." The man finally stood to shake her hand, and introduced the other men. They all had regular-Joe kind of names. Actually one of them was Joe. She didn't bother to remember them, as their names weren't as important as getting them off their asses and out the door to get something done.

"So how are we coming with the schedule?" she asked when no one moved. She knew the answer, but she wanted to force them to address the issue.

"We'll be done with time to spare," the man on the counter said.

"Really? Will you be working nights then?" She raised her eyebrow, causing them to finally move into action.

"Zane said the boats wouldn't be here until Thursday."

"Yes. That's right. But it's Tuesday now, and unless you plan to unleash a few fairy godmothers and a flock of helpful bluebirds, you're not going to be done by Thursday." One of the men laughed, the rest didn't.

She might have come off a little bitchy, but she didn't care. Her life was falling apart, and this was the one thing she thought she could keep together and on track. And these idiots had messed it up.

One by one they headed for the door while they grumbled things she could hear but ignored.

When they were gone she opened the curtains to let in the sunshine and pulled out the files to get started. The loud hum from the pressure washers coming to life made her relax a little. It was going to get done in time for the grand opening. That was what mattered.

She was busy the rest of the day, setting up the computer and getting the files organized. She checked in with the temp agency to see that her interviews were all set up for the next day. She'd made progress with the team outside. The small building had been cleaned and they were going to start painting in the morning.

Feeling like she'd accomplished something, she went back to the hotel and had a drink in the lounge before going to her room to watch television.

She should have been using the time to search for a new job, after all she'd just quit and didn't have anything else lined up. The thought of going back to Hasher and Borne didn't appeal. But that would be her back-up plan. Resigning before knowing her next step might have been a stupid thing to do, but so was sleeping with her boss.

It didn't matter. It was done. She would find something better and she wouldn't ever have to see Zane again.

On Wednesday morning, she was happy to see the crew busy working when she arrived. Her little rant must have motivated them somewhat.

She conducted interviews and called references between setting up the office and the computer system.

Brady showed up with the boats, as expected. She took him up on his offer of dinner. It was clear he'd meant it in a friendly way. They spent most of the evening talking about Hunter. It was obvious he loved his brother.

"It's weird when you think about the paths you end up on," he said, taking a sip of his beer. "Hunter was only eleven when he was injured. He could have turned into anything. He could have been a nuclear physicist or he could have ended up in a gang and in prison at eighteen. I have no idea what path he was on before the accident."

"Does it matter?"

"I guess not. All this time I've just been happy he was alive. But recently I've been thinking about his life. And how to make it better for him."

"He seems happy, Brady. He loves you very much."

"When I left for basic, he was nine. I remember him waving to me from the front window until I couldn't see him anymore. He told me he was going to join as soon as he was old enough and then we would be able to save the world together."

"I think maybe you're saving each other's worlds."

Brady nodded and sniffed, his eyes bright. "Zane's a good guy."

She sat up at the abrupt change in subject. "I know."

"The thing is, he doesn't date. So he pretty much sucks at it. I'm not trying to make excuses for whatever stupid thing he might have done to mess things up with you. All I'm saying is, try to look past it to see that he's not a dumb shit on purpose. He's really into you. I don't know if he said it, but there. Now you know." He grinned and she nodded and rolled her eyes.

"Fine. I'll consider the possibility he's not actually a dumb shit."

"That'a girl."

By Friday when it was time to go home, she had everything ready to go. The feeling of accomplishment as she looked at the pristinely painted building fell when she realized she would be giving up her job. The job she loved.

* * *

On Monday morning, Kenley went in to the Connecticut office with a determination she had never felt before. She was literally fighting for her life. She'd spent the weekend figuring out exactly what she wanted from Zane, both personally and professionally.

She wasn't surprised he wasn't there by eight, but when ten rolled around and he still wasn't there, she sent a text.

*Are you coming in today?*

*No. I'm in Florida. Last minute thing.*

She didn't know whether that was true or not. She threw a crumpled coffee cup across the room at the moment a well-dressed man stepped inside, causing the bells above the door to ring.

The startled man looked over at her and she winced.

"Sorry about that. Can I help you?"

"I'm here to pay a bill."

"Sure. Your name?"

Kenley pulled up Mr. Fortney's account and applied his five-hundred-dollar payment, which he made in cash. Who used cash anymore? She studied him for a moment while his receipt printed out. He didn't look like a mobster. But did the real ones look like the ones on television?

Letting it go, she handed over his statement with a smile and thanked him for stopping in. When he was gone she took the money back to the safe in Zane's office and found there was more cash there from payments made while she was away.

"Does he even know how to fill out a deposit slip?" she grumbled as she closed the safe and spun the dial. She'd have to go to the bank on her way home.

Back at her desk she started going through the pile of new invoices that had come in. It was enough to keep her busy and focused for the rest of the day.

When the bells above the door chimed the next time, she looked up from her work with a smile on her face.

"Can I help you?" she asked the pale, shaky man as he stepped closer to her desk.

"Yeah," he said. "Give me all the money." He pulled a gun out of his waistband and pointed it at her.

# Chapter 15

Zane was arguing the value of a boat with its owner when he got the call. Happy for a distraction, he stepped away and answered Brady with more enthusiasm than he really felt.

"What's up?"

"We have a big problem," Brady said, sounding out of breath. His first thought was that Kenley had bailed. That she hadn't even given him a chance and had gone back to Hasher Bourne. But he hadn't thought her loyalitis, as she called it, would allow her to abandon him.

"What's wrong?"

"I got in late this morning. I parked out back to load up the boat that's going to Toms River." So far nothing was out of the ordinary. "I went into the office to take a piss before I left and I heard Kenley. She was upset and yelling. When I looked in through the window on the door, I could see a guy holding a gun on her."

Zane zoned out for a full minute. When he was back Brady was going over the facts. Kenley had been robbed while on the job. Someone had hurt his Kenley?

He would kill them.

He was just formulating a plan when he caught the word *bail* and he snapped to attention.

"Wait. What about bail?" he asked.

"I need you to bail me out of jail. I freaked out when I saw her in danger. I guess my training kicked in without me knowing it, and I kind of, I don't know, lost my shit. The asshole was unconscious and bleeding when the cops got there. Scott was off duty. They took me in."

"Where's Kenley now?"

"They took her to the hospital. She was really shook up. The officer said they would probably release me if my story checks out with hers or the other guy, but I need to get out of here so I can get to the hospital to make sure she's okay."

"All right. What do I do?"

"Here. Talk to this nice lady," Brady said before Zane could get any more details. There was a shuffling sound and then a woman's voice came on the other end.

A few minutes later he had posted bail and Brady was released.

Zane explained the situation to his customer as he booked a flight. He hadn't unpacked. His bag was still in the rental car. Within ten minutes he was driving back to the airport. He needed to get to Kenley.

Zane checked in with Brady a few times during his delay in Charlotte. Kenley had been given some anti-anxiety meds and discharged. Brady had taken her home so she could sleep. Brady had a busted-up hand and would need to check in with the police again in the morning.

Zane was already planning to give him a large bonus for beating the hell out of the guy and for saving Kenley. Every time he thought about what could have happened he felt sick. Once he even picked up his airsickness bag.

This was all his fault.

He'd left her there by herself. He should have been there with her. He should have been there to protect her. Despite Brady's reassurance that she was fine, Zane wouldn't relax until he'd seen her for himself.

Without a second's hesitation about the time, he knocked on Kenley's door late that evening. He heard the clanking as Kenley disengaged all the locks, and when she opened the door his heart took over.

* * *

She wasn't sure how she felt about Zane being there as she unlocked the door and opened it. Without asking, he stepped into her home, closed the door behind him and pulled her into his arms.

He felt so good. So safe.

She cried into his big chest uncontrollably as he apologized and kissed her hair. She wanted to ask him what he was apologizing for, but she couldn't stop sobbing. She'd held it together all day, but now that he was here, she broke down.

Their misunderstanding seemed so stupid and petty now.

"I should have been here with you. I shouldn't have left you on your own. I should have security or something."

"You couldn't have known this would happen. It's not your fault."

"What about the other things I've done? The hiding and avoiding you. Am I allowed to apologize for that?"

She let out a sigh. "You didn't do anything that horrible, Zane. I think I freaked out. I got spooked and I used it as a reason to push you away before you could hurt me. I'm the one who should apologize."

It was easier to speak her mind in light of what had happened. Having a gun pointed at you put things in perspective.

"I acted like a dick."

Somehow she was laughing at the same time tears leaked from her eyes. She looked up at him and watched as the smile on his face faded into something more serious. More intense.

Then he leaned down and kissed her. It was a soft touch of lips. At least for the first time. When he bent down the second time, he pulled her closer and kissed her more urgently. His arms encircled her body, holding her against him, and she remembered a flash from earlier in the day when someone else had grabbed her arm and shook her. Threatening to shoot her if she didn't turn over all the money they had. The man's breath had been foul—beer and stale cigarette smoke. She didn't want those memories to intrude on this happy moment with Zane, but she couldn't fight it off.

He pulled away slightly when she froze.

"I'm sorry," she whispered, looking up at him. His eyes got wide.

He muttered a curse. "I'm such a jackass. I'm sorry, Kenley. I can't believe I was so—" He shook his head and took a step back. "After what nearly happened to you today, now I'm here pawing all over you and forcing my way into your home." More curses she couldn't quite make out.

"No. It's not like that," she assured him. "Not exactly." She sat on the edge of the sofa and he sat next to her, his hand resting on her shoulder to offer comfort, but nothing more.

"Do you want to talk about it?" he asked. His words were soft and kind, but she noticed his other hand was clenched so hard the knuckles were white.

"It seems like a bad dream. Like it didn't really happen." His hand clenched even harder. She didn't want to think about it anymore.

It could have ended differently for her. Brady could have been delayed somewhere along the way or not even come in to the office.

But that hadn't happened. He'd walked in and stopped the man with the gun.

Though *stopped* was not really the word. She'd always seen something scary lurking in Brady's eyes. That thing was unleashed on the scrawny man, who hadn't known what hit him.

She knew that man couldn't hurt her anymore. Brady said he was in the hospital. What she was afraid of was being haunted by the memories for the rest of her life. Up until that morning she'd been fine to be alone at the office and in her home. Now she didn't know if she'd ever feel safe to be alone again. She didn't want to think about the gun or the man or the fear anymore. She wanted to think about something else. Something good.

"I need you."

"I'm sorry?"

He obviously didn't understand, and why would he? It was an unusual request. "I need you to help block out what happened."

"Oh." His brows rose in surprise. "I'm not sure if that's a good—"

She didn't wait for him to argue whatever point he may have had, valid or not. She kissed him. This made sense to her. She wanted Zane to push the bad memories away. She wanted someone to touch her, whom she trusted and… loved. Yes, she did love him.

"Please," she begged, hoping she could convince him by pressing closer. "Just for tonight. I don't need any promises. Touch me. I don't want to think about that man anymore. Take it away."

"I don't want to hurt you," he said. "It would kill me if I did something else that caused you pain."

"Then don't say no. Help me. Please. I want you to be the last person who has touched me."

She looked into his eyes, testing his resolve. He glanced away from her with a look of pure torture, then with a groan he pulled her against him and kissed her hard.

\* \* \*

Zane couldn't believe he was going along with this. He knew better, but she was convincing. He'd flown home to do whatever he could to help her. He surely wasn't expecting this.

But as she tugged up his shirt and ran her hands along his bare chest, he wasn't going to stop her. He would go along with her plan and hope she didn't regret it afterward.

She pulled her clothes off as if she was in some kind of race and then lay back on the bed, waiting for him to catch up. As he climbed on top of her he noticed a slight flinch and he pulled away. She was still frightened.

"I'm not so sure this is a good idea," he said, though his body urged him—no begged him—to move on. But this wasn't about his body or about him at all. This was about Kenley and what she needed.

"I'm fine."

"You flinched."

"It was because I felt kind of trapped for a second, but I'll get over it. I want to power through."

"It's not even been a day. Maybe you should give yourself some time to—"

"No. Please just try again. It will be okay. I want this. It's important. I want something good."

Instead of moving over her again, he came up with a different plan. One where she could be in complete control of the situation.

He flopped down onto his back next to her and pulled her on top of him.

"I'm here. Do whatever you want," he said, pleased with himself for coming up with such a great alternative.

She sat up, her thighs straddling his waist and then looked down at him nervously.

"I—I don't quite know how to do this," she confessed. She winced again, but this time it wasn't with fear as much as embarrassment. He brought her hand to his lips and kissed her palm. She was so sexy, even in her inexperience.

"Just do whatever feels good to you, and I guarantee I'll like it," he said with a grin. "There's no wrong way."

She might not have much skill, but her instincts were sound. She moved on him like a professional. He put his hands on her hips to help guide her, not that she needed his guidance. He was actually trying to slow her movements as she fought to quicken the pace.

"Kenley..." He groaned out her name and clenched his fingers into her flesh. "Slow," he begged. "It's too much."

Her hair fell like a curtain around them, and there was a very naughty smile on her face.

"I kind of like being the one in control. I feel so powerful," she said wickedly.

"I might not have the power, but I can do this." He pushed up off the bed to meet her thrust. The smirky little grin left her face, replaced by lust and pleasure.

She was getting closer. He could feel it with each thrust.

He raised his hips higher from the bed to enter her deeper. That was all it took and she collapsed on him. He could feel the tremors in her body as they matched his own pulses.

This was where he belonged. He would never be so stupid again as to think he could live without her.

She slid to the side and he turned so they were facing one another.

He trailed his fingers along the side of her face, down her cheek to her lips, which pulled up into a smile under his touch.

"Are you okay?" he asked as worry intruded on the moment. This seemed like a very unorthodox method to get over being robbed at gunpoint, but he was confident she knew what she wanted.

"I'm fine. A little tired. Thanks for making me do all the work." Her grin told him she was joking. "I'm lucky. Things could have ended up differently for me today, but they didn't. I want to move on and put it behind me."

This sounded like a good plan, but now that he was thinking clearly again, he worried it wouldn't be as easy as she made it sound.

He saw the bruises on her arm now. Where that man had touched her. Brady had mentioned the guy having the gun to her head. She must have been so scared, waiting for the last sound she would ever hear.

She had been attacked. Maybe it had been stopped before it became a higher offense, but the man—whenever he woke up in the ICU—would be charged with armed robbery and assault with a deadly weapon. Deadly.

He shuddered while trying to push the thought away.

He remembered his sister telling him once that people handled things differently. It wasn't his place to tell someone they weren't coping with something correctly just because it was different than how he would have dealt with it.

"Get some rest," he suggested, hoping her wish to move on was as easily said as done, but he still had his doubts. He'd seen what Brady had gone through while wrestling the demons from his past. He squeezed her closer, wanting to protect her from her own demons.

"Will you stay?" she asked. He sniffed. As if there was any question as to where he would be spending the night.

"Of course. I would sit outside your door if you didn't want me in your home, but I'm not leaving you."

"I want you here. I feel safer with you here."

"I want to be here." It seemed like it was the easiest thing to say now. Ever since that morning in the hospital he'd been trying to avoid wanting her. He didn't want her to hold any power over him or make him feel small. Now he realized it was him who had made him feel small and powerless.

Kenley wasn't to blame for that.

She nodded and snuggled in closer before falling right asleep. He wasn't quite ready for sleep yet. Instead he lay there with her in his arms, listening to her even breathing and feeling the steady rhythm of her heart beating against his ribs.

He'd felt trapped by his feelings for her before, but as he held her something changed. There was no more one-sided obsession, and he didn't feel like he needed to keep her at a distance to prove to himself he was stronger than her charms. He kissed her hair, finally feeling free of all of that stupid, juvenile crap, and fell asleep more content than ever before.

He woke in the dead of night to a horrible sound. Retching. Light peeked out from under the bathroom door. He tested the knob and found the door unlocked.

Kenley was a mess. Tears streaked down her red cheeks. Her hair clung to her face and neck in sweaty clumps. Her skin was pale and seemed too tight for her body. As she moved her hand up to block the light he noticed how badly she shook.

"Oh, baby." He felt his heart break for her as he ran a washcloth in cool water and went to her. He pulled her into his lap as he cleaned her up and held her close. "Are you okay?" It was probably a stupid question, but he didn't know what else to say to get her to start talking.

"I'm f-f-fine," she sobbed. Obviously that wasn't true. He wondered if she would ever be fine again.

He held her while she cried for what felt like hours. It was a small blessing he sat next to the box of tissues.

When the last of her tears fell, he turned on the shower and helped wash her hair and body. He didn't linger, or try to make it sexual, but he didn't shy away from touching her either.

He understood her desire to feel something other than the harsh touch of that man's fingers or the chill of the gun against her temple. He would do whatever he could to take her fear away. To anyone else it might have looked like a washing of bodies, but in reality it was an inner cleansing.

He whispered things to her. He told her she was strong and safe and wonderful. He kissed her softly when she looked at him in need. She didn't have to speak to tell him what she wanted.

After drying her off, he carried her back to bed and held her until she fell asleep. But in the morning, she was gone.

There was a split second of panic before he heard the roar of the shower running and he relaxed again. Until the knock at her door.

"Kenley? It's Brady. You okay?" Brady's voice filtered through the door while he tapped again.

Zane pulled on his boxers and ran a hand through his messy hair as he went to the door to open it. Brady jumped back in surprise and then a slow, knowing smile came over his face.

"Morning, boss."

"Morning." Zane frowned at the other man's grin. "Don't start. I swear if you say I'm diddling my secretary, I will fire you." Brady held up his hands.

"I would never say that. Mostly because I would never use the word diddling. No, I would probably say you're—Oh, hey!" he said as Kenley came out of the bathroom.

Zane turned to make sure she was dressed. She was. She pulled the fuzzy robe closer around her. "How are you feeling today?" he asked with the smile still on his face.

"Pretty good. Thanks again for yesterday." She didn't look at their guest, just stared at her bare feet.

"No problem. Although I couldn't help but notice how I was your hero and did jail time for you, but yet you sleep with this guy." Brady thumbed over to Zane. He was joking, but Zane still felt like throttling him.

Kenley smiled at Brady's joke with pink cheeks, her eyes still fixed on her toes. Maybe she was embarrassed that Brady was here while she was only wearing a robe? Or maybe she'd seen him in action and was now afraid of him too. As far as Zane could tell, Brady had handled himself very professionally. Well, except for beating the piss out of the suspect. But Zane didn't fault him for that.

"Thank you." She nodded in Brady's direction.

"Well, speaking of the jail time, I need to head over to the precinct. Scott called and said they would most likely be dropping the charges this morning. There was a witness from the bar who heard him planning something. They thought he was just drunk and high. It looks like the guy is going to make it. Though he has a broken jaw and ruptured spleen. I don't really remember anything after I stepped into the lobby. When I saw Kenley and the gun... I just reacted." Brady shrugged as if what he'd done was no big deal.

It had been a very big deal. He knew Brady struggled with issues from his past service. Zane hoped this event hadn't brought up bad memories.

"I appreciate what you did, Brady. You will be compensated for the inconvenience of being held in jail, but there's really no way to thank you enough."

"She's okay and that asshole will think twice before trying something stupid like that again. That's all I need. I guess you got this from here." He nodded to Kenley who was tucked under his arm. "I'll go take care of my legal issues and get on the road as long as I'm allowed to leave the state."

"You can put it off until tomorrow or Thursday."

"Can't." Brady smiled. "I have a date on Friday night. I need to be back."

Zane had never heard Brady refer to one of his hookups as a date before, nor had he ever seen that sparkle in his eye. That look of anticipation was new. Before he could question him, Brady was gone.

"I should get dressed. I'm late for work."

It was the second shock in five minutes. Was she crazy?

"You're not working today." He could tell by the way her spine stiffened that he'd made a mistake.

"Really, I'm fine," Kenley said sternly with her arms crossed over her chest. "I have work to do."

"What if I asked you to take an extra day as a favor to me?" He tried a different tactic.

"Hmm. Maybe." She walked closer and wrapped her arms around his waist. "I'm sorry Brady found out about us."

"I'm not. I'm glad there is an *us* to find out about." He brushed a strand of wet hair from her cheek.

"But he could tell everyone. I said I didn't need any promises last night. I meant it. What happened doesn't change things."

"It doesn't change how I feel about you at all. But I wanted to be with you since you left me at the hospital with the worst parents in all the world. I want to be with you, Ken."

"I don't expect anything from you."

"You should." Zane smiled down at her. "I don't care who knows about us. You can't back out now. Please don't quit. And please, please say you'll stay with me."

"I will."

He kissed her, feeling like his life might finally be on track.

# Chapter 16

Kenley noticed she was smiling as she got ready to go to the office the next morning. Zane was lying on the bed watching her. His bags sat by the door where he'd dumped them the day before.

Thinking of him rushing to her side made the smile bigger.

She knew how lucky she was. She tried not to think of what could have happened the day before, but occasionally her mind would flash to something. A smell, or a sound. She pushed it away, knowing it was over. She was fine. She was safe.

Zane stood and took her in his arms. He bent to kiss her as if he'd done it every day for years. Her stomach gave a little flip at the idea of him doing it for years to come. It was only natural to think about what came next. Near-death experiences made you think about the future.

Soon she was getting carried away and had to pull away.

"I have work to do," she told him.

"Would you think I was being over protective if I decided to stay with you?" She could see the worry in his eyes.

"I thought you're supposed to deliver Wes's boat this week."

"And Wes would kick my ass if I left you for a boat delivery. He'll understand."

"I'll be fine."

"I'd like to make sure of it. Besides I need to meet with Scott and the guy from the security company."

With his hand protectively resting on the small of her back, he led her out to his truck. They held hands for the drive to the marina and she couldn't help but think things were really going to be as fine as she kept insisting.

That was until she walked into the office and saw the aftermath from the robbery.

The office chair was overturned, and the curtain from the window lay in a pile on the floor. There were two distinct puddles of blood, not huge but enough to know someone had lain there for a while bleeding. Her coffee cup was nearly full, as if she were coming back to finish it.

If it hadn't been for Brady, she might never have come back. She could have died here.

She hated the way her hands shook and she couldn't seem to swallow. Why was she freaking out now? It was ridiculous. It was just a coffee cup and a little bit of blood. She was overreacting.

The man had frightened her and grabbed her arm. He'd put the gun to her head and shouted in her ear. But she wasn't permanently damaged. The bruises on her arm had already turned yellow at the edges.

She would be fine.

*   *   *

Michaela got dressed for her date on Friday, even though she hadn't heard from Brady since he'd left her office on Monday morning after dropping off Hunter. They'd made the date as he'd tried to leave. The third time.

She smiled, remembering how he'd said he needed to get enough of her kisses to last him all week. The smile faded when she looked down at her phone. The thing had been silent, despite the texts and voicemails she'd left for him.

If she'd spent more time dating instead of going to med school, maybe she'd know how she was supposed to handle such a thing. Up until last year she'd had the same boyfriend for six years. It had turned out he was also someone else's boyfriend. What a shock that had been.

Almost as big as the shock she'd gotten when Brady had kissed her. She hadn't minded one bit. After all, he was incredibly sexy. But he was also kind of scary. Or so she'd thought until he'd kissed her.

While his lips were firm on hers, and their shared attraction had them grasping at each other to get closer, there was a tenderness in his touch that made her feel safe. She didn't know much about Brady Martin, but she knew he wouldn't hurt her.

She frowned at her phone again, noticing the time. Ten minutes before he was supposed to pick her up. Looking down at her carefully planned outfit she felt silly for hoping. As she turned to go back to her room to change into her comfy clothes, her doorbell rang.

After glancing out the window to make sure, she opened the door to find Brady standing on her porch. There was a pizza box in his hand, a six-pack of beer hung from his fingertips, and a bottle of wine was tucked under his arm. He grinned and she smiled back as she opened the door wider.

"I know I said I wanted to take you out for dinner, but I've had a hell of a week and I was hoping I could talk you into staying home instead."

She nodded and took the pizza box from him.

"That sounds great."

He leaned down and kissed her. "Thank you. You look beautiful and you smell amazing. I'd say I'm sorry no one gets to see you but me, but screw them. I want you all for myself."

She couldn't help but laugh at the compliment.

"Pizza and wine are perfect." It wasn't about the where or the what she was eating as much as the who she was eating it with. She didn't know much about Brady, and she was looking forward to hearing his story.

He did the honor of opening the wine, while she got plates down for the pizza.

"So, you said you had a bad week?"

"Yeah. I was in jail." The cork popped and he sniffed it, not with any real skill, just as if it was the thing a person did when they pulled the cork from a bottle of wine.

She laughed, expecting it to be a joke, but he went on.

"Just for a few hours. The charges got dropped, but I'll need to testify if the slime ball doesn't plead guilty."

"You're serious? You were in jail?"

He filled her glass almost to the top, not realizing he was supposed to have stopped at the widest point of the glass.

"Yes." He twisted the cap from a bottle of beer and took a long sip.

"Why?"

"A junkie tried to rob the company I work for. He had a gun pointed to Kenley's head when I walked in." He shook his head and took another drink. "I lost it, Mick. Kenley is the office manager. She doesn't look anything like you, but for a split second I saw you in danger instead of her and everything went red rage. I don't know how long I was out of touch. When I came back everyone was still breathing, though the guy was only making gurgling sounds."

She gasped and reached out to put her hand on his arm. His knuckles were covered with cuts and bruises. She could only imagine what the man looked like. Not that she had much sympathy.

"Kenley got sick and I called 911. When the cops showed up they found me holding her, and the other guy bleeding and unconscious. I guess it looked bad, so they took me in."

"I can't believe a hero showed up at my door with pizza."

He grinned and shook his head. "I'm not a hero."

"All heroes say that." She stood on her tiptoes so she could kiss his cheek. "I knew you were a great guy when I saw how much you cared about your brother, but now it's confirmed." He let out a sigh, but gave up arguing. "Did you stop to help any old ladies across the street?"

"No. Sorry."

"Well, there's always next time."

"Eat your pizza before it gets cold," he ordered, slipping back into that scary façade for a moment. But it no longer had the same level of intimidation she remembered from their showdown before.

She complied easily, eating her pizza and sipping her wine as he went on.

"My boss, Zane, has it bad for Kenley. He flew back to take care of her. It was a classy move. I hope it pays off."

"I would definitely be touched if someone jumped on a plane to come to my aid."

"I would be there in a second if you needed me," he said, his grin downplaying the intensity of his statement. She didn't doubt him.

"How is Kenley?"

He shook his head. "She says she's fine, which is bullshit. I know because when I got my foot blown off in Iraq, I said I was fine too." She swallowed a sip of wine, hoping it covered her surprise.

She'd noticed he had a limp, but she didn't realize he'd lost his foot.

"You weren't fine?" Her voice betrayed her fake calm.

"Not even a little bit. I ended up breaking down, falling into a deep depression. I was hoarding my pain meds so I could end it all. The only thing that saved me was Hunter."

"Hunter?"

"I had to get better so I could come back to the states to take care of him. I was still learning how to walk with my prosthetic when they came to tell me my mother was dead and that Hunter had been severely injured. I needed to get my shit together so I could help him."

And this man didn't think he was a hero? Was he kidding?

They chatted easily until the wine was gone and it was late. She loved listening to his stories, even the bad ones. It was nice knowing he wasn't perfect.

When the conversation slowed, she wasn't sure what to do next. In a date situation, it would be time for him to drop her off. She would kiss him at the door and tell him she'd had a nice evening.

But Brady was already in her house. Was he expecting an invitation to spend the night? Did she want that? What if it made their relationship with Hunter's care uncomfortable?

As if he'd read her mind, he let out a breath and leaned close to her, brushing a piece of hair behind her ear as he studied her face.

"I should go, but I can't seem to make myself leave."

"Oh." Her heart pounded. She didn't want him to leave, either, but she didn't have the courage to say it.

"I know we're not ready for the next step, but can I stay with you tonight? If I go home, I'll have bad dreams all night. Let me hold you, so I know you're safe. I'll stay in my clothes and I won't touch anything I'm not allowed to." He put his hand up, pledging an oath.

She trusted him completely. It was herself she wasn't sure about. Every time he kissed her or even looked at her in that way, she felt like throwing her panties at him.

"Okay," she managed to get out.

"Just to sleep. I'm beat. When we do get to that step, I want it to be really good." She had no doubts about that. But that didn't mean she didn't have a question.

"How will we know when we get to that step?"

Brady burst out laughing.

"I have no clue. I thought you'd know. I've never taken more than one step with a woman before you, Mick."

She laughed along, but her heart throbbed happily in her chest. He cared about her. She'd tried her best to keep her feelings for him at bay, but now they flooded in.

"I guess we'll figure it out when we get there."

"I have to say…" He leaned down and kissed her neck, under her ear. "I hope that step isn't a long time away."

"Me, too."

\* \* \*

Kenley closed her carry-on and rolled it to the door where Zane took it from her. Over the last two days, he'd been treating her like she would break at any moment.

Maybe that was because she kept breaking.

After the episode in the office when he'd sent her outside so he could clean up, she thought she'd dealt with everything. She was able to go back into the office without any problem, but as soon as Zane left her alone to go in his office, she'd experienced chest pains and couldn't breathe. Zane said he thought maybe it was a panic attack, but she brushed it off.

Whatever it was, it was unnecessary. She was fine. Or she would need to be. They were going to Ohio for the grand opening of the new shop. She needed to get herself together.

Zane had his fingers through hers as they boarded the plane.

"You okay?" he asked. It was becoming their motto.

"I'm great. There's going to be cake at this shindig."

They got there a day early so they could meet the new hires and set up the decorations. She didn't have any issues being alone in the new office. She seemed to have broken out of whatever shackles had held her captive back home. Maybe she really was getting better.

One part of her life that was definitely better was her love life.

Rather than find more reasons why they wouldn't work out, she'd decided she was going to go for it.

As Shelly, the new Executive Production Coordinator, entered the few invoices there were for the new location, Kenley pulled out her phone to send Zane a text. He was out at the dock, but she didn't think she could wait another second.

*I changed my mind about no promises.*

Thirty seconds later he wrote back:

*Good. I want to make some.*

Followed by:

*I'll be done here in a half hour.*

* * *

Fortunately, his new service manager wasn't a big talker and didn't need a lot of instruction. He'd done the job for sixteen years, so there wasn't much Zane could tell him he didn't already know.

"If you have any questions, you have my number." Zane wrapped up his speedy training session, eager to get back to Kenley. The text she'd sent seemed simple, but he knew what it meant. They were moving things along. This wasn't just casual anymore. It meant something.

For him it had meant something from the first time they'd kissed.

She smiled when he walked into the office. It was so good to see her smile. Her real smile. She'd been forcing them for his benefit since the robbery, but he could tell the difference. He could also tell when she felt anxious about being alone. And he'd noticed the way she flinched when someone stepped too close to her.

She'd insisted she was fine, but he knew it wasn't going to be easy to forget having someone put a gun to her head and threaten her life. It made him crazy just thinking about it and he hadn't even been there.

"You feel better here?" he asked as they locked up the building to go back to the hotel.

"There are no bad memories. I guess that makes it easier."

"If you want, we could always move here."

"Move? Together?"

"You said you changed your mind about no promises. To me, that means considering the possibilities of cohabitation." He laughed, but she looked a little stunned.

"But move the whole way out here? You would miss all the things your niece will be doing in the next five years. Trust me, it's like every day there is a new event."

"There are other ways to keep in touch. If you want to stay here, I'd be willing to at least think about it."

The smile she gave him was real and full of some emotion he'd never encountered before. While neither of them said the words, he thought she might be at the same place he was.

"Thank you for the offer, but I don't want to run away from this. I'm stronger than this silly fear."

* * *

"I have bad news," Zane said as he got off the phone and fell into bed next to her that night after the party. She could already tell by his end of the conversation that he was being called away on a job. "I have to take a detour to Michigan before going home tomorrow."

"I'll take care of changing your flight." She reached for the laptop.

"Do you want to change both flights so you can come with me?" While she was happy he'd invited her along, she knew the reason. He knew she was frightened to be alone. She couldn't follow him around the country like a scared puppy forever. It was time to face it head on.

"No. I'll be fine."

"I didn't ask because I think you're weak, Ken. I do like having you with me. And maybe it makes me a little nervous when I'm away from you."

Well, that was better than feeling like a burden. "Thank you. I appreciate it. But I do need to take the next step toward getting past this."

"I'd feel better if you told your friends."

"So they will fuss over me? No, thank you. I'll tell them later."

"Okay. If you're sure."

"I am."

"Have I told you how amazing you are?"

"A few times."

"Yeah, but before I was mostly saying it to get myself out of trouble. I really mean it now." He winked and pulled her in for a kiss.

\* \* \*

Her apartment felt different as she stepped inside and parked her suitcase by the door to her bedroom. She then spent a good ten minutes checking the closets and under the bed for intruders before she went to unpack.

Zane called to check in three times. She hadn't used the word *fine* so much since her mother died.

It would be difficult to convince anyone she was fine when she jumped a foot into the air at the sound of her own doorbell.

Scott Porter waited on the porch in his uniform.

"Hi there," she said, hoping he wouldn't ask her out again. At least this time she had an excuse. She had a boyfriend.

"Zane asked me to stop by to check on you."

"Wow. He must really be worried if he called you."

"He is." He looked past her into her apartment. "Did you want me to do a sweep while I'm here? Just to be sure?"

"Actually, I just did it."

"Okay." He turned and she felt her chest freeze.

"But since you're a professional, maybe you could look too. Just to be sure." She had checked out the place thoroughly, but a sweep sounded more official.

"Can do. It won't take but a second." He looked in all the places she'd looked. But there was something about the gun hanging on his belt that made her feel more secure.

"All clear."

"Thank you."

"Not a problem. I'll keep an eye on your place when I'm doing my patrol. You don't have anything to worry about. The guy is still in the hospital and hasn't made bail, so he'll be in jail as soon as he can walk. You're safe."

"I know. It's silly. It's not like he could find me here. I'm just kind of nervous."

"I'm not surprised. You'll probably be rattled for a while."

"I'm fine." That word was getting old.

She texted Zane to thank him for sending Scott over.

She didn't hear back, but he would have been in the air, so it wasn't surprising not to get a response. Several hours later he finally called back.

"Hello."

"Why aren't you asleep? It's after eleven."

"It's also a Saturday night and I'm only twenty-eight. If I go to bed before midnight on a Saturday, I'll wake up an old person. That's how it works."

"Huh. You might be right about that. We're the same age, but I'm way older than you."

"I don't know about that. During sex you're still going strong while I'm exhausted and can't catch my breath."

"That comes from practice."

She heard the smile in his voice. They'd been getting a lot of practice over the last few days. She couldn't seem to get enough of him. When he was touching her, and making her body feel good, it was impossible to think about what happened.

"I'm not going to see you tomorrow. And I'm not going to be in the office on Monday. Something came up and I need to stay out here."

"Okay."

"I just want you to know I really do have to stay out here. I'm not staying on the road so I can avoid you. I won't ever do that again. I swear."

"Thank you."

"If you need anything, call Brady. He's back and he'll help."

"Okay."

The empty bed spawned fitful dreams and restless sleep. Sunday she went to visit her parents. They asked how work was going and she told them it was... fine.

The armed robbery report was just a small blurb in the newspaper, and since her friends and family lived in another town, no one noticed. She knew they would be upset and worried if she told them what had happened. She would tell them when she knew she could answer their questions without breaking out in a sweat. Speaking about it now still made it too real.

While Vanessa hadn't read the paper, she did know something was wrong as soon as Kenley stepped into her house the next day. Vanessa had been her friend for a very long time, and could read her like a book.

"What is it? Something's wrong. Did Zane do something stupid?"

"No. He's amazing." She did her best to act normal, but she was too conscious of everything she said or did.

"What is with you? You're skittish."

"I'm not skittish."

"You jumped out of your seat when Hannah's toy hooted."

"I had a run-in with some guy at the office. It was nothing."

"Did he hurt you?" Her laser focus was on Kenley, no doubt watching for clues.

"No. Someone came in and stopped him." Stopped him was not really the right word. From what Scott had said, the guy still couldn't walk. Brady had been a mad man—his eyes unfocused on anything but the man with the gun. She couldn't say she was sorry.

When it was over, she'd said Brady's name, and it was like a light came back on. He'd looked around the office as if he was confused about how the guy had ended up bleeding on the floor.

"What happened?" Vanessa said, pulling her out of the memory.

"Can I get a pass for now? I promise I'll tell you. Just not today. I need some time. The important thing is that I'm…" She swallowed. "Fine."

"Uh-huh. Fine like you were when your mother died and you came back to school the next week?"

"It was finals. She didn't want me to miss them."

"Still, you weren't fine then and I know you're not fine now."

"Okay. Maybe I'm not. But I need to be. I want to be. So just let me be fine until I really am."

"Whenever you're ready, I'll be here."

"I know. Thank you." They hugged it out and she left to go home. She had made sure to be home before dark. After checking the place over she settled in with a book and twitched at every noise her home made.

The next morning she went in to work and followed her normal routine. She started the coffeepot, and greeted the men before they went out to the shop.

She was busy, which made the day fly by. It was after three when Brady came in.

"Hey, how you doing?"

"Good," she said, keeping her eyes on her screen.

"Ken?"

"Yeah?"

"Look at me."

"I really have to get this in."

"Look. At. Me." The demand in his voice made her head jerk up. He smiled, but his eyes were hard and intent. He reminded her of a wolf.

"Yes?" she squeaked.

"Can we please talk this out? I know I must have scared the shit out of you when I started whaling on that guy. I lose it sometimes. That was one of those times. But I swear to you, I'm not so bad that I would ever hurt you, okay?"

"Sure. I know that." She still couldn't look at him.

"You're not looking at me again. What is it?"

"Nothing."

"Bull shit. Tell me, or I'm just going to sit on the edge of your desk until you do. And I'm going to eat your candy stash from your second drawer while I wait."

"Fine." She reached out to stop him from touching her candy. "I just—I wish you hadn't had to see me throw up."

After the incident, Brady had taken her outside until the police came. It was a good thing too, because she'd tossed her lunch in the bushes in front of the building. He'd held her hair and gone back inside to get her a paper towel.

The confession of her humiliation was met with laughter. She glared at him and he did a fair job of trying to get himself together.

"Sorry. Here I thought I'd freaked you out, and you're worried about me seeing you throw up."

Yes. Did he need to repeat it?

"Sweetie, I was in the military. Between injuries, drinking too much, or being scared out of our wits, vomiting was pretty much a daily occurrence. I don't think any less of you because of it."

She couldn't help but chuckle at his little speech. She nodded. "Okay. Thank you."

"You have to stop thanking me. You've thanked me six-hundred-and-twenty-four times."

"No, I haven't. It's maybe six-hundred twenty-one at the most." It felt better to joke about it.

"I'm going to hug you, and we're going to call it good. Then I'm going to ask you for a favor, but you shouldn't feel obligated because I saved your life or anything."

Again she chuckled as he wrapped her in his big arms. It was completely friendly. His hands stayed where they belonged.

"I want you to know I have a girlfriend now, which is why I'm not using my gallantry to weasel my way into your bed."

"A girlfriend? Really?" She stepped back when he released her.

"It's new. I'll probably fuck it up, but I like her. She's a doctor."

"Get out."

"No, really. And she even knows I'm an asshole. She's seen me at my assiest and yet she still let me make out with her."

"Wow. I'm impressed." She nodded. "So what's the favor?"

"Hunter is going through occupational therapy. Michaela thinks he'd be able to have a job. I wasn't so sure until he stayed with you and polished up the fittings. I was wondering if you might be able to find more work for him. Odd jobs he'd be capable of doing. Zane said he'd find a place for him, but I don't want it to be an inconvenience."

"Of course it wouldn't be an inconvenience. I like having him here."

"Maybe make a list of things you think he'd be good at. I'll run it by Mick and make sure he can handle it."

"Sure thing."

Brady turned to leave but came back.

"There's one more thing."

"I'm not hugging you again."

"Would you stop throwing yourself at me, woman? You're dating my boss and I told you I have a girlfriend." He chuckled at his joke, but turned serious. "I do need you to do something for me."

"Okay."

"I want you to talk this out with someone."

Kenley let out a sigh. "Everyone is worrying about nothing. There's nothing to talk about. Nothing happened. So the guy threatened me. He didn't have a chance to hurt me."

"Do you dream about it?"

She shrugged and then, when he kept watching her silently, nodded.

"I know about the dreams. Trust me, they start to become more real if they aren't dealt with."

She opened her mouth to put him at ease, but he cut her off again.

"I'm not trying to boss you around or stick my nose in your business, but you should talk to a professional about this."

"You mean a shrink?" Kenley shifted to her other foot. She'd spoken to a grief counselor after her mother died. It hadn't helped. Time helped the most. Besides, she was… fine. "Nothing happened, and I have you to thank for that."

"Something *did* happen. If the guy hadn't done anything, I wouldn't have beaten him into the ICU. Something happened. It might not be the thing that could have happened, but it was something."

"Okay."

"These things have a way of sneaking up on you when you think you're fine. I know firsthand how hard it can be to keep things locked away, no matter how much you don't want to think about them."

"I'll keep that in mind," Kenley agreed, though she knew she would be okay. The guy had been desperate. She knew it from the way his hands shook and the panic in his bloodshot eyes. He probably wouldn't have shot her. He just wanted the money.

She shuddered at the memory. Would he have let her live after he'd taken the money? He'd done nothing to hide his face. She would have been able to identify him. Would he have taken out the witness?

"I know what I'm talking about. I'm still haunted by things I saw in Iraq. It comes out of nowhere. I sure as hell didn't want to chat about it, but talking does help. Just remember that."

Kenley nodded and watched Brady leave. She went back to her bills and thought about other things. Nice things.

Cookies, her niece's hugs, margaritas, and Zane's kisses. She suddenly realized she hadn't heard any sounds coming from the back. She opened the door to the shop to check on the other men and found the place was dark.

Checking the clock, she realized it was after five. She hadn't even noticed. Spooked to be alone, she hurried around the building, locking all the doors.

* * *

Unable to wait another second to get back to Kenley, Zane caught a late flight that night and got to her house a little after eleven. He had flowers in his hand and a big smile on his face when she opened the door.

"I thought you wouldn't be back until tomorrow," she said, smiling back at him. She was dressed for bed in a pair of cotton shorts and a T-shirt. He could tell there was no bra. One less thing he'd have to take off. But first they needed to talk.

"I missed you, so I came home as soon as I could."

"Thank God," she said as she stood on her tiptoes to press her lips to his. She took his hand and led him to her bedroom where he stopped. He almost gave in, but he knew he needed to stand his ground on this.

Instead of going inside he picked her up and carried her back to the sofa. With her on his lap he kissed her until she pulled back to look at him.

"You didn't want to…" She nodded in the direction of her bedroom.

"I do. Very much. But I want to talk with you first. I don't want this to just be about sex." They'd been having a lot of sex. Part of him expected this since their relationship was new and she was making up for lost time on the sex front. But he wasn't stupid. He knew she was also using sex to cope with what had happened. No doubt she thought if she could have sex with him she must be fine.

*Fine.* That goddamned word. He'd heard it so much he wanted it stricken from the English language. The worst part was that people didn't seem to know what it really meant. All his past girlfriends had used it as a curse when he'd asked if something was wrong. They'd said they were fine, but what they meant was they were holding in their anger with plans to unleash it at a more inopportune time.

Kenley also had difficulties with the definition. She seemed to think it meant she would ignore the problem until it got easier to deal with.

"Okay. We can talk if you want."

She pouted, which almost made him give in. But he needed to do the right thing. Brady had warned him of the dangers of letting her brush it off as nothing. He'd been there. He'd seen what happened. Zane trusted his judgment.

"I got a naughty cheerleader outfit. It took me forever to muster up the courage to take it to the counter and pay for it, but I did. Three cheers for me."

He sat up straighter and looked at her. Was that what she thought this was about? She wasn't just a fantasy come true. She was his reality.

"I'll admit, maybe at first I just wanted to have sex. But now it's about you. I want you, Kenley. The real you. Not the woman I made up in my head. I like so many other things about you."

"Were you planning to list them now, or can I kiss you?" she asked with a grin.

"I'm planning on completely ruining the mood to talk about how you're holding up. And if you use the word fine, I'm going to hold you down and tickle you until you hurl, and we already know how much you hate that."

"Brady told."

"Yes. He thought you were terrified of him. He was so happy it was just embarrassment."

"He's going to be terrified of *me* when I get hold of him."

"He cares about you." He kissed her hair and pulled her closer. "Not as much as me, of course."

"He thinks I should talk to a professional."

"I don't want to take sides here, especially if it will wreck my chances of seeing the naughty cheerleader outfit, but I have to agree with him. Even if it's not a miracle cure, it can't hurt. I don't like you being afraid. I can't handle the guilt of leaving you alone, knowing you're scared."

"Okay. I guess I'll give it a try before you stage an intervention."

"I already ordered the banner."

She smacked him and then kissed him in that way that melted his soul. She was done talking about it. He decided he would let it go for now.

After making out with her on the sofa for a while they talked about their day. She wanted to go to New York to visit her friend the next weekend. He was happy to see she wanted to go out. Maybe he'd been wrong. Maybe she would be okay after all.

"I have an idea," she said as she bit her lip.

"I love your ideas. They make me more efficient, and in turn, make me money." He kissed her neck, making her giggle.

"You know the app I made with all the pictures of items in the shop?"

"Yeah. I've been cleaning it out as I have time during layovers. I think it's pretty up to date now."

"There are things in there you're not using."

"Right."

"What if we link the app to a website where people can buy the things you won't use? Like a retail site."

"Huh. I never really thought about it. It's a good idea."

"I don't know if I can make the site though."

"Don't worry. I can hire someone to do it."

"Maybe you can give the person a discount on a boat in exchange for the website."

"I am amazed by your mind. I am so glad I talked my sister into hiring you." She laughed and rolled her eyes.

* * *

Someone kicked him, waking him from the most peaceful sleep of his life. Before he had fully woken he was scratched across his chest and kicked again.

Kenley was thrashing around in her sleep. Her mumbled cries of "No" twisted his gut with worry.

He turned on the light by her bed. "Kenley?" he said, shaking her awake.

She woke immediately, blinking from the light. Letting out a deep breath, she reached for him and began sobbing as he held her close.

"You're not fine, are you?" he whispered into her hair.

The only answer was a shake of her head and another quiet sob.

# Chapter 17

After a recommendation from Brady, Kenley sat in Dr. Fulmer's office as the doctor read the police report out loud.

"So that is officially what happened. Those are the facts," the woman said as she crossed her arms on her lap.

"Okay," Kenley said. She was there. She knew what had happened.

"Was anything missing?"

"I don't know. I don't think so. The police were pretty thorough with their questions."

"And your subconscious is taking the facts and twisting them into something horrible."

Kenley nodded. That was an adequate description. Over the last two weeks she'd been having more bad dreams. The anxiety of being alone in the office was getting worse too. Zane was doing a good job of having excuses to stay in the office, but he still needed to take Weston's boat up to Boston.

"When you're awake, do you seem fixated on what could have happened if Brady hadn't come in?"

"I try not to think about it. If I start thinking about all the potential risks of going anywhere alone, I'm afraid I'll become a prisoner in my apartment." She swallowed. "But it does pop into my head when I'm not concentrating on other things." And it had kept her from going to the city to meet up with Alyssa last weekend. She'd come up with a last-minute excuse and gone home.

"If you don't deal with it, it could sneak up on you at any time. You could become a prisoner in your own head."

"I feel very fortunate nothing happened. I just want to focus on that."

"Nothing happened?" Dr. Fulmer repeated her words while holding up the three-page report. "This happened. It's real. It was bad. Yes, it could have been worse, but don't downplay what took place."

Kenley swallowed and nodded again. Why couldn't everyone just let it go? Why couldn't she? She hadn't been shot or hurt in any way. So he'd grabbed her arm. So he'd shouted at her with his nasty breath fanning across her face. That happened a million times to people in the subway.

"I'm going to read the report again so you know what happened. They are facts and they are in the past. Do you understand?"

Kenley nodded and listened to the words this time instead of trying to block them out.

When she was done she passed the papers to Kenley.

"You're going to be called to testify on these facts. While you're in the courtroom you are going to hear this again. I want you to be prepared and comfortable with the facts so you don't break down on the stand. Can you read them out loud to me?"

She stumbled on the words *armed robbery* all three times they came up. Apparently the doctor noticed.

"You were robbed at gunpoint."

"But I wasn't hurt—"

"It's true you weren't shot, but the fear of the possibility brings out the same feelings of helplessness and loss of control."

Kenley nodded in understanding. She had felt helpless and out of control. That was the part that still haunted her even when Zane was close by.

She took the papers home and read them out loud twice a day, per the doctor's orders.

By the third appointment Kenley was able to read through the report and admit that she had been threatened at gunpoint without making other excuses or trying to brush it off. It was progress.

She was healing. Maybe someday soon she would even be fine.

\* \* \*

Zane was following Kenley's lead as far as her recovery was concerned. And it was a recovery. The night she'd pulled out the tattered police report and read it to him out loud had nearly killed him. But he'd listened and held her close afterward, feeling as if she'd made some giant step forward.

Inside he'd raged for the chance to hurt the man who had terrified her this badly. If he'd actually pulled the trigger, Zane would have ended him and not cared about the repercussions.

Fortunately that hadn't happened.

He felt relief wash over him at the sound of her giggle when he picked her up to set her on his desk. They'd been working, but when they got to the bottom of the pile, he'd pushed his laptop and a few other things out of the way to make room. A few papers scattered and fell to the floor as he reached for the button on her blouse.

He couldn't resist pulling her close and kicking the door shut for a little fun. He paused, worried about their venue. Just down the hall she'd been threatened. Would the memories intrude on this moment?

She laughed and wiggled closer. The sweet sound pushed his concerns away. That first night she'd wanted him to touch her. To make new memories. This would be a new memory. A very nice memory.

"What's so funny?" he asked when she giggled again.

"I was just remembering how I was fired from my last job because my boss thought I had sex with her husband, and now here I am having sex with my boss on his desk."

"I'm not your boss right now. It wouldn't be right." He pulled her nipple into his mouth and let go with a pop.

"What are you then?" He noted the challenge in the question. As if he'd be too big a coward to confess his feelings.

He shrugged. With anyone else this question might have freaked him out, but this was Kenley. It was so easy to give her an answer.

"Your boyfriend. Or if you need an official title, may I suggest 'The Guy Who Makes My Knees Weak'?" She giggled again until he ran his thumb over her erect nipples. The giggle was abruptly cut off by a gasp.

"Wow. You're right. My knees are weak."

He bent to take another swipe when the phone rang.

"Crap. I have to get that," she said as she stopped working on the button on his jeans to reach for the phone.

"No. Don't touch it."

"But it's my job to answer the phone."

"Not right now it isn't." He couldn't wait out any long-winded customer. They would have to call back. He unzipped his pants and tugged them down along with his boxers. He loved that Kenley was on The Pill. It made having sex anywhere a lot easier.

He kissed up her neck while he worked the zipper on her jeans. He was just about ready to slide them over her beautiful ass when they heard someone come in the back door.

"I didn't lock the door. Shit!" he cursed and pulled his pants back up as Kenley hopped off the desk. She had just finished buttoning her shirt when

Sidney opened the door, carrying a bundle of blankets. A murmur from the bundle indicated his niece was inside.

"Why the hell didn't you answer the phone if you were here?" Sidney snapped. "I have the tax forms you asked about. It would have been easier for you to walk out to my car instead of making me get Paige out of the car and—" Sidney stopped and concentrated on them.

Kenley's cheeks were bright red and he wasn't able to look his sister in the eye. Not good.

"Oh my God! Were the two of you…?" She laughed loud enough to cause a disgruntled sound from Paige. "Wow. Sorry. I didn't mean to interrupt. I'll just set these…" She glanced at his desk which was still in disarray, then looked behind her at the guest chair. "Here looks good. I guess I'll let you get back to *work*."

Zane let out a sigh, knowing he wouldn't be able to avoid the misery his sister was sure to inflict every time they met.

"Come on, pumpkin. Uncle Zane is… busy."

"Christ," Zane said. "Give her here." He never wanted to be guilty of being too busy for his niece. Besides, there was no way he would be able to get back to business with Kenley now that his sister had caught them.

Kenley chuckled as Zane dug through the light pink blanket to find the little person inside.

"Hey, sweet pea," he said with a smile. "Please don't spit up on me like the last time, 'kay?" He looked up to tell Kenley how Paige seemed to have a problem with his flannel shirts, but he stopped.

She was staring at him with some look on her face he didn't recognize. It wasn't bad. It was kind of dreamy. Like she was happy to watch him holding the baby.

*Oh.*

He looked at his infant niece, seeing her as the promises-of-things-to-come she was. It wasn't as if he hadn't thought of marriage and a family. He did want kids someday. He'd even considered the idea of having them with Kenley, but that look on her face caused his flight instincts to kick in for a second. It was the look men were taught to evade for as long as possible. To his surprise, once the initial fear abated he felt comforted by the idea.

He'd suggested they move in together. At the time it had been a desperate attempt to take her away from her fears. But now he realized how much he meant it.

Standing there next to the woman he had feelings for while holding his adorable niece, he wondered why men saw this scenario as a trap. If getting married and having kids was so horrible, why did so many of them do it?

There must have been some secret to it. He surely couldn't ask his father—he'd failed miserably on all levels.

He handed the baby back to his sister with a smile in his heart.

"I forgot, I have a few calls to make."

Sidney and Kenley gave him a look, but left him in his office alone.

* * *

"So how long has *this* been going on?" Sidney asked as they walked to Kenley's desk. Kenley knew there would be no way to get out of the conversation. Strike that—interrogation. "Last I heard, he'd messed things up when my parents were being their horrid selves."

"It wasn't him. We worked it out."

Kenley glanced down the hall, remembering Zane's sudden need to be alone. Maybe it wouldn't matter. She'd seen his skittish look enough times to know when he was ready to bolt.

She knew she loved him, and she wondered if he was the type who would ever be able to love her back. She had to admit she'd felt a little twinge in her heart as well as a jolt to her biological clock as she watched him holding Paige. It was easy to see how much he loved the little girl.

"I'm glad he fixed things. My brother's never been really serious about anyone before. He had a few girlfriends during college. He's dated, but nothing long-term."

That should have make Kenley feel better. He'd never had a serious relationship, either. But instead she felt more anxious. She'd never wanted to have more with anyone. She'd seen the pain her father had endured when her mother died. The pain that was still in his eyes whenever anyone spoke of her. She'd spent the last several years thinking love meant pain. Now she realized it might be worth the risk.

"But now I think," Sidney continued, "he needed to get his business started first. So he knew what he was capable of. What's important is what happens now."

"You're right." Kenley perked up. The past was the past. What mattered was if Zane was ready for a relationship now.

They chatted until closing. Sidney had called her many times since the robbery, but this was the first time they'd seen each other. Sidney looked around the innocent-looking space and shook her head.

"I can't believe we could have lost you here in this spot where I once told Zane he was acting like a poo-poo head." Sidney wiped under her eye and pulled Paige a little closer. "I'm so glad you're okay, Kenley."

They attempted an awkward hug that included the baby and ended up laughing.

Kenley locked the door behind Sidney. It was way after quitting time when she walked into Zane's office.

He'd put everything back on his desk. Too bad.

With a confidence she didn't quite feel, she strode over to him. Rolling his chair back, she straddled his thighs.

"I want you, Zane Jackson." Her voice only shook a little as she unbuttoned her shirt, trying for seductive. "Right now."

With nothing but a low groan, he moved his laptop and papers out of the way again. In one swift movement he stood and placed her on the desk.

They made quick work of each other's clothing, and seconds later he slid into her with a hard thrust that pushed her across the desk. Undeterred, he simply moved her back into position and drove into her again.

She loved how her sweet, shy Zane turned into this sexy, aggressive creature when she touched him.

He licked and nipped at her skin everywhere at once, and yet she wanted more. Two more thrusts sent her over, and she shouted his name, or something close to it, as he let out a moan of surrender and fell heavily on top of her. His chest heaving against hers, his breath against her neck.

"You know there is a perfectly good bed in your apartment a few blocks from here. And you are officially off for the day," he said, kissing the place under her ear.

"What about you? Are you off for the day?"

"I have a few things I should finish, but I could be persuaded."

"Why don't I go start dinner and I'll call you when it's ready."

He shook out her shirt and passed it over.

"You're perfect, you know that?"

She hid the frown. She didn't want him to think she was perfect. She wasn't. She didn't want to be on a pedestal. The only place to go from up there was down.

"I'm afraid you're delusional." She sat up and looked around for her jeans, but he stopped her.

"What's that supposed to mean?"

"I'm not the perfect woman you had fantasies about when I started here. I have faults and problems. If you keep me on a pedestal I'm bound to fall off."

A smile started on one side of his mouth. "If you'll recall, I just had you on my desk, not a pedestal."

She found her pants and pulled them on.

"Ken?" She paused. "I see the real you. The stubborn, workaholic, borderline-neurotic you, as well as the kind, sweet, sex-on-a-stick you. And I think you're even more perfect. So get over it."

Her heart filled with love as he bent to kiss her.

"Okay," she said, pulling herself together as she slipped on her shoes. "I was going to make meatloaf."

She watched as Zane set the picture of his sister back up on his desk, adjusting it slightly to the side. Then he turned to her with a smile on his face.

"Sounds good," he said. "Call me and I'll be there."

\* \* \*

Zane was still smiling and straightening things on his desk when Brady came in and flopped down on his sofa.

"I have a big problem, boss."

"I was having an awesome day. Please don't come in here with bad news," Zane begged.

"You have the same shit grin on your face that Ken had when she left. Does that have anything to do with your awesome day?"

"The awesome day you're about to ruin?" Zane deflected the question. Brady laughed it off instead of persisting.

"Actually, my problem is of a personal nature."

Zane sat up, wanting to help. He'd already agreed to bring Hunter in three days a week, but if he needed something else, Zane would be there.

As much as he and Sidney tormented each other, there was an important bond between siblings. He knew he would be there for Sid, the way Brady took care of Hunter.

"What do you need?"

"I think I'm in love."

Zane couldn't help the burst of laughter that escaped. "And you think I can help you with that? I've messed up so many times with Kenley, I'm barely hanging on."

"From the look on her face when I passed her, you're holding your own."

"But sex is different than real feelings. I don't have to tell you that."

Brady frowned and shook his head. "No. You don't. I haven't even had sex with Mick yet. I guess I just need to know what happens if you tell a girl you have feelings and find out she doesn't."

Zane squirmed a bit in his seat and then shrugged. "I'm not sure. I've never told Kenley I loved her."

Brady's eyes went wide before he tilted his head and squinted. "But I thought you—"

"Yeah." He'd tried to tell her less than fifteen minutes ago, but he still hadn't managed to work up the nerve. Every time he thought he was ready, he'd think of how awful his parents' marriage was, or how Kenley was out of his league.

"You may be even worse off than me."

"Possibly."

"I think I want to go for it."

"Let me know how it works out." Maybe he could get some pointers on love from the playboy.

* * *

Michaela smiled as she stepped into the lobby of the place where Brady worked. She hoped she wasn't making a mistake, but she had a good excuse. It was her job.

He'd stopped by her house the night before. He'd said he wanted to talk to her about something, but then he never said anything. Instead, they made out on her sofa until she thought they might take that next step. But he'd left with an apology and an excuse about getting up early the next day.

She didn't know what was going on.

"Hello. How can I help you?" the woman at the desk asked with a friendly smile.

"Hi. I'm Dr. Walker. I spoke with Mr. Jackson about doing an evaluation for job placement for Hunter Martin."

"Oh, yes. Zane isn't here, but I should be able to answer any questions you have." She gestured to a chair. "Can I get you anything to drink? Tea, water, coffee?"

"You must be Kenley?" Brady had told her every detail of that day. At least the ones he could remember. The darkest parts were shrouded in rage. Probably for the best.

"Yes." The woman looked surprised. "Sorry." She held out her hand to shake. "Kenley Carmichael."

"Hunter has told me a lot about you."

Kenley answered her questions and took her for a tour of the facility. When they were walking back into the office, Brady was heading out and they stopped, staring at each other.

"Hey, baby. I didn't know you were stopping in," he said before he bent and brushed a kiss of happiness over her lips. She'd intended the visit to be a professional one, but at the sight of him, that all went to hell.

"This is your doctor girlfriend?" Kenley smiled.

"Yep. Didn't she tell you?" Brady's brows pulled together in question.

"No. I was here on official business." She hoped her excuse took that look off his face, but it didn't work. "Are you done for the day?"

"Yeah. I was going to wash up and head home." He left before she could say anything.

"I think I hurt his feelings."

"That can't be. Men always act like they don't have any feelings." Kenley snickered at her joke, but Michaela could only manage a smile. "He likes you a lot. He's pretty excited to have a girlfriend. I don't think he's ever had one before."

She swallowed and went to wait in the hall for Brady to come out.

"Good luck," Kenley called.

"Hey," Brady said when he emerged from the restroom, drying his hands.

"I was wondering if you would be interested in coming home with me for dinner."

"Are you trying to make it up to me?"

"I don't have anything to make up to you since I was here to do my job and I know you respect me and my job. But now that I'm done with my evaluation, I'd like to take you home with me."

He nodded and grinned. "Sure."

* * *

Brady followed Mick to her house. The second they were inside he pulled her against him and kissed her. He still felt a little thrown by his reaction to her dismissal in the office. Now he wanted to claim her, and make her feel so good she'd want to shout their relationship status from the rooftops. Or at the very least, social media.

"I'm sorry," she whispered by his ear as he moved her backward toward the stairs that would take them to her room.

"You don't want to?" He stopped in his tracks. They still hadn't taken that step yet. He didn't want to rush things. But he felt like now was the time.

"I do. I'm saying I'm sorry if I made you feel like I didn't want Kenley to know we were dating. I'm not sure why I didn't say anything."

"You wanted to keep it professional." He repeated her excuse back to her.

"That is the truth, but not all of it."

"Do you want to tell me the rest?"

"I think I was trying to convince myself you don't matter as much as you do. When I found out my ex was cheating on me, I was devastated because I'd let him become so important to me. I didn't want that to happen with you."

"Baby, I think the problem wasn't that you let him become important to you, it was that *you* weren't important to *him*. Trust me, you are very important to me. I would never be so stupid. Please let me be important in your life. You won't regret it."

She smiled and nodded. They continued their way up to her room and he unbuttoned her shirt while kissing her at the same time. He might be considered disabled, but he had some skills.

That thought stilled his lips and fingers.

"What is it?"

"I'm going to be taking off my pants."

"Yes. That's how it works."

That's not how it had worked for him since he'd lost his foot. His MO had been to get a woman so worked up before they got to her place that he could do her on the table, counter, or even a wall without getting undressed. Then with the right excuse and a smile he was out of there. Even when he'd stayed with Michaela that night, he'd kept his jeans on.

But Michaela was not going to be satisfied with that. He wasn't going to be either. He wanted to take his time and worship every inch of her body. That would mean she would want to reciprocate on some level.

"I have a prosthetic."

"Your foot. I know. You mentioned it."

Right. He'd told her. And she was still turned on. "Are you one of those women who get off on that?" He'd met a devotee once. Scary shit.

She blinked at him and frowned as she pulled her shirt together and sat up. "I'm one of those women who gets off on the guy she likes kissing her. At least until he says something stupid."

So that was a no. "I'm sorry. I'm trying to figure out why you're with me." Best to just cut to the chase. If she would just spit it out, he could decide if her answer repulsed him enough to make him leave or not. If he knew how she felt, it might be easier for him to tell her how he felt. God, this was hard.

"I'm with you because I thought you were a great guy and we have a lot of chemistry. But maybe I was wrong."

"You're a fancy doctor. I move boats around. There has to be something else."

With a determined look in her eyes she reached up, put her hands on the side of his head, and yanked him down to her lips. There she proceeded to kiss the hell out of him, until he moaned and gave in.

Right when he was ready to drag her back down on the bed she pulled away, her chest heaving and her eyes bright.

"That is the something else. Is it enough for you?"

"Yeah." He nodded. "It is."

"Besides, I'm not a real doctor."

"Is the certificate in your office a fake?"

"No. I did finish med school. Though it was the hardest thing I've ever done. I did it even though I didn't want to."

"You didn't want to become a doctor?" She was great at what she did. She really cared about the patients.

Hell, he must really be in love if he'd chosen to learn more about her over getting in her pants. He wanted the whole package with her, which meant getting to know everything. He turned to face her on the edge of the bed and took her hands in his, urging her to continue.

"My parents are the best. They would have encouraged me to be anything I ever wanted. Apparently, at some point when I was a child, I told them I wanted to be a doctor. After that, everything I did, every class I took was influenced by a decision I don't even remember making. But I went along with it. I didn't know I was unhappy with the idea until I was there, elbow deep in a cadaver trying not to gag." She shook her head. "And failing most of the time."

He managed to hold back his laughter.

"After a long time and a lot of money, I graduated, but realized I'd never enjoy being a doctor. I couldn't handle those kinds of things up close. But I still wanted to help people. After going back to school on my own dime for business, I was able to get the job as director. I'm really excited about it. But the doctor part is a lie in my heart."

Brady's earlier worry was back.

"Mick, my leg is not pretty. If you can't stand to look at it, I would understand." She slapped him on the shoulder.

"Stop it. You're not going to be able to scare me off. There is a huge difference between me seeing your healed amputation and me being the one who does the amputating. I can handle it. Now, take off your pants and shut up."

"Yes ma'am."

He decided to table the emotional stuff until he had a better handle on it. For now he'd rely on their chemistry to guide him.

# Chapter 18

"You're leaving already?" Wes said as Zane handed him the keys to his new boat. "I thought you were planning to stay for a few days."

That had been the plan, but as soon as Zane arrived he'd been itching to get back to Kenley. It wasn't just protectiveness anymore. It was something else. Something he needed to deal with. Soon.

"I'm sorry. I need to get back. Work stuff."

Wes didn't fall for it. Maybe because Zane couldn't make eye contact. "You're ditching me for a girl."

"Not just a girl. *The* girl."

"Oh." Wes's eyes went wide. "Really?"

"I think so. I just need to find a way to take that next step."

"I've never taken that step, so I won't be much help." Instead of giving him crap, his friend drove him to the car rental office and wished him good luck.

"I just don't want to end up like my parents, you know?"

"Trust me, I know. Neither one of us had very good role models in the happy marriage department. I still have to hope that means we'll know how to do it better. If anything, we'll be more selective in who we chose to spend our lives with."

\* \* \*

Zane invited her over to his house the next evening. He was going to make her dinner and tell her how he felt. Maybe.

As he cooked she wandered around his kitchen, taking in the photos on his fridge. She'd offered to help, but he wanted to take care of her needs. All of them.

Besides it was his turn. She'd made him a wonderful meal at her apartment the week before. One that ended with them in her bed.

He hoped this dinner turned out the same way. It was a warm June evening, and he was looking forward to sex on the deck.

"Are you going to your reunion?" she asked, pulling his attention away from cutting up basil and thoughts of her naked body. She was standing at his message board where the invitation was pinned.

"I haven't decided."

"It says you need to RSVP by tomorrow."

"Other things came up."

"It's not too late."

He shrugged and she came closer.

"You're not going?" She sounded disappointed.

"I hate all those people, Kenley. I promised myself I'd never have to see them after I graduated."

She nodded. "I don't believe you hate *all* those people. You had to have had friends in high school. There had to be good memories too."

"Let's say I decided to go. Would I have a hot woman as my date?" He tilted his head.

She shrugged. "It's kind of short notice, but you could probably put out an ad."

"Very funny." He dropped the knife so he could chase her around the island. He caught her easily and pinned her to the counter for a deep kiss. He'd already found the girl of his dreams by placing an ad. "Will you go with me?" he asked.

"Yeah." Her face lit up before she pushed him away playfully. "Are you going to feed me or what?"

\* \* \*

"You've got it bad," Brady teased him as he dropped some forms on his desk.

"I do not," Zane made a lame attempt to defend himself, but deep down he knew it was true.

"You told me you were going to be in Boston dropping off your friend's boat until Thursday. I believe it's only Tuesday."

"So? I got done early." Zane shrugged it off, but the sound of the other man's laughter told him he hadn't been convincing.

"There's nothing wrong with wanting to be with your girl," Brady allowed with a sympathetic smile and a pat on the shoulder. "I miss Mick when I'm out on the road."

"Are you thinking of doing something about that?" Zane asked. If the King of the Bachelors could settle down with one woman, anyone could do it.

"Maybe. What about you?"

"I invited Kenley to my ten-year high school reunion in a few weeks. I hated the people I went to school with, and I don't want to go."

"Go." Brady pointed at him as if he were the boss. "Trust me. Facing things puts you in control." Zane was surprised by the in-depth advice. "Plus, when women dress up, they always wear sexy underwear. You won't want to miss it."

"You know this as fact?"

"It's a gift." He laughed. "Going to this lame-ass reunion might bore your balls off, but you can deal with anything for one night. Especially when there's sexy underwear waiting at the end."

"That's the thing. It's not one night of my life. It's dredging up my old life. The one I hated."

Brady patted him on the back. "This time you'll have a smart, sexy woman next to you who only wants you. Go stick it to them. Give yourself some closure on that part of your life, so you can move on to the better part."

The better part.

Zane could see himself being happy with Kenley for a very long time. But there were no guarantees. His parents were the perfect example of how bad a marriage could be.

Forever was a very long time to be miserable.

* * *

"I just don't understand what the big deal is," Kenley told Alyssa that weekend. After talking it over with her therapist, she'd managed to go to the city alone. She was feeling pretty proud of herself. Zane, however, had texted her three times to make sure she was doing okay. "It's just a reunion. We can make fun of people, and then go home and forget about them. I'm not sure why he's so worried about it." Kenley snorted and then finished off her second margarita.

"You said he didn't have it easy in high school. Take it from someone who knows what that was like. I have never gone to my reunions."

"But don't you want to show everyone how awesome you turned out?"

"Easy for you to say, Miss Cheerleader. The people who made me feel small back then still wield a lot of power, silly as that might be. Whenever I visit my mom and run in to someone from back home, it's like I'm transported back to that time, and I feel just as vulnerable. It's one of the reasons I don't put myself in that position often."

"I guess I didn't think of it like that."

"Why is it *really* important to you?" Liss was not one to play games or beat around the bush. She was always up front, even if it hurt.

"It's going to sound stupid."

"Undoubtedly."

"I told you I was adopted."

"By two loving parents, while I only ever had one, yeah." Brutal. Kenley knew there was some dark thing in Alyssa's past that she kept secret, but Liss had always talked happily about the relationship with her mother. Considering all she'd ever said about her father was "Spawn until dawn, then gone" Kenley wondered if that was the reason Liss had adopted such a businesslike approach to relationships, but she'd never probed.

"I was too young to remember anything about my parents, but still, knowing someone gave me up because they didn't want me... I always wonder if I'm good enough."

"That is the most ridiculous thing I've ever heard." The margaritas were making Liss even more up front than usual, but Ken already knew it was ridiculous. It didn't change things though.

"Everyone has a story, Ken. Everyone has a list of things that have happened to them that mold who they are. In the end it doesn't matter. You still have to deal. He's invited you to go someplace he doesn't feel comfortable. Be there for him when he faces his demons."

"Demons?" She gave a look of mock fright. "Surely they can't be that bad."

"Let's hope not. I hear they prey on the orphans first." Right for the kill.

\* \* \*

He followed Kenley into her apartment feeling like a weight had been lifted. She was home safe.

He'd tried not to make a big deal about her trip to New York. She needed to go as part of the healing process, but God had he been worried.

Having her away for the weekend made him realize what his life would have been like if that strung-out junkie had pulled the trigger. And while his biggest fear was that she could have been taken away from him that day, it didn't mean he couldn't still lose her in a different way. He needed to tell her how he felt.

He'd not had the best role models when it came to relationships, and he'd never had a desire to have one before now. He had a lot to lose, and no skills to keep that from happening.

The desire to avoid her—and the pain that seemed inevitable—reared its head. But he'd promised her he wouldn't run away from her again. From them.

So instead he pulled her close and kissed her.

"I'm glad you're back," he whispered, meaning it down to the depths of his soul.

He was determined to enjoy the moment.

In bed together, he took the most direct route to pleasing her so they could go to sleep. It was late, and they had to get up early for work. He held her as she slept, the moonlight coming in through the window, casting her face in a warm glow.

Had he really thought she looked like Courtney? The memories of his old crush were ten years old, but he didn't think Courtney was ever this beautiful. In fact, other than the long blonde hair, they didn't look that much alike. Thinking back to the day she'd walked into his office, he'd though she was the girl who had haunted him in high school, but it was more about the way she carried herself with confidence, or a convincing version at least. The way she'd seemed out of his league, and the feeling that had inspired in him.

Fear that he would once again fall short in the eyes of a beautiful woman. He pulled Kenley closer, reveling in the fact she was there, naked, in his arms.

In some ways she still scared the bejesus out of him. But he wouldn't let that destroy this moment.

She had invited him into her bed and her heart.

\* \* \*

It seemed like only an hour later when Kenley was waking him. He'd eventually fallen asleep after giving himself an intense lecture on living for the now.

After a quick shower, coffee and a kiss, she walked him to the door.

"I'll see you in a little while. Are you sure you don't want a ride?" he asked as he picked up the mail they had stepped over in their rush to get to a bed the night before.

Resting on top of a sales flyer was a thick envelope. He couldn't help but notice the return address.

*District Court of the State of Connecticut.*

She took it and swallowed.

"It must be the information about the trial," she said, running a finger under the flap of the envelope.

"Let me know when, and I'll go with you."

She shrugged. "You're busy. I don't expect you to take off to go."

He stepped closer and looked down into her eyes.

"Kenley, we're together now. I *will* be there next to you when you face that man." It was an easy thing to promise. He'd been making things more difficult than they needed to be. He needed to stop thinking so much and just go with his heart.

"Thank you," she whispered as he held her tightly and kissed her hair.

They were together. And there was nothing to fear. He would see her through this trial and then, when there was nothing else standing in their way, he would tell her he was ready to take the next step. Together.

\* \* \*

Brady showed up at Michaela's duplex a little after three. When he told Zane he'd received a subpoena to appear in court, Zane had given him the rest of the day off.

He'd begged Mick to spend the afternoon with him. It didn't take much persuasion. She opened the door when he knocked and ran upstairs, with him chasing behind.

"Damn, woman, slow down. I only have one foot."

"Please! I'm not falling for that trick." He laughed as he caught her at the top of the stairs. He picked her up and carried her the few feet to her room, throwing her on the bed and falling on top of her.

She giggled until he kissed the laughter into a low moan. As she reached for his pants someone banged on the wall with a hammer.

He jumped back at the sound, his heart rate soaring from the fright.

"What the hell?" he said over the sound of an air-nailer.

"Renovations." She pulled him back down, catching his ear with her teeth. "They'll be done by next week."

"You're getting new neighbors?"

"I guess so. I'll have to run an ad."

He pulled back to look at her.

"You're a landlord?"

"I'm going to try it. My father is an investment broker." She shrugged it off and then her eyes went wide. "I just had a great idea."

"What is it?"

"The place would be perfect for Hunter."

"You want Hunter and me to move in next to you?"

She shook her head slowly, a crooked smile on her lips. "I want Hunter to move in next to *us*."

*Oh.*

He felt himself pulling away both physically and emotionally. He knew how he felt for Mick. She was great, and he'd never been so happy with a woman before. He'd been ready to tell her he wanted to commit, that he loved her, but shacking up? That was more than he was ready for. It meant more than just sharing the things he wanted to share and having a standing date every weekend.

Living together meant day in and day out. It meant her seeing him when he was in pain, or when he was dealing with bad memories. He wouldn't be able to hide the truly frightening things.

No way were they ready for that. And if she left, where would that leave him or his brother. It wasn't safe for Hunter to get too attached. He'd lost enough in his life already.

Brady shook his head.

"Thanks for the offer, but we're not ready for that." He'd meant him and Mick weren't ready, but she misunderstood.

"It would be perfect. Hunter would have his independence, but we'd be right here if he needed us. He's ready, Brady."

"I'll make that decision if and when the time is right. It's not right." He stood and ran his hand over his hair. He felt trapped. "I need to go."

"Go? What's wrong? It's okay. We don't have to do it. It was just an idea."

An idea that would continue to grow until it became a reality. While she might brush off the idea of moving Hunter in next door, she was thinking of Brady moving in with her. She was at that level and he wasn't. No matter how much he might want it, he couldn't just slip into a normal life.

He panicked.

Without being consciously aware, he was suddenly in his truck, driving away.

* * *

Zane gave the waitress a nod—the nod that meant he wanted a beer—and sat between Brady and Josh at the bar. Brady wasn't looking so good as Josh went on with his story about how his daughter had made him a sandwich for lunch.

"It looked like a regular PB and J but when I bit in, there were M&Ms and a slice of bacon." He tilted his head to the side and smiled. "It was actually really good."

"I have a big problem," Brady said out of nowhere.

"What's up?" Zane automatically assumed it would have something to do with the trial.

"No offense, boss, but you're not going to be able to help. You're worse off than me." He rubbed a hand over his face. "I thought maybe I was in love with Mick, but the second she mentioned moving in together, I turned into a pussy and ran off. I've faced down enemy fire, and the first time a woman shows serious interest in me, I practically pissed myself."

Zane held up his hand. "I could use some help in this area too. I'm going to be making a move soon. Any pointers would be appreciated."

Josh and Paul looked at one another for a second before bursting out in laughter. "Rookies," Paul said.

"Pull up your panties, boys. Love isn't for sissies," Josh warned before going into a step-by-step tutorial on how to survive having feelings for someone.

By the time he got to childbirth, Brady was looking a little green, and Zane couldn't blame him.

"The basic point he's making," Paul interrupted, "is that you can't be afraid to just go for it and know the other person has your best interests at heart. If she's the one for you, she'll take special care of your heart. Always."

Zane had no doubt that Kenley would take special care of his heart. He worried he wouldn't be able to take care of hers. Especially while she faced her biggest fears—a courtroom and the man who had threatened her life. She would be depending on him, and he didn't want to let her down.

\* \* \*

It was July.

Kenley should have been enjoying the summer with Zane on his boat. She should have been picking out a dress for the reunion they were going to in a couple of weeks. But instead she was in the courthouse, getting ready to come face-to-face with the man who frequented her nightmares.

Dr. Fulmer had prepared her for this day, and Zane was with her. She was as ready as she would ever be to get this over with so she could truly put it behind her.

She was fine.

They walked into the courtroom hand in hand. Brady was already sitting toward the front so she and Zane went to sit next to him. Brady's knees were bouncing, the only outward sign of his anxiety.

She glanced down at her dress pants and brushed off a piece of lint with a steady hand. She was completely fine, as she'd told Zane and everyone else since it had happened. But now, with Dr. Fulmer's help, she felt it might actually be true.

Nothing had happened to her. The man had grabbed her arm and yelled at her. It was no big deal. Except she knew this was just the lie she'd told herself when she was trying to hide. She couldn't hide anymore.

The door along the wall opened and a man was escorted into the room. At first she didn't recognize him. He looked like a normal guy in a dress shirt and khakis. His hair wasn't in wild disarray as it had been that afternoon. Her blood turned to ice water when she heard him speak to the man next to him. It was suddenly difficult to get air into her lungs.

When the bailiff said, "All rise for the honorable Judge Margaret Billows," her legs wouldn't move. All this time she'd thought she was fine.

She wasn't fine at all.

* * *

When the scrawny man walked into the courtroom, it took every bit of control Zane had to stay seated next to Kenley and not fly over there to start whaling on him. Then he took a good look, and realized he still looked a little roughed up from the encounter with Brady. The man was on crutches, a cast running from his toes to his hip.

"I thought I remembered the sound of a femur snapping," Brady said with a low chuckle. Zane had already given Brady a raise, which he'd tried to refuse since Zane had agreed to employ Hunter. Hiring Hunter hadn't just been a favor to Brady. He did a good job and was a valued employee. Not to mention Kenley seemed to feel better when someone was in the office with her.

When the bailiff ordered everyone to rise, Zane moved to stand, but was weighed down by Kenley grasping his hand. She wasn't standing, instead she was staring at the man on the opposite side of the room, panting and looking pale.

"Ken?" Brady said while motioning for her to stand. She didn't move. It was as if she was frozen there.

With a nod to Brady they pulled her to her feet so she wouldn't be in contempt of court. A serious-looking woman in a black robe came in and told everyone to be seated.

Kenley slumped back in her seat and blinked up at him.

"I can't do this," she whispered. "I have to go. I have to get out of here." Her eyes were frantic, which made telling her she couldn't leave almost unbearable.

"You have to stay. If you don't he could be released without so much as a fine." The district attorney had told them the man hadn't taken a plea, because he didn't have much to lose. He'd robbed a few other people and would be going to jail no matter what. He'd pleaded not guilty in the hopes of some miracle. Kenley not testifying would put him on the path to that miracle.

"But he—The gun—I couldn't—"

"Shh." He pried her fingers from his leg before she drew blood. The district attorney glanced over his shoulder and gave her an encouraging look, but she couldn't have seen it with her gaze still fixated on the man who had hurt her. "Look at me." He had to place his fingers on her chin and guide her face up to make her take her eyes off her attacker. He'd wanted her to be here for Brady's testimony so she knew what to expect.

Her therapist suggested she be in the room before her testimony so she had time to adjust before having to go up on the stand.

"We only need to stay until you go up there and tell them what happened. Then we can leave. You'll never have to see him again. I'll be right here the whole time. He can't hurt you. You can do this. I know you can."

"...and our testimony will prove beyond a reasonable doubt that this man threatened the life of Ms. Carmichael. Had it not been for the heroic bravery of Lieutenant Brady Martin he might have killed her for a few hundred dollars. I assure you her life has more value than that. The defense will paint this man as a victim of his addiction, and that may well be. But Ms. Carmichael is the victim in this case and I ask you not to forget that."

The district attorney wrapped up his opening remarks to the jury. While his words were true, and had a certain dramatic flair that might help get a conviction, Zane felt a need to protect Kenley from hearing them. And maybe himself.

He wasn't foolish enough not to know what could have happened. It was obvious when you combined a desperate heroin addict and a loaded gun, the outcome could have been deadly if Brady hadn't come in. But still, sitting there in the same room, hearing it spoken as fact while Kenley trembled beside him, he felt completely helpless.

"The defense calls Lieutenant Brady Martin to the stand to testify."

"Christ," Brady muttered as he squeezed out of the row. He patted Kenley on the shoulder before he walked to the front of the room. With his hand on a Bible he repeated the oath that assured everyone he would tell the truth.

The truth Zane wasn't sure he wanted to hear.

Brady spoke about how he had originally planned to leave, but he'd decided to drop off the paperwork before leaving for the day.

"I heard shouting as I walked from the shop up to the door to the office. It was a man's voice. I didn't recognize it, so I stopped outside the door and only opened it enough to see into the lobby."

"And what did you see?"

Brady swallowed and ran his hand over his hair.

"I saw that man with his arm across Kenley's throat and a gun pressed against her temple." Brady swallowed again and kept his eyes on the attorney.

"He was yelling at her to give him the money, and Kenley was telling him she didn't have any money. He pulled her off her feet and told her he knew a man had come in with cash that morning. He called her a liar and said he was going to blow her brains out if she didn't give him the money."

Zane hadn't known it was this bad. He'd heard the police report, but it sounded more clinical when not told with Brady's personal experience. Zane looked at Kenley, who was sitting beside him with an eerie calm. A hint of anger stirred. Why hadn't she just given him the money?

It wouldn't have been any guarantee of safety. The man still could have shot her if she had given it to him, but still for her to put herself at risk rather than give up his money...

"And then what happened?" the attorney prompted when Brady didn't continue on his own.

"I—I'm not exactly sure."

"According to the eyewitness, you grabbed Mr. Grubb by the arm and dislocated his shoulder before pushing him to the ground and kicking him in the ribs. When he attempted to kick you away, you seized his leg and broke it with your elbow before choking him until he was unconscious."

"I don't recall," Brady said.

"Are you saying you didn't touch this man?" the judge asked.

"No, ma'am. I'm saying I don't remember the details. When I realized what he was doing to Kenley, I kind of... snapped."

"But you were able to call an ambulance."

"That was after I calmed down."

"And you assisted Ms. Carmichael until help arrived."

Brady shrugged it off. "She was shook up, but didn't seem injured. Except for the marks on her arm and temple."

"Ladies and gentleman, a skilled marine doing what he was trained to do."

Brady looked more and more uncomfortable as his testimony wore on. He seemed to be struggling to keep his language in check when the defense attorney painted him as a menace to society.

Eventually he was done and he took his seat next to Kenley again. Brady put his arm around her shoulders and pulled her over so he could kiss her head and whisper something in her ear.

She nodded and relaxed slightly. Until her name was called.

Kenley made no move to get up. His earlier anger had faded. He realized she hadn't done anything different than what he would have done in her place. He couldn't fault her for her determination and loyalty. They were two of the many traits he loved about her.

"You can do this," Zane whispered. "You are the strongest person I know. Go up there and keep your eyes on me. Don't look at anyone else but me, okay?" She nodded and stood.

While she was being sworn in, Zane leaned over to Brady.

"What did you say to her?"

"I told her Mr. Grubb was too busted up to hurt her, and if he tried, I'd be more than happy to break a few more of his bones."

Zane watched as she sat in the same seat Brady had just vacated. She looked so small. Her gaze was on him the whole time she told her story. He'd heard it already, but it affected him the same way. He felt utterly helpless.

He worked to make sure he didn't show his anger, since she was watching him. He needed to be strong on the outside, even if he was falling to pieces on the inside.

# Chapter 19

That night when they got back to Kenley's apartment, she didn't talk about the trial and he didn't have the courage to bring it up. She crawled into bed next to him and ran her hands up his chest. He knew what she was doing. He'd allowed her to do it many times because he'd honestly thought she was okay. But after seeing the way she'd reacted in the courtroom, he couldn't let her hide anymore.

"We need to talk," he said. The look of horror on her face clued him in that he'd said something terribly wrong. "Oh. No. Not that kind of talk." He shook his head and waved his hands in front of him, hoping to erase the concern on her face.

"What do you want to talk about?" She still looked worried.

"I think it's time to admit that you're not as fine as you thought you were." She frowned, and he wanted to give in and just love the hurt away, but that wouldn't work. Not in the long run.

She let out a sigh and nodded.

"I was okay until I saw him. In my memories he was a lot bigger. I remember being scared. But then I saw him and I felt so weak. The guy was barely bigger than I am and I couldn't defend myself."

"He had a gun, Kenley. He was also high, which would have made it difficult to fight him off." He brushed a piece of hair behind her ear. "I know you're strong enough to heal from this. I just don't think it's a good idea to use sex to block it out."

She nodded. "Okay. You're right. Dr. Fulmer and I prepared for this, but I don't think anything could have readied me to see him again. I'll talk to her about it at my session next week."

Instead of sex, he held her close to him all night, glad her part of the trial was over. She didn't want to hear the rest, so the next day they planned to go out on the boat and move on with their lives. If only he had a clear idea of what to do next. She'd assured him they didn't need to worry about the future. They only needed to live for now. He'd been planning to take the next step after the trial, but was she ready?

\* \* \*

Stepping into Dr. Fulmer's office made her feel stronger already. She was determined to get through this so she could be free. She didn't want to cringe when she saw someone who reminded her of the man who had scared her. She didn't want to have flashes of memories that terrified her. And she didn't want to obsess about what could have happened until she was afraid to be alone. She wanted to take back her life, and assure Zane that she wasn't using sex to hide from what happened.

After the meeting with Dr. Fulmer, Kenley felt better about the trial, though she was still not clear what her next steps with Zane should be. She just knew she wanted more.

Zane was supportive, and Brady was a huge comfort in that he came up with new and inventive ways to inflict bodily harm on anyone who would try to hurt her, and shared them with her to make her laugh. It probably wasn't the healthiest of ways to deal with things, but it made her feel better.

She liked having Hunter in the office on the three days he worked for them. It was fun watching him take ownership of his new duties. It was also nice to have company when Zane was away on business, which wasn't as often as it had once been.

She and Zane were making out in his office the next week when someone came in the front door.

"I swear if that is my sister I'm going to kick her out."

"You can't, she's going shopping with me, to help pick out something to wear to the reunion."

"You're sure you want to go? I can think of other things to do that night." He nibbled the skin under her ear, making her shiver in delight.

"You stood by me when I faced down my fears. I want to help you do the same."

"Fine, but I'm warning you, your man with a gun has nothing on a ballroom full of bullies." He winked at her as they heard footsteps in the hall.

"I'm walking very slow and loud so as not to catch you unawares," Sidney called from outside the door.

"Come in!" Zane yelled.

"Everyone's properly clothed?"

"Yes. It's safe." Kenley laughed and scooted off Zane's lap.

Sidney stepped in, still covering her eyes.

"Of course it's safe," Zane said, acting smooth. "Just taking care of some business."

"Right. Business." Sidney laughed. "You ready to go? I'm eager to do something fun with someone who doesn't go in their pants."

"I'm ready." She kissed Zane goodbye, who kept the PDA to a minimum in front of his sister.

"Have a nice time. I'll see you on Friday when I get back from North Carolina. Don't worry about locking up. I've got it."

"All right. Have a safe trip. I'll miss you." Kenley bit his earlobe and Sidney made a gagging sound.

"I'll miss you too."

With a wave they left him at his desk and headed for the mall.

* * *

"What do you think of this one? Too much?" Kenley held up the proverbial little black dress on steroids. The last party she'd been to hadn't ended very well. She hoped she wouldn't be accused of adultery.

"Does it come with a can of Insta-Pimp?" Sid smirked.

"You could just say no. You don't have to come up with a clever insult for every dress."

"It's a gift."

Kenley laughed.

"I want to look really good so Zane isn't embarrassed to have me with him. I know he's nervous about seeing his old classmates."

Sidney let out a laugh at this. "You're kidding right? He will be thrilled to have you with him. Even if you wore a burlap bag. Besides, you're already fulfilling his wildest dreams by looking like the girl he fantasized in high school."

"I am?"

"Didn't he tell you? It was the reason he didn't want to hire you at first. Because you reminded him of the girl who wouldn't give him the time of day back then. She broke his little heart." She shook her head. "I think he gave in and hired you because it was his way of taking the power back or something like that."

"Oh," was the only thing Kenley could say.

"But that doesn't matter now. You two are great together."

"Right." Kenley hadn't realized Zane was with her because she looked like someone he'd once loved. This information made it suddenly hard to breathe. All this time, she'd thought Zane cared about her, and here he was only living out a fantasy that didn't have anything to do with her.

An hour later, they agreed on a different black dress. They went out to dinner, where Kenley pretended to have a great time. But the truth was, Sidney's words had taken root and doubt was growing quickly.

She knew how she felt about Zane and he made her feel special when they were alone. But was he only with her to live out some fantasy?

He called the next day, but she was in the middle of showing Hunter how to use the microwave to heat up his lunch.

She called him back later.

"How did the shopping go?" he asked.

"I found a dress."

"You would be beautiful in a paper bag."

"You think so?" She wasn't trying to hit him up for a compliment, but she wanted to know if he really felt that way or if he was just saying what was expected. One off-hand remark from Sidney and she was beginning to question everything. She hated it.

"Yes. And not just beautiful, but smart and funny." He sounded completely sincere and her heart relaxed a little. Surely that didn't have anything to do with an old fantasy. "Plus, I think you're beautiful in nothing at all."

"Yeah, well, you're the only guy who's ever seen me in that."

"I'm the luckiest man on the planet."

She smiled, feeling special. She almost asked him about the girl from his past, but couldn't bring herself to do it.

"I'll see you tomorrow."

"Good night."

She sighed as she went to bed, trying to put her insecurities aside. Zane was with her because he liked her. Not because she looked like someone he never had.

Unfortunately her subconscious wasn't on board with the plan to move on. She woke from a dream in which Zane walked into the reunion, and spotted his long lost love, who ran straight into his arms. The two of them ran off together, leaving Kenley standing there in a room full of strangers. Alone.

\* \* \*

Brady pulled in at Elmhurst late on Friday evening. He'd missed his visit with Hunter last weekend, because of catching up on the time he took off to attend the sentencing. While Zane and Kenley didn't care about the outcome of the trial, he needed to see it through. To make sure that guy wouldn't be out there hurting other people.

People like Hunter or Michaela. He hadn't seen or spoken to her since he'd fled her home after her invitation to move in with him. A lot of people thought of him as a hero. He'd saved some of his men in Iraq, and Kenley had told him how much he'd changed her life.

But Brady knew what he was underneath. A coward.

He was afraid of loving someone who might not always love him back. Hunter was safe. He would always be his brother. Everyone else was an unknown.

Taking a left onto Hunter's floor he took the corner and stopped at the door to his brother's room. An older man sat in a hospital bed, struggling to get a spoonful of green Jell-O up to his mouth.

Brady backed up and looked at the number beside the door. Was he on the wrong floor?

No.

He hurried to the nurse's station, worry making his stomach turn. Surely if he'd been injured they would have contacted him.

"Where has Hunter Martin been moved?" he demanded.

The nurse's smile faded as confusion set in.

"Hunter moved to a personal residence last week."

"Personal residence?" Brady said at the same time it clicked. With a terse "Thank you" he rushed out of the facility and hopped up into his truck.

She'd gone too far this time.

\* \* \*

Michaela didn't have to look to see who was pounding at her front door. She'd been waiting for him to show up for the last week.

With a deep breath she pulled open the door and braced herself.

"What the hell are you thinking?" he started.

She put up her hand and shook her head.

"You can either calm down to talk about this rationally, or you can leave. The choice is up to you."

"Apparently the choice isn't up to me at all. You'll just do what you want behind my back when I'm out of town."

"I didn't do anything behind your back. And the choice of whether Hunter came to live here wasn't yours to make. He's an adult. It's his decision."

"I want to see him."

"I want you to see him too, but before that happens you need to calm down."

"The hell I do."

"Brady, you need to stop using your brother to punish yourself. It's not fair to him."

Brady stepped back, eyes wide, as if she'd slapped him. She was sure it probably felt that way to him. She wanted nothing more than to hug him and ease his pain, but she needed to stay strong. She couldn't back down now. Not if she wanted to help these men.

"I'm not—"

"You are. You want to take care of him as penance for not being there to take care of him before the accident. But you're suffocating him. You need to let him go and let go of the guilt. He's happy here. Please just see for yourself with an open mind before you drag him back to a half-life in some home."

He blinked a few times and walked in a slow circle. When he was calm he came to stand in front of her. His lips were pressed together in a firm line, but he nodded once.

He was listening. She took a breath. This was her chance.

"He doesn't have a lot of furniture right now. I redirected your last payment to Elmhurst into a checking account for Hunter. We went furniture shopping, but he insists on having furniture like he had at home, and we haven't been able to find the right thing yet. We moved the bed from my spare room, and he has a card table in the dining room for now."

Brady said nothing as he followed her into her kitchen and through a door that led into Hunter's new home.

Hearing her enter, Hunter glanced up and said, "I still have four hundred ninety-two dollars and forty-six cents after I paid this bill." Hunter happily held up a check before he noticed his brother. "Brady! Look! I'm paying bills."

"You have bills?" Brady's voice was tight.

"Yep." She still found his excitement over bills amusing.

"When he decided to move in, he had two requests. That he get to pay bills like you, and that he could have you over for dinner."

Brady swallowed, but remained silent.

"I promise you, his bills are minimal. Enough to give him his independence and build some credit without being overwhelming."

"I also paid for my bus pass," Hunter announced while holding up another check. There was no way Brady could misinterpret the excitement on Hunter's face. "Brady, can you stay for dinner?"

"Sure thing. What are we having?" Brady's voice wavered as he moved closer.

"I'm not allowed to use the stove. It's not even plugged in. But I have meals ready." Hunter opened the refrigerator. "You can have barbeque chicken with rice and broccoli. That one takes four minutes to make. Or you can have fish with roasted potatoes and green beans. Or there's a turkey salad wrap. Or we can get pizza."

He moved to the envelope hanging on the refrigerator with the correct amount of cash for the delivery and tip.

"I can only get pizza once a week. The rest of the time I have to eat healthy."

Brady choked down his obvious emotion in order to answer. "I think the fish sounds good."

"That takes five minutes." Hunter nodded and removed the fish dinner. He opened the lid and held out the directions. "Then I will let it set for a minute before you can eat it."

Brady remained silent as Hunter put the meal in the microwave and said. "Five-oh-oh, and start."

When Hunter got two plates out of the cabinet and put them on his temporary card table, Brady sucked in a breath and stepped back.

"I'm going to go wash up," he managed to get out before he fled down the hall.

"The soap in my bathroom smells like apples!" Hunter called.

He hadn't shut the bathroom door completely, so she pushed it open to find Brady bent over the sink sobbing. She moved her hand over his bowed back and he turned in a quick move to pull her into his arms.

"I'm so sorry. I've been such an ass to you and you've been so wonderful. He's so happy, Mick. I have been holding him back. I guess I did want him to need me, but that was a dick move. I shouldn't want him to need me or anyone. I've been so selfish."

"Shh. You've done everything you knew to do to take care of him."

"It was all wrong."

"It wasn't. You love him. And that can't ever be wrong."

"But look at him." Brady pointed toward the kitchen as he wiped his eyes with the back of his hand. "He's making me a fish dinner, and setting the table."

"And he still needs you to be his brother."

Brady choked up again and then ran some water to splash over his face. He dried his face and hands on one of the towels Hunter had picked out because they were the same color as Brady's.

When he was collected he pulled her close and rested his forehead against hers.

"I love you," he whispered.

Her breath caught and she moved away, but he held her tighter.

"I'm not just saying it because of what you've done for my brother, though that in itself would have been enough. I love you because of the way you're willing to stand up to me for my own good."

She opened her mouth to protest, but he cut her off with a kiss.

"Brady. Your dinner is ready." Hunter knocked on the door.

"I'm coming." Brady smiled.

"How many minutes?"

"Just one."

"Okay." When Hunter's footsteps retreated he gave her a quick kiss.

"Come on, woman. My dinner is getting cold."

He opened the door and took her hand as he led her to the kitchen.

"Mick, what do you want to eat?"

"I think I'll let you boys have dinner alone."

"Please stay," Brady asked. Squeezing her hand. "This is a family dinner, right Hunter?"

"Yep."

"I'll take the turkey wrap."

"I knew you were going to pick that," Hunter said with a smile as he got it out. "That doesn't take any minutes."

He put it on the table and put the chicken in the microwave.

"Why are we eating our nice family dinner on this card table?" Brady asked Hunter when he sat down.

"We couldn't find a table like the one at your house."

Brady nodded and took a bite of his dinner.

"What would you say if we moved all the furniture from my apartment in here?"

"Are you going to move in with me?" Hunter asked.

"No. I'm going to move in next door with Mick."

"But you can come over sometimes for dinner, right?"

"Yes. I'll definitely come over sometimes for dinner." Brady gave her a wink, and she knew she'd done the right thing.

For all of them.

* * *

Kenley was only wearing her slip when Zane knocked. He'd had a delay and didn't make it home on Friday. He'd barely made it in time to change and come pick her up. She let him in and his mouth dropped open.

"Is that the dress?" he asked.

"No. It's my underwear."

"Okay. I was a little nervous for a second."

She laughed as he held out a bouquet of flowers for her.

"Thanks. What are these for?"

"I was thinking about you while I was away and I wanted you to know." He leaned over and kissed her. His hand trailed down her back and rested on her rear end.

"You promised," she reminded him. "I need to get ready." Despite the fact she would have liked to claim him as her own before they tempted fate at the reunion, they didn't have time.

"Fine." He let his head fall back. He was wearing a suit, but his lack of a tie said, *I don't give a damn about you people.*

He followed her into the bedroom and talked to her about work as she went into the bathroom to put on her makeup and do her hair. It was a comfortable conversation. One she imagined having with a husband. She frowned at herself in the mirror. She hated when she jumped too far ahead. It only led to disappointment. After discussing it with Dr. Fulmer, she realized it was one of the reasons she'd never gone further in her past relationships. She worried about getting emotionally attached too soon. That kept her from becoming emotionally attached at all. Like her virginity, it was another of those vicious circles she couldn't escape.

She walked back out and slipped the dress up her legs, turning so he could zip it.

"And then Paul pointed out that the boat was one—" He stopped talking when she turned around. "Wow." He looked her up and down as she slipped on the heels.

"It looks okay?"

"There's not a lot more fabric to the dress than the thing you have on under it," he noted, making her laugh.

"I guess not, but this is really a dress."

"Are you sure?" He was still checking her out, peeking down the front. He frowned. "I don't know, Kenley. I might need a sharp stick to keep the guys away from you."

Despite his reaction she still felt a little self-conscious about the dress by the time they got in the truck and he started the vehicle. Before he backed out, he leaned over and kissed her painted lips, taking a bit of it with him.

The closer they got to the hotel the more tense he became. His knuckles were nearly white when he finally parked and jumped out to come help her down. This was it.

At the doors to the building he paused and smiled down at her.

"You're absolutely gorgeous. Stop fidgeting."

"You look pretty scrumptious yourself."

He tilted his head to the side and then looked toward the doors.

"I'm not trying to impress anyone in there, Ken. I know they don't matter. But you do. And I don't want you to get a bad impression of me from the way these people treat me. I was no one to them. I doubt they'll even remember my name."

Despite his claim not to care, she knew he did.

"You're not that boy anymore, Zane. You're better than those stupid people who picked on you. You are now, and you were back then. For your own happiness, let the bad stuff go. Either because of, or in spite of those people you became the man you are now. The man I—" She stopped before she said too much. "The man who owns his own successful business."

"The man who is walking in there with the most beautiful woman on his arm who plays a key part in making his business such a success?" He held up his elbow and she tucked her hand around his arm so he could lead her inside.

They moved into the large room, crowded by people their age. Right inside the door was a table covered in name badges and manned by three women. One of those women looked very familiar to Kenley.

"Name please?" the woman said with a bright smile.

"Zane Jackson."

The woman stood up straighter, her smile glowing at maximum level.

"Zane? Is it really you?"

"Hi, Courtney." The woman wasn't wearing a name badge, but that didn't keep Zane from remembering her name.

The woman clapped in glee and came around the table to hug him. Zane's expression was pure shock as he hugged her back and then stepped to the side.

"Look at you! I can't believe how tall you are." She'd mentioned his height, but had her hand on his arm. As if what she'd wanted to say was that she couldn't believe how filled out he was.

Thanks to Sidney, Kenley had seen a photo of Zane from high school. She knew he'd been kind of skinny.

"You look good," Zane managed to say.

"Thanks. How are you? I always think of you when I come home to visit. Me and my two boys live in Denver now." No mention of a husband. No ring on her finger.

Kenley fidgeted again, causing Zane to remember her existence.

"This is Kenley Carmichael. My girlfriend."

"It's so nice to meet you," Courtney said, as friendly as could be. "You have the sweetest guy for a boyfriend. No matter how bad of a day I was having, Zane always had a smile for me when we passed each other in the hall."

"Yes. He has a great smile." Kenley resisted the urge to step between them. She was not going to be petty or jealous. Even though she'd banked everything on the hope that this woman would be a vile bitch, instead of a completely pleasant person.

Another person walked in so Courtney was forced to return to her post.

"You two go on and have a great time. I'll try to catch up with you later, Zane."

"O-okay," Zane stammered and moved into the room while affixing the sticker with his name printed on it.

"So that's her?" Kenley said.

"Her who?"

"The girl you're pretending I am?"

# Chapter 20

As Kenley's words sank in, so did his heart. She somehow knew Courtney was his weakness. No, not somehow. Sidney must have told her.

He loved his sister, but he really wished she would learn to keep her mouth shut. Especially about things that were sure to get him into a heap of trouble.

The sight of Kenley biting her lip and looking around the room caused the air to get stuck in his chest. She was upset. She looked unsure of herself. He knew what that looked like because he'd felt the same way all through high school.

Ignoring the wave from his old friend, Dan, he took Kenley's hand and led her outside to the large patio, moving to the darkest corner so they could have some privacy.

"You seem to have some information." He wasn't angry, but his words came out rather harsh. She pressed her lips together and looked away from him.

"I know you used to fantasize about a girl when you were in high school, and that girl looks like me. You thought we looked enough alike that you passed me over for a job I was qualified for so that you wouldn't have to feel rejected all over again."

Christ. She had a *lot* of information. But not all of it.

He nodded before he spoke.

"Yes, I had a crush on Courtney a long time ago. Yes, when I saw you I felt vulnerable and weak all over again. I was wrong not to hire you because of it, and I did the right thing eventually, which is how you came to work for me."

"Because you wanted to use me to feel like a big guy now." Her words stung and he tried not to lash back at her, though he didn't like being accused of using her, for any reason.

"At first I tried to stay clear of you, because I didn't want to feel like the nerdy kid drooling over the hot girl again. But then I got to know you and I tried to stay away from you for a different reason. You are my employee and a damn good one. I didn't want to risk messing that up." How futile that goal had been.

"But eventually, I realized I couldn't stay away from you. I didn't want to. Because I like you. You, Kenley. Not the girl I originally thought you looked like. In truth, I don't see a lot of similarities between the two of you anymore. She's very pretty, but you... you have my heart, Ken. You're the woman I love, now that I've finally figured out what love is really about."

Finally, he'd said the words that had been building in his heart for months. To his surprise, it wasn't difficult at all.

He smiled down at her smile.

"You love me?"

"You. Only you."

"Am I being stupid?"

"A little bit, but I still love you."

She reached for him as he bent to press his lips against hers.

When he kissed her, everything changed. The people from his past faded into nothing and the only thing left was her and their lips pressed together, and the feel of his hand on her back through the thin fabric of her dress.

She was gasping for air when he finally released her, eyes blazing with some emotion he'd never seen before. He remembered her almost confession earlier and swallowed.

"I love you too." She whispered. "I figured it out a little while ago."

"And you didn't say anything."

"I was going to. I was waiting for the right time."

"We're so bad at this. I'm shocked we've gotten this far," he said, causing them both to laugh. She leaned up to kiss him again.

He looked around the patio. Some people were staring at them. Ellen Dunning, whom he remembered had once told him she would go out with him if he stopped hanging with the losers. Those losers had been great friends.

"I thought I had something to prove to myself by coming here, but I was wrong. I'm happy with my life now. I don't need my past to remind me of that."

"We're free to focus on our future?" This question might have freaked him out earlier, but now he had the answer.

"Yes. We're free."

"So what do we do now?" she asked.

"Do you want to get out of here?"

He kissed her again, in case there were any questions, and then she whispered in his ear, "I thought you'd never ask."

They were officially in love. He'd told her and she'd said it back. They'd both survived the ordeal.

It didn't matter how he'd gotten there. He was on the right track now.

* * *

*Zane will be home tomorrow*, Kenley told herself as she trudged in to work Wednesday morning.

After the reunion they'd gone back to his house, where they'd stayed the rest of the night and all day Sunday. But Monday he had to go out to Ohio to meet with a few clients. She was counting down the hours until he returned.

She was in this new relationship with all her heart. She wasn't holding back anything from fear. There were no guarantees in life, but she was going to live hers to the fullest.

She was thinking of the reunion with Zane when Officer Porter walked in. A genuine smile lit up her face at the sight of him. Now that there was no pressure of romantic involvement, she found Scott to be a great friend.

He always seemed to drop in to visit at the end of her shifts when Zane was out of town. She might have been irritated, but she knew Zane had probably asked this of his friend out of concern for her safety. She couldn't be angry at him for caring about her.

"Officer."

"It's Scott."

"You're still wearing your uniform. I can't tell."

"I'm definitely here in the capacity of a friend right now. And I hope you'll still want to be my friend when I leave." At his words she noticed how nervous he appeared.

"Is it bad news? Is Zane okay?"

"I'm sure he's fine. It's not that. And I don't think it's bad, or I would have just kept it to myself."

He sat down on the guest chair across from her desk and took off his hat.

"I did a stupid thing." He let out a sigh, but didn't say anything else.

"I'm going to guess there's more to the story. If you want me to help, you're going to have to tell me the stupid thing you did."

"Remember when we were on the date to nowhere and you told me about how you were adopted?"

"Yeah." Unease twisted her stomach.

"I offered to run your DNA to see if it got any hits and you said you didn't want to know."

"Right."

"Well, Kenley, I'm a cop who's training to become a detective, and you were an unsolved case."

"You didn't." She gasped.

"When I went through your house after the robbery, there was an empty soda can and well…" He winced. "I was supposed to pick a case from the files we were given, but I wanted to see if I could figure out yours."

"And did you?"

He peeked up at her. "Do you want to know?"

"You said it wasn't bad."

"It's not bad, but there's no happy ending either."

Did she want to know? All her life—despite her loving parents—she had wondered what had compelled someone to leave their child in a library. It had shaped her in some way, however minor. But now she might be able to finally know what had happened. If she was courageous enough.

"Tell me."

She sat down in the other chair, just in case she wasn't as ready as she thought. Scott shifted toward her and took her hands in his.

"It's not as easy as it sounds. There's not just one database for fingerprints and DNA that you put it in and it shoots out a match." Hmm. That was exactly the way it worked on television.

"Okay."

"First I looked back to articles and stories about missing persons the same time you turned up in Pennsylvania. I found something in New Mexico. A woman had filed a report that her daughter had taken her granddaughter away and when she returned the little girl was missing. The police questioned the mother of the toddler, but all she would say was that her daughter was safe. I spoke to one of the detectives who questioned her and they said they tried everything to get her to confess to doing something to her child, but she remained adamant that the little girl was safe.

"When the woman died a few months later from cancer, they suspected she had killed the little girl in a drastic attempt to keep them together in the afterlife or something."

Kenley's bare arms were covered in goose bumps.

"I read through the reports and contacted some of the woman's friends. They were more forthcoming with the details now than they had been back then. Apparently this woman was afraid of her mother and did not want the grandmother to have custody of the little girl. They said the older woman was cruel and abusive, but was the next of kin.

"She also had enough money to fight for custody, so even if the woman, Martina, had left the child with someone else, there was no guarantee the grandmother wouldn't have gotten custody at some point. According to Martina's friends she wasn't willing to risk it. No one seemed to know for sure where she went, but she was gone for two weeks.

"Once I had a scenario that matched, it was simply the matter of running your fingerprints against those of the missing toddler." He swallowed. "It was a match."

"Oh God." She covered her face with her hand in shock. She was originally from New Mexico and her mother's name was Martina. "What was my name?"

"You were born Amanda Marie Jennings. There is no father listed on your birth certificate."

"And my grandmother?"

"Died two years ago. From the sounds of it, she only got crazier as she got older. You were lucky, Kenley."

"My mother abandoned me to protect me, not because I was bad."

"Is that what you thought?"

He leaned over and put his arms around her as she started to cry. Why, she wasn't exactly sure. She must not have known how much this mattered to her.

"You didn't do anything wrong. Sometimes things just don't work out the way you think they will."

"What's not working out?"

It was Zane's voice. She hadn't heard him come in. Scott released his hold on her and she stood, realizing how this might look if someone had just walked in.

\* \* \*

Finding Kenley in Scott's arms was a bit of a jolt, but he trusted his friend, as well as the woman with the tears dripping off her chin.

"Porter, why have you made my girlfriend cry?"

"It's not his fault," Kenley defended the other man. The ring box in Zane's pocket felt heavy. He'd been planning this moment since that day she'd looked at him with forever in her eyes while he'd been holding his niece. He'd been practicing what he would say since he picked up the ring. He'd been sure he was ready. But now it would appear she wasn't.

"Kenley, are you angry at me?" Scott asked, his face pale. "I completely overstepped and you have every reason to hate me or report me."

"*Report* you? What the hell did you do?" Zane stepped closer. While he trusted Kenley, he was now having doubts about Scott. Kenley moved with him, staying between the two men.

"It's not what you think. It has nothing to do with us," Kenley said.

"I was hoping we would share everything," he told her, his glare still on the policeman.

"I'm not going to report you. I'm actually glad you did what you did. Now I know the truth. So, thank you."

"If you're sure?"

"I am. But I think you should probably go," Kenley suggested.

"I'll stop by tomorrow to check on things. Let me know if you need anything."

"Thanks."

Scott nodded at Zane before Scott pulled his hat on his head and walked out of the office. Kenley locked the door behind him and turned the sign to say they were closed.

"You're being ridiculous," she said while rolling her eyes. "There is nothing going on between Scott and me."

He followed her to his office where she sat on the sofa and patted the seat next to her. He didn't want to sit. He needed to walk.

She let out a breath and said the one thing he never expected her to say.

"My real name is Amanda."

* * *

An hour later, Kenley finished the story and leaned back against the cushions, feeling exhausted. Zane mirrored her pose and shook his head.

"That is some story."

"I still can't believe it's *my* story."

"The thing I really find unbelievable is that you ever thought it was your fault. You're an amazing person. And even if you were the brattiest three-year-old in existence, it still wouldn't have been reason for someone to cast you aside. How could you ever think such a thing?"

"I guess the same way I thought you only wanted me because I looked like the girl of your dreams." It did seem silly now. She knew Zane loved her.

"You *are* the girl of my dreams, Ken." He kissed her and she knew exactly who she was and what she wanted. "Would you consider changing your name?" he whispered.

She shook her head. "I couldn't do that to my father. I'd always complained about the name Kenley because it was unconventional, but it's who I am. I can't think of myself as Amanda."

"It wasn't your first name I was talking about." He pulled out a square velvet box and got down on one knee. With a snap, the box opened to reveal a diamond ring. "Will you marry me, Kenley Rose Carmichael?"

On the same day she'd been given her past, she was also given her future. Who knew getting fired could turn out to be such a great thing? She went to his desk and pushed the papers to the side before turning back to him with a big smile.

"Sure thing, boss."

# Epilogue

"Hunter? You ready to go? Come on, man. We only have thirty-two minutes." Brady stepped through the door that separated their kitchen from his brother's.

"Can you help me with my tie?" Hunter asked as he hurried into the room in his dressy new clothes. He'd decided he wanted to use some of his money on new clothes so he would look nice at Kenley and Zane's wedding. Michaela had taken him shopping and the results of her effort looked pretty nice.

"Yeah. I think I remember how to do a tie."

"You're not wearing a tie?" Hunter gave him a look that had judgment written all over it.

"I'm not. I'm wearing khakis and a dress shirt. That's good enough for a wedding on a boat."

"You look nice." Hunter shrugged.

"You look even better," Brady allowed as he pushed his brother's chin up so he could see. A few slashes of silk between them and the tie was snug and straight around his neck.

"Don't you boys look handsome?" Mick said as she stepped in wearing a low-cut dress and highheels. She didn't dress up for work, and he never took her to the kinds of places she'd need to wear something like the ensemble she was wearing now. He made a mental note to change that in the future.

"You look pretty," Brady said.

Hunter followed his complement with, "You're so beautiful, Michaela."

"Are you trying to one up me in front of my girl?" Brady teased his brother, though Hunter didn't understand the joke.

"Oh! I almost forgot my gift for them." Hunter ran off.

"Hurry up!"

"I am!"

"You did a great job with his clothes. He looks like a player."

"That wasn't my goal. I was just happy to find something that didn't have itchy tags. He hates itchy tags." When she smiled at him, something in his chest leaped with happiness. Michaela had opened her heart and her home to him and his brother.

She was an amazing person and sexy to boot. He couldn't wait a second longer to make her his.

\* \* \*

Brady gave her a look she hadn't seen before. He was rarely serious, with exception to the few times she's seen him mad. He was serious now.

"What? What's wrong?"

"Nothing. At least I hope not." He bit his bottom lip and tilted his head as if listening for Hunter's return. "I was planning to do this later. Maybe when we were alone and somewhere more romantic than my brother's kitchen, but I can't wait."

He pulled a small box from his pocket. The velvet cube was dwarfed by his large hand, but she knew exactly what kind of box it was.

A ring box.

He snapped it open to reveal a diamond.

"Will you marry me, Mick?"

"I thought you weren't the marrying kind."

"It turns out I am the marrying kind, as long as I'm with someone who is *my* kind."

"And I'm your kind?"

"You are better than my kind, but I'm hoping you'll say yes anyway."

"Yes."

"Really?" He didn't even attempt to hide his surprise, which made her laugh.

"Are you going to try to talk me out of it?"

"No ma'am. I'm going to get this ring on your finger before you change your mind." He pulled the ring from the satin and slid it in place before he kissed her, complete with his usual moan of happiness.

"Eww. Stop kissing on my side. You guys said you wouldn't kiss over here anymore," Hunter complained, making them both laugh.

"Fine. I'll kiss her later on our side. We have to get going."

"We only have twenty-one minutes left."

"Good thing it only takes nine minutes to get there."

They got to the marina in plenty of time. Hunter was excited about all the decorations and getting to ride on the boat. Brady winked at her as he rested his arm around Hunter's neck.

"How would you like to be in a wedding?"

"In Kenley and Zane's wedding? I don't know what to do. I didn't get to practice." Michaela patted his arm to calm him.

"Not this wedding. Brady was talking about *our* wedding."

"I'm going to marry you?" Hunter's eyes went huge and he stepped away from her. Brady just laughed at the miscommunication.

"No. I'm marrying Brady. Which means I will be your sister. Do you want to be my brother?"

"I'm already Brady's brother." He twisted his lips to the side.

"I'm willing to share you with Mick, if that's okay with you."

Hunter nodded. "That's okay with me. Can I go look over the edge?"

"Yes. Keep both feet on this side of the ropes."

She wrapped her arm around Brady's waist as they kept an eye on Hunter.

"Are you sure you want to sign up for this? I mean he's my brother and I'm committed to taking care of him for the rest of our lives. But if it's too much for you, I would understand. That ring wasn't meant to be a trap."

"It doesn't feel like a trap. I knew when I said yes I was making a commitment to both of you. I understand the two of you are a package deal." She didn't want him worrying about this. "I have enough room in my heart for both of you."

He relaxed in her arms and rested his forehead against hers.

"You're an amazing person." He pulled back and looked down at her, his lips pulling up on one side. "I get more room in your heart than Hunter, though, right?"

"I don't know. You only said I was pretty."

They laughed and kissed until the music started for the service.

"It's beginning," Hunter said as he sat next to her. She looked up into Brady's eyes and smiled.

"Yes. It's beginning."

# Keep an eye out for

*GETTING DOWN TO BUSINESS*

The next in

Allison B. Hanson's

On the Job romances

Coming soon

From

Lyrical Press

# About the Author

**Allison B. Hanson** lives near Hershey, Pennsylvania. Her novels include women's fiction, paranormal, sci-fi, fantasy, and mystery suspense. She enjoys candy immensely, as well as long motorcycle rides and reading. Visit her at allisonbhanson.com.

# NEVER LET GO

# ALLISON B. HANSON

## A Blue Ridge Romance

NICK
OF TIME

ALLISON B.
HANSON

A Blue Ridge Romance

# WHEN LEAST EXPECTED

*First in a new series!*

LYRICAL
shine

*Sometimes happily ever after takes a major swerve…*

# ALLISON B. HANSON

A Blue Ridge Romance

Printed in the United States
by Baker & Taylor Publisher Services